WITCHING ON A STAR

A WICKED WITCHES OF THE MIDWEST MYSTERY BOOK FOUR

AMANDA M. LEE

WINCHESTERSHAW PUBLICATIONS

Copyright © 2014 by Amanda M. Lee

All rights reserved.

No part of this book may be reproduced in any form or by any electronic or mechanical means, including information storage and retrieval systems, without written permission from the author, except for the use of brief quotations in a book review.

❀ Created with Vellum

PROLOGUE

When you're dead, time has no meaning.

Days come and go. Weeks come and go. Maybe years come and go, too. I really have no sense of time. I just mark it in the back of my mind.

Sunrise is like a gift and sunset is the inevitable curse that follows.

I don't like the dark. I never liked the dark, even when I was alive. The only company I have at night is the stars – and I do love the stars. I wish on them every night, just like my mama told me to do when I was alive. I wish for someone, anyone, to see me. For someone to talk to me. For someone to remember me. No one ever does, though.

So I spend my days watching the water and the nights wishing for something I can never have. I like the way the water laps at the beach – when it's not frozen in the winter, that is. I never got to wade in these waters when I was alive, but I could hear it brushing the bottom of the boat. It became soothing.

Now that I'm dead, though, I can't feel anything. Except loneliness, that is. I feel a profound sense of that.

Most of the time, I wander around this place – which is literally falling apart due to the ravages of time and inclement weather – and I wait. What am I waiting for? I have no idea. I have no purpose, so I have nothing to look forward to. I just am.

The few people that visit this place where woods and water meet don't notice me. They can't see me. That's how I know I'm dead. I tried to talk to them at first, the ones that looked nice anyways. Most are armed with cameras and picnic baskets and they never see me as they spend an afternoon traipsing around my own personal hell – and then leave again. I have no idea where they go.

Some that come to this area aren't nice, though. I don't know how I know that. Maybe it's in the way they talk to each other, or in the way they look at each other – like animals ready to prey on the weak. I stay away from them. I never try to talk to them. They scare me.

There's a memory I'm trying to hold on to – and these people trigger it whenever I see them. I just can't quite grasp it. All I know is that I don't want to be here when they're here. They say you can't recognize evil in someone's soul – but I can.

I've started to branch out from this little area, though. I've seen all there is to see here and boredom still exists – even when you're dead.

Just over the bluff, there's a small little town. It's called Hemlock Cove. I've heard some of the hikers and picnickers call it that when they pass through. I don't know why, but I feel that whatever I'm supposed to be doing is there. Whatever person I'm supposed to be looking for is there, too.

I just have to figure out exactly what – or who -- that is. I wish I had a little magic to help me out.

ONE

"We're at war!"

"Great. I can't wait," I replied distractedly.

"I'm serious. This is a war and I need my best soldiers. Bay Winchester, are you even listening to me?"

I glanced up from the magazine I was idly flipping through and met my Great Aunt Tillie's hostile countenance with a mixture of amusement and dread. "No, I got it. We're at war. I didn't realize I was one of your soldiers, though. I thought you could do this all alone. Isn't that what you said last night?"

Aunt Tillie was standing at a chalkboard she had erected in the living room of the family quarters at The Overlook – the bed and breakfast she ran with my mom and her two sisters – and she was clearly in a state.

On the best of days, Aunt Tillie is a little persnickety. The past two months, though? Aunt Tillie was at the abject worst a person could possibly be. She was angry. She was vengeful. And, man, was she crotchety.

At four foot, eleven inches, and eighty-five years old, the casual observer wouldn't exactly be quaking in their shoes when they went toe-to-toe with Aunt Tillie. Anyone that's spent more than five minutes with her – and, in my case, twenty-seven years – would know she's scarier than any mass murderer could ever be.

I come from a family of witches, you see. Real witches. We're not like fairy tale witches with magic shooting out of our fingertips – at least most of the time. We all have abilities, though. And Aunt Tillie's abilities were used to wreak havoc, more often than not, on anyone that got in her way.

Currently, she was in a right proper snit about a competing inn that was being constructed on the other side of Hemlock Cove. Under normal circumstances, this wouldn't be cause for alarm. Hemlock Cove is a tourist destination in Northern Lower Michigan – and another inn wouldn't actually hurt The Overlook's business. The fact that my father and two uncles were opening the inn, though, was the bone of contention for Aunt Tillie. She had spent the past eight weeks drawing up battle plans for her assault on the Dragonfly Inn – and they were getting more and more elaborate. That's why she needed the chalkboard – to keep track of her diabolical schemes.

"I *can* do it on my own," Aunt Tillie said bitterly. "I just thought, since one of the evildoers was your own father, that you would want to help."

"Evildoers? When did you stop calling them *bastions of hell*?" I focused back on the magazine wearily.

"Your mother said I'm not allowed to call them that anymore because it's disrespectful," Aunt Tillie sniffed.

I cocked an eyebrow from my place on the couch. "And you listened? That doesn't sound like you."

"Are you going to make fun of me or help me? You can't do both."

"I'm a multitasker," I countered. "I think I can probably do both."

"So, you'll help?" Aunt Tillie's face lifted hopefully.

"No," I shook my head, my shoulder-length blonde hair shaking around my shoulders as I did. "I'm not going to help."

"Why not?"

"My mom told me that if I helped you that I would be grounded," I responded truthfully.

"You're an adult. You can't be grounded. You need to tell her that you can make your own decisions and that you can't be controlled."

"You're trying to control me," I pointed out.

"That's different," Aunt Tillie said evasively. "I'm in the right. It's okay to be bossy when you're in the right."

"Ah, good to know."

"So, are you going to help me or not?"

"No."

"You're dead to me."

"Fine."

"No, you're really dead to me."

"It's still fine."

"If you're not going to help, then get out!"

I looked up from the magazine again and fixed Aunt Tillie with a hard stare. Her close-cropped hair, which had been black in youth, was now totally gray and standing on end. Her round features – which I always likened to those of a hobbit – were pinched and ferocious. She clearly wasn't letting this go.

"You want me to leave?"

"If you're not going to help," Aunt Tillie said stubbornly.

"I was invited for breakfast," I reminded her. "If I just leave, my mom will be ticked – and nobody wants that." Least of all me. My mom was master of the guilt trip. And, while Aunt Tillie was scary, there were some ways that my mom managed to be even scarier – like when I purposely ignored a direct order. And I, along with my cousins, Thistle and Clove, had been expressly ordered to be at the inn for breakfast this morning. There was some big announcement my mom and aunts were all atwitter about.

"Breakfast is in the kitchen," Aunt Tillie said, turning back to her chalkboard and away from me. "There's no need for you to be in here with me if you're not going to help."

I couldn't agree more. I got up from the couch, casting one last look at her board, and then went in the kitchen to join my mom, aunts, and cousins in their breakfast preparations.

My mom, who was busy ladling pancakes into the cast iron griddle, gave me a hard look when I entered the kitchen. "I thought I told you to watch your Aunt Tillie?"

"I was, but she ordered me out if I wasn't going to help her," I shrugged, plucking a strawberry off the fruit plate and popping it into my mouth. Since spring was finally here – after a really long and hard winter (both on the weather and emotion fronts) – we were getting good produce again.

My mom narrowed her eyes. "What's she planning now?"

"She wants to enchant a bunch of moles to create a series of holes under the Dragonfly and make the ground underneath unsteady," I replied. "She thinks, if they dig enough holes, the inn will just collapse into them. Problem solved."

My cousin, Thistle, stopped cutting the tops off strawberries at the cutting board and laughed. Her hair, which changed with the seasons, was currently a bright purple (she said it was for Easter, but I knew it was just an attempt to irritate her mother). Her doe eyes were filled with mirth. "That's actually not a bad idea."

"Where is she going to find the moles to enchant?" My other cousin, Clove, asked from her spot next to the sink. While I was blonde and fair, and Thistle was currently purple and fair, Clove had been blessed with olive skin and black hair like her mother and, ironically, Aunt Tillie in her youth. She was short like Aunt Tillie, too, while Thistle and I were several inches taller.

"I don't have any idea," I replied. "Maybe she's going to order them off the Internet. She always says you can buy anything on the Internet. She's bought other animals online."

Aunt Twila, Thistle's mom, involuntarily shuddered at the memory. A few months back, Aunt Tillie had ordered a scorpion named Fred with the intent of putting him in a guest's bed. Fred had managed to escape, and my mom and aunts were convinced that Fred was still loitering around The Overlook somewhere.

"We'll have to make sure she doesn't get any deliveries," Aunt Marnie, Clove's mom, sighed. "She's always trying to sneak things in here."

"Hopefully that will change after this morning," my mom said primly, tucking a strand of blonde hair behind her ear wearily. "She'll be too distracted with other things to plot the downfall of the Dragonfly."

I glanced at my mother curiously. She'd been decidedly tight-lipped about the goings on at the Dragonfly Inn since she heard about it. She acted fine with everything, but I had a feeling that wasn't true. While she and my father hadn't parted on ugly terms, there had to be some sort of emotion roiling about inside of her now that he was back in Hemlock Cove. She never said anything to indicate that, though. In fact, Marnie and Twila had been quiet about the fact that their ex-husbands were involved with the new inn, too. I couldn't help but wonder if the three of them were plotting something themselves.

My mom glanced up and met my gaze. "What?"

"Nothing," I shook my head. "I was just wondering why you, and Marnie, and Twila haven't really talked about the Dragonfly."

My mom pursed her lips. "What is there to say?"

"Have you seen Dad?"

"No."

"Not even once?"

"No."

"It's a small town. That doesn't make a lot of sense to me."

"Well, I'm sorry I can't quench your curiosity with a bit of ugly gossip," my mom said snidely. "There's nothing to say. Why don't you ask your father about it?"

I had. He'd been as stingy with information as she was being. The truth was, though, while I had been out to the Dragonfly to visit my dad on several occasions, the conversational topics hadn't run any deeper than the weather and construction updates. I wasn't sure I was ready for any deeper conversations.

"Winnie, don't be mean to her," Marnie chided her sister mildly. "It's not her fault that Warren, Teddy, and Jack are back. You shouldn't take it out on her."

I raised my eyebrows at Clove behind her mother's back. It wasn't like Aunt Marnie to be the voice of reason. They were definitely up to something. One glance at Thistle's suspicious face told me she was thinking the same thing. Now wasn't the time to talk about it, though. We would tackle that situation later. When we were alone.

"I'm sorry," my mom apologized stiffly. "That was uncalled for. Your Aunt Tillie is just driving me crazy."

"What else is new?" Thistle asked. "She's always driving you crazy. That's what she does best."

"She's being really bad right now, though," my mom muttered. "She got a big box delivered the other day. She wouldn't let me see inside of it. I just know she's got something big planned. It was probably filled with dynamite or something."

"She needs a license to order dynamite," I said pragmatically. "She doesn't even have a driver's license. I don't think you have to worry about that."

"Besides," Thistle interjected. "She could make her own explosives here. She doesn't need dynamite."

That thought didn't make anyone feel better, so we just ignored it. "So, what's the big surprise?"

"You have to wait until your Aunt Tillie is in here," Twila said, pushing her flame-red hair off her forehead as she finished arranging the fresh-baked bread on a tray for the main dining room.

"Go get her," I instructed Clove. Despite myself, I was curious about their big announcement. It had to be something huge to distract Aunt Tillie.

"Why me?" Clove visibly blanched. She was more fearful of Aunt Tillie than the rest of us.

"Because you haven't pissed her off today," Thistle said sagely.

Clove blew out a sigh. "Fine. But if she curses me, I'm blaming you."

What else was new?

After a few minutes, Clove and Aunt Tillie made their way back into the kitchen. Aunt Tillie didn't look thrilled to be there. "I'm here. What do you want to tell me?"

My mom turned to her beloved aunt and fixed her with a hard glare. "You could at least try to be nice."

"Why? You're never nice to me. Why should I be nice to you?"

"We just bought you a really big gift," my mom countered. "I think that deserves at least a modicum of respect."

Here's the thing about Aunt Tillie: She's spoiled rotten. She might be set in her ways, but she's also someone that is open to a good bribe. She obviously doesn't want to risk losing something really good.

"Fine. You have my respect. Now, what's the big announcement?"

"Well, we were going to wait until after breakfast ... ." Marnie hedged, exchanging a doubtful look with her sisters.

Aunt Tillie's newfound "respect" wasn't going to last long; that much was obvious.

"We decided, that since you lost your wine closet this winter for the new furnace," my mom started.

"And you handled that so well," Thistle said bitingly.

"That we were going to build you something new that would be all your own," my mom continued, shooting Thistle a dark look.

"A new wine closet?" Aunt Tillie looked less than impressed. "You called me in here to tell me you're building me a new wine closet?"

Aunt Tillie's homemade wine was famous around Hemlock Cove. While we couldn't prove it, the assumption was that she had a thriving side business selling the wine to guests and adventurous townspeople. Since she'd lost the space she used to make the wine two months ago, Aunt Tillie had been the queen of the perfected pout whenever the subject was broached. It was getting tiresome.

"No, not a wine closet," my mom said hurriedly. "We're building you a greenhouse."

"A greenhouse?" Aunt Tillie looked dubious.

"You've always wanted one," Twila said hurriedly, frowning at Aunt Tillie's less than stellar reaction.

"You said it was too expensive," Aunt Tillie reminded her. "Why now?"

"Well, we've been saving up our money," Marnie said evasively. "We've got a spot picked out at the back of the property and everything."

"It's going to be big," my mom said excitedly. "There's going to be plenty of room for you to grow whatever you want."

"Whatever she wants?" *Uh-oh.*

My mom realized what I was referring to immediately. "No pot," she said. "You can't grow pot in there."

Aunt Tillie also had a magically hidden pot field on the east side of our property that no one was supposed to know about. Unfortunately, almost everyone in town knew it was there – including local law enforcement. Aunt Tillie had cast a spell, though, that protected the field – for all intents and purposes. You could still see it, but only family – and a chosen few, like Thistle's boyfriend, Marcus – could actually get to it.

"There will also be plenty of room for you to make your wine," my mom continued. "We're going to have everything you need all in one place for you. Won't that be convenient?"

Aunt Tillie considered the offer. Only people that really knew her would be able to tell how excited she really was. She hid it well. "Fine," she said finally. "I think a greenhouse is a good idea."

"Good," my mom said, relief washing over her face. "Let me show you where we were thinking of putting it. You're going to be able to have input on every little decision. It's going to be a greenhouse entirely of your making."

"What about breakfast?" Clove whined. Like everyone else in my family, she was food-oriented above all else.

"After breakfast," my mom conceded.

Once everyone had filed out into the dining room and only Aunt Tillie and I were left, I turned to her curiously. "You know they're only doing this to distract you from your battle plans, don't you?"

"I do," Aunt Tillie nodded.

"Is it going to work?"

Aunt Tillie shrugged mischievously. "Who knows?"

I knew. There was nothing that was going to distract Aunt Tillie when she set her mind to it. She was just letting my mom and aunts think she was focusing on the new greenhouse.

It was going to be a long couple of weeks.

TWO

After breakfast, my mom led us to the spot she had in mind for the greenhouse. The Overlook property is hard to explain. Our family has owned the parcel the inn currently sits on for centuries. The first homestead on the property was a cabin, which was later expanded into a Victorian home – which was used as a small visitor lodging when I was a child.

A few years ago, my mom and aunts decided to expand the property into a full-fledged bed and breakfast, taking advantage of their kitchen and organizational skills. This part of Michigan doesn't have a huge industrial base, so when the town leaders decided to rebrand Hemlock Cove as a "fake" witch town years ago – as a way to keep the town viable and take advantage of the local ski and golf facilities – my mother and aunts had embraced the idea and expanded (and renamed) The Overlook to reflect that rebranding.

Most of the town doesn't realize that they have real witches living amongst them. They know we're weird, but they don't know we're magical. I'm fairly certain most of them believe that Aunt Tillie is abject evil, though. That has more to do with her personality than her powers, though.

In addition to the main house – which kept the bones of the older family dwelling at the back, where my mom and aunts still reside – the property also boasts a guesthouse that was utilized for tourists in the 1970s and where Clove, Thistle and I currently reside.

The greenhouse was going to be constructed at the back edge of the main property – which abutted several acres of wooded land we also owned – and overlooked a small creek and was nestled next to a large bluff.

It was actually the perfect spot for a greenhouse.

Aunt Tillie didn't look convinced – or maybe she was just being difficult, it's hard to tell. "How big is it going to be?"

"How big do you want it to be?" My mom asked warily.

"Big," Aunt Tillie said honestly. "There's a lot of stuff I want to grow."

"No pot," my mom reminded her.

"I'm not stupid," Aunt Tillie blew out a frustrated sigh. "You don't grow pot in a greenhouse anyway. That's the first place the cops will look."

"Always good advice," Thistle said sagely.

"Are you being fresh?"

My attention was momentarily distracted from the burgeoning fight between Aunt Tillie and Thistle by a hint of movement at the edge of the woods. At first, I thought it was an animal, but the closer I looked, I realized that it was a little girl.

Under the bright sky, it took my eyes a second to register what I was seeing. The little girl was dressed in a plain white dress and her dark skin helped hide her from prying eyes. She must be lost, I realized. Why else would she be here?

The little girl's dark eyes met mine, our gazes locking together. She seemed surprised when she saw I was staring directly at her. That surprise washed over her face quickly. She glanced to the trees behind her and then turned back to me curiously.

I took a step toward her, smiling warmly. I didn't want to scare her. "Are you lost?"

"Who are you talking to?" Thistle asked curiously, her eyes following my sight line.

"There's a little girl over there," I said, pointing to the clump of trees. "I think she must be lost."

Everyone turned in the direction I was looking. When I turned back, though, the little girl was gone.

"There's no one there," Clove said.

I walked over to the area, which was only starting to show the signs of spring growth, and frowned as I looked around. The little girl had disappeared – and there was nowhere within a reasonable distance for her to be able to hide. "I swear I saw a little girl."

"Did you recognize her?" My mom asked.

"No."

"What did she look like?" Marnie asked worriedly.

"I don't know," I shrugged. "I think she was about eight or ten. She had black hair, in braids, and she was wearing a white dress. She was black."

"Black?" My mom raised her eyebrows in surprise. I didn't blame her. While some black families resided in this area, they were still the rarity – not the norm. "Are you sure?"

"I thought so," I bit my lower lip.

"Light was probably just playing tricks on you," Aunt Tillie said, turning back to the spot where her greenhouse was to be erected. "That happens to me all the time. I have glaucoma."

My mom frowned at Aunt Tillie. "Since when?"

"Why do you think I need the marijuana?"

"Because you just like breaking the law?" Thistle suggested.

"I knew you were going to be a problem today," Aunt Tillie grumbled. "I just knew it."

I cast one last glance back at the spot where I had seen the little girl and then moved back to my family. Maybe they were right. Maybe I had imagined her.

AN HOUR later I managed to extricate myself from Aunt Tillie's grand greenhouse plans and make my way to work.

The Whistler is Hemlock Cove's only newspaper – and it's really only a newspaper in the loosest sense of the word. It's more like a weekly advertorial, with one main story and a bevy of birth announcements and area happenings intermixed.

I had actually gone to college and earned a journalism degree. After graduation, I had moved down to the Detroit area to work at a "real" newspaper for two years. While I had liked the excitement of the city and the rush I got when covering something of actual importance, the miles and miles of pavement and the stifling buildings made me feel like I was suffocating. I found I wanted to be home more than I wanted to chase a big story.

When I got back to Hemlock Cove, William Kelly, a local businessman that my family had dealings with throughout the years, gave me a job as editor of the paper. Several months ago, William had died, and his grandson, Brian, was the current owner of The Whistler.

Brian Kelly was handsome and charismatic. He was also a royal pain in the rear with delusions of grandeur that far outweighed his skill set. Basically, I tolerated him and he tried to bulldoze me. It wasn't a great combination.

When I got to my office, I found Edith waiting for me – and she didn't look happy, not that she ever did. Edith is The Whistler's resident ghost. Back in the day, she wrote the local advice column. She had died at her desk, after eating what I suspected was a poisoned dinner, and she'd been haunting The Whistler ever since.

Oh, yeah, I can see ghosts. That's my special talent. No one else in my family, with the exception of Aunt Tillie, has that particular gift. In the past, I'd thought of it as a curse more than anything else – especially when the townsfolk thought I was wandering around Hemlock Cove talking to myself -- but I was starting to rethink that avenue of thought in recent months.

"What's up?"

"He's up to something again," Edith said.

"Who?"

"Brian," Edith replied grimly.

The truth is, I have suspected Brian Kelly of a number of nefarious things since he came to town – including murder, on occasion. While he's proven to be a duplicitous businessman, I've come to the realization that he's not capable of much else. He's just too much of a ninny.

"What's he doing now?" Since Edith was a ghost, and Brian couldn't see her, I'd often utilized her busybody nature to spy on him. What? I'm not proud of it. I'm not ceasing that particular action anytime soon either.

"He's been on the phone with someone about a new plan," Edith whispered conspiratorially. I have no idea why she whispers. It's not like anyone but me can hear her.

"What kind of plan?" Edith always thinks something evil is afoot when, sometimes, Brian is actually just conducting legitimate business.

"If I knew that, don't you think I would have told you?"

She had a point. "Well, if you hear anything else, let me know."

"I'm not your slave," Edith reminded me.

"I know."

"I help you out of the goodness of my heart, because I'm a good Christian woman." And because she had nothing better to do with her time.

"I know."

"You should at least thank me for my efforts."

"Thank you."

"Thank me, for what?"

I looked up in surprise to see Brian standing in the door to my office. Edith looked horrified as she shrank into the corner. She obviously hadn't heard him coming either. I tried to pretend like Brian's sudden appearance hadn't thrown me for a loop. "Sorry, what?"

"Who were you thanking?" Brian glanced around my empty office, his eyes flashing over Edith but not seeing anything.

"I was just talking to myself," I lied.

"Oh, I do that sometimes," Brian said, although his face belied that statement. "What were you talking about?"

"I was just thinking about Aunt Tillie," I said.

Since he was staying at the inn until he found a place of his own – something I was starting to doubt would actually happen – Brian was familiar with Aunt Tillie. If Clove was scared of Aunt Tillie, Brian was terrified of her. He continued to stay at the inn, though, because my mom and aunts doted on him.

"What about your Aunt Tillie?"

"She got a big gift this morning," I said with a small smile. "My mom and aunts think it's going to keep her busy for months."

Brian looked relieved. "Oh, yeah, and why is that?"

"They're building her a greenhouse on the property."

"A greenhouse?" Brian looked confused. "Why?"

"So she can grow things." Just not pot. "And make her wine in her own space."

"Oh," Brian nodded. "They're trying to appease her. She's been upset about that wine closet thing for months."

"Yeah. This will make her happy for a little while."

"And keep her busy."

"And keep her busy," I agreed. "Was there something you wanted?"

"Oh, yeah," Brian ran a hand through his blond hair haphazardly. "I have a new idea."

Oh, good. Brian was always coming up with ideas for the paper. Most of them weren't feasible in this area. "What's that?"

"We're expanding," Brian announced happily.

"Expanding how?"

"We're going to start printing three times a week. Isn't that a great idea?"

That was a terrible idea. "There's not enough news in Hemlock Cove to put out three editions a week." Not to mention there were only two full-time employees and two part-time employees to handle all these new editions.

"Oh, I think you're wrong there," Brian said. "This town is happening lately. There have been murders and drug kingpins. It's just as busy as Detroit."

Not exactly. "Those were isolated incidents," I reminded him. "We've had three big stories and nothing else. It's been quiet for months."

Brian frowned. "Why are you trying to talk me out of this? I thought you would be excited to be the editor of a real newspaper?"

"Brian, I don't want to diminish your dreams," I said carefully. "But, in a normal week, we don't have enough news to fill one edition. Last week, the top story was a feature on the stables changing the feed for the horses."

Brian waved off my statement. "It was just a down week."

"The week before I wrote about the fact that it was spring. That was it. That it was spring."

"So? People liked that story."

I decided to try a different tactic. "News print is expensive. How can you justify two more editions of the newspaper and no more news?"

"The ads will make up for it," Brian said.

"We don't exactly have an expanding ad base," I reminded him, the arrival of the Dragonfly Inn notwithstanding.

"But we're always full of ads," Brian countered.

"Once a week, yes," I said. "However, the paper is really just printed for the tourists and that's why we get ads once a week. Why would the local businesses, which have a captive audience with the tourists, place ads more than once a week?"

"Why wouldn't they?" Brian had no idea how a newspaper actually worked, especially one like The Whistler. That much was obvious.

"Good luck," I said finally. I figured that the minute he actually got someone in here to tell him how much this was going to cost, he would change his mind. I was done trying to make him see reason. It always proved to be fruitless. He had to learn things on his own.

"Now that's what I want to hear," Brian said with a bright smile as he turned to leave my office. "I'll keep you updated as things move forward."

"I can't wait."

THREE

After a couple hours of work, I decided to join Clove and Thistle for lunch. As I made my way down Main Street, I couldn't help but relish the feel of the sun on my face and the warmth on my skin. The days were still only topping out in the fifties, but that was a marked improvement on the bitter winter we had just survived.

As a denizen of Northern Lower Michigan, I was used to snow. This past winter, though, had been brutal beyond belief. Not only had we set snowfall records, we had also set low temperature records – on almost a weekly basis. This spring had been more welcome than a steaming bowl of my mother's homemade stew.

Downtown Hemlock Cove is as quaint as they come. We're talking cobblestone streets and kitschy businesses that cater specifically to tourists. We've got a livery, a bakery, a hardware store and a pewter unicorn store. There's also a new corner store, featuring homemade quilts and afghans, and a new pizzeria that made some of the best pizza I had ever had the pleasure of eating.

My favorite store on the main drag, though, is the local magic store, Hypnotic. Thistle and Clove had opened the store while I had been down in Detroit. Now it was a thriving business, and one of the main tourist destinations in Hemlock Cove. I was proud of what they had accomplished.

When I entered Hypnotic – the wind chimes over the door announcing my presence – only Clove was in the front of the store. She glanced up when I entered and then turned her attention back to the ledger she was balancing.

"What's going on?" I asked as I slid onto the overstuffed couch in the middle of the retail area.

"Nothing," Clove said nervously, smoothing down her shoulder-length hair as she averted her gaze from mine. "Why do you think anything is up?"

I hadn't meant the question as an inquisition. Clove's reaction, though, made me realize that something really was up. She was a terrible liar.

"Where is Thistle?"

"She's in the back," Clove said. "We're getting ready to do our spring ordering and we have to take stock of what we need."

That sounded plausible – except I knew that Thistle was obviously doing something else given Clove's nervous demeanor.

"Huh," I said. "So, are you guys going to be carrying anything special this spring?" I was going to play the game until Clove folded. She always did.

"What? Oh, I don't know. We've found some new candle wax we want to try and Thistle has ideas for some flower candles she wants to make. She's going to branch out and start making those scented wax melts, too."

"That sounds cool."

"Yeah," Clove continued, casting a quick glance over her shoulder at the curtain that separated the main store from the storeroom at the back. "And we've ordered some cool new voodoo dolls from New Orleans. They're really neat."

"Those should be a big draw."

"Yeah," Clove nodded. "And more herbs and crystals, of course."

"Of course," I agreed. "And Thistle is doing inventory?"

"What?" Clove looked surprised. "I told you she was doing inventory. Why did you ask me that?"

Because you're a big fat liar. "I just forgot."

"Oh, okay."

"What is she inventorying again?"

Clove pursed her lips and furrowed her brow. "You're trying to trip me up."

"That's an ugly thing to say." *True, but ugly.*

"I'm not doing anything," Clove whined.

"I didn't say you were," I said. "I want to know what Thistle is doing."

"Why do you think Thistle is up to something?"

"Because you're acting all squirrely," I replied succinctly.

"I'm not acting squirrely," Clove countered. "You're just suspicious by nature. It's not a very nice trait."

Well, that did it. Thistle was definitely up to something. I got to my feet and started moving toward the storeroom. Clove blocked my entry behind the counter. "That's for employees only."

"What are you hiding?" I grabbed Clove's shoulders and tried to physically move her. She was small but strong.

"Hey, don't do that," Clove protested, reaching up and grabbing my hair angrily. "You can't go back there."

"Ow! Let go of my hair." I reached over and yanked Clove's hair for good measure.

"Ow! That hurts!"

"It's supposed to," I gasped as Clove gave my locks a particularly vicious yank. "Stop that."

"You stop it," Clove seethed through clenched teeth.

"You stop it first," I ordered.

"No, you stop it first."

This was getting us nowhere. "At the same time."

Clove met my gaze, searching my blue eyes with her brown for hints I was lying. "On the count of three."

I nodded. "One."

"Two," she gritted out.

"Three," we both said at the same time and then took a step back from one another.

"Well, that was undignified," Clove said finally, never moving her wary glance from my face.

"You started it," I grumbled, turning away from her and moving back toward the couch. I wasn't giving up; I was just regrouping and rethinking.

I didn't have long to wait. Once I was back on the couch, the curtain to the storeroom was dramatically thrown open as Thistle flounced her way out. "What are you two doing?" Her tone was accusatory.

"What were you doing?" I asked suspiciously.

"She was taking inventory," Clove said hurriedly. "I already told you that."

Thistle cast a sidelong look at Clove and just shook her head. "I was on the phone."

"With who?"

"Good news, I've been selected to be a contestant on *America's Next Top Model*. I'm very excited," Thistle said blandly.

"Oh, well, that will be fun," I replied, matching her tone. "I hope they make you pose with sharks."

"That's your fear, not mine," Thistle reminded me.

"Fine, then I hope they make you pose with snakes," I countered.

"That's Clove's fear."

Crap, she was right. "Then I hope they make you pose with monkeys," I said triumphantly.

Thistle narrowed her eyes. "That's just mean."

"And I hope they're picking bugs out of your hair and eating them while it happens." I have no idea why Thistle is scared of monkeys. Visits to the zoo as kids were terrifying for her, though. Maybe it's because *King Kong* had scarred her like *Jaws* had scarred me.

"You're getting more and more like Aunt Tillie every day," Thistle grumbled.

"So, what were you doing?" If she thought that little display was going to distract me from the original question, she was sadly mistaken.

"I was talking to my dad on the phone," Thistle said angrily. "Is that a crime now?"

"No," I shook my head. "I just can't figure out why Clove was hiding it."

"Because she freaks out about weird things," Thistle replied, moving around the counter and throwing herself onto the couch next to me. "You know that. She's a little dramatic."

This was true.

"I am not dramatic," Clove shot back. "You guys always say that, but it's not true."

It was totally true. "So, what did your dad want?" I turned to Thistle in an effort to avoid Clove's overt pout.

"He wants us to come out to dinner at the Dragonfly," Thistle replied cautiously.

"Us? Which us?"

"You, me, and Clove," Thistle said. "They all want us to come out."

"Why?" While I had been on a few jaunts to the Dragonfly a few times over the past two months, which had all resulted in tense and uncomfortable interactions between me and my father, a dinner sounded just horrible enough to make me balk at the suggestion.

"He said that he wants to get into a rhythm," Thistle said.

"A rhythm?"

"His word, not mine."

"I don't know," I hedged.

"He says that all three of them want to be able to spend more time with all three of us," Thistle continued. "He thought that, if we were all together, it might be more comfortable."

"For them or us?"

"Both, I think," Thistle nodded.

"I think we should go," Clove announced, widening her eyes as Thistle and I both turned to regard her coldly.

"Of course you do," Thistle scoffed.

"What's that supposed to mean?"

Thistle ignored Clove's whine. "What do you think?" She turned to me.

I shrugged noncommittally. "I don't know."

"We can't just ignore them," Clove said. "They're our fathers."

"Yes, and our mothers are going to look at it as if we're betraying them," Thistle said honestly.

"You don't know that," Clove countered. "They've been acting fine."

"*Acting* being the operative word," I supplied.

"Yeah, they're definitely up to something," Thistle agreed. "I just can't figure out what."

"It's got to be hard on them," I replied. "They raised us alone for a long time, with just each other to rely on. Now, our dads are back and they're feeling threatened by that – and it's not just because they're our fathers but because they're their ex-husbands, too."

"Yeah, it's a whole pile of crap," Thistle agreed.

"What do you want to do?"

"I don't know," Thistle said. "In an ideal world, I'd want to know my dad. There's so much water under the bridge, though. They chose to leave us here with our moms. They chose to move away."

"Because Aunt Tillie scared them," Clove said bitterly.

"You can't blame it all on Aunt Tillie," I reminded Clove. "They let her push them around."

"She's scary, though."

"She's also loyal," Thistle said pragmatically. "She was loyal to our moms because they were her family. She didn't owe our dads any loyalty. They weren't her family."

"What about us, though?" I countered. "Didn't she owe us some loyalty? They are our fathers, after all."

"Yeah, but her loyalty to our moms outweighs her loyalty to us," Thistle said, clearly lost in thought. "I think we should go," she said finally. "They're obviously staying here for the long haul this time. We can't ignore them. We should try to forge some sort of relationship with them."

The truth was, I had enjoyed a better relationship with my father after he had left Hemlock Cove than either Thistle or Clove had. While things were uncomfortable right now, at least I knew him. Thistle and Clove had almost no memories of their fathers from childhood – or their teen years. They deserved more. "Okay," I blew out a sigh. "Let's do it."

"Really?" Clove looked elated.

"Why not? How bad can it be?"

Thistle shook her head in disgust. "You just jinxed us. You know that, right?"

Whoops. "Yeah," I grumbled. "I know it. Let's do it anyway."

"How bad can it be?" Clove asked brightly.

Famous last words.

FOUR

Despite our bravado after agreeing to a family dinner with our fathers, the three of us were too scared to admit to our mothers that we were going to the Dragonfly. Magically, we all found enough to keep us busy in town until fifteen minutes before dinnertime.

We met in front of Hypnotic, deciding to drive separately (but still together) for what was sure to be a tense evening.

I followed Thistle and Clove in my own vehicle, using the ten-minute drive out to the Dragonfly to try and relax. It didn't exactly work. I parked outside the refurbished inn and moved up beside Thistle and Clove, who were both waiting for me on the front porch. I could tell they were equally nervous.

"We could still cancel this," Thistle whispered.

"No," Clove protested.

I was about to agree with Thistle when the front door of the Dragonfly popped open and my Uncle Teddy darted his head out. "Oh, I thought I heard a car."

"We're here," Clove announced enthusiastically.

So much for cancelling. I forced a smile on my face by way of greeting Teddy and then waited for him to usher us inside. Once we had shed our coats in the front lobby, Teddy turned to us nervously.

"Jack and Warren are just finishing some stuff up upstairs," he said. "They should be right down." I could tell he was just as agitated as we were.

"You've done a lot with the place," I said, in an effort to maintain polite conversation. "It's looking good."

The three of us glanced around the lobby appreciatively. While The Overlook was home, the Dragonfly also had a homey feel. The wood was dark and polished and the hardwood floors had been finished and glazed since the last time I had been out here. The walls were still bare – and it looked like a color-wheel sample with paint options was sitting on one of the end tables in the mostly furniture-bare space. Still, though, they'd made impressive headway in just two months.

"Do you want a tour?" Teddy asked.

"Sure," Thistle said.

"Well, this is obviously the lobby," Teddy said. "We're still waiting for a front desk and we're trying to decide on a color to paint it."

"It looks nice," I said honestly.

"Most of the upstairs bedrooms are still a mess," Teddy continued. "There's a lot of work to do up there. The kitchen is mostly finished, though."

We followed Teddy through the swinging doors that led from the dining room into the heart of the house. I was surprised when I saw the work they had done. The last time I had been in this room, the back wall had been burnt from a previous fire and the laundry room on the other side of the wall had been exposed to the elements. All of that had been fixed.

Since the Dragonfly was an older space, a lot of modern improvements had taken place in the kitchen to bring it up to code. All of the appliances were shiny and new and the countertops had all been refinished and replaced – along with the cupboards.

"This is beautiful," Clove breathed. "You guys did a really great job. When we were here in the winter, this place was a hole."

Teddy smiled tightly at Clove. When we'd been here in the winter we'd been spying. That probably wasn't the best memory to revisit.

"Do you guys have a projected opening date?" I asked, hoping to remove the onus of conversation catastrophe from Clove's shoulders.

"No," Teddy admitted. "We were hoping to have everything done by the first of June, but we can't find a construction company that can guarantee that date. We thought we had one for the upstairs rooms, but they suddenly came up with another project – a greenhouse or something – and that's looking less and less likely. It must be one heck of a greenhouse," Teddy offered lamely.

Thistle and I exchanged a dubious look. So the greenhouse wasn't just something to appease Aunt Tillie after all. They were sneaky.

"Have you tried checking construction companies over by Traverse City?" Thistle asked wanly. "I'm sure that, if you pay enough, they'd be willing to drive over here. There's more than one construction company in the area."

"That's a good idea," Teddy said. "Thank you."

"No problem," Thistle said uncomfortably. It's not like she wanted to admit that the reason they were having trouble finding contractors was due to our mothers.

"Oh, good, you're here."

I glanced to the swinging door and saw my father and uncle, Warren, enter the kitchen. They both had big smiles plastered on their faces. They weren't alone, though. There was a woman with them.

My father walked over to me and gave me a warm hug. I reciprocated and then turned to Warren and the guest. "I'm Bay," I extended my hand for the woman to shake.

"I'm Karen," the woman introduced herself, shaking my hand warmly. "It's so nice to meet you. All three of you."

"This is Clove and Thistle," Warren introduced Karen. I took the opportunity to look her up and down as she greeted my cousins. She was an attractive woman, about forty if I had to guess. She had shoulder-length reddish hair and a trim figure. I figured she must be their interior designer, after a few minutes. She had that look about her.

"Are you the interior designer?" Thistle asked the question. I could tell she'd been thinking the exact same thing I had.

"I am," Karen said after a second, turning to Warren with a question in her eyes.

Warren stepped forward nervously. "She's also my fiancée," Warren said, glancing at Clove worriedly.

Oh, well, great!

Clove looked flabbergasted. "You're engaged?"

"I am," Warren said carefully. "I was looking for the right time to tell you."

"And ambushing her at a family dinner sounds like a great way," Thistle said sarcastically, moving over to Clove's side protectively and glaring in Warren's direction.

Uncle Teddy started wringing his hands as he glanced from one surprised face to another. "Let's everyone just stay calm."

I looked over at him. "No one's going to freak out, so you can calm down."

"I just want to make sure that no one ... does anything."

It took me a second to realize what he meant. He was worried one of us was going to somehow hurt Karen magically. Well, now I was pissed off, too.

"What did you think we were going to do?"

Thistle glanced up when she heard the tone of my voice. She realized, right away, what her father had been insinuating. "Really? What did you think we were going to do?"

Uncle Teddy looked lost. "Nothing. I was just ... this is all going wrong."

"Let's all just take a second and relax," my dad said amiably. "This is just a misunderstanding."

"What's a misunderstanding?" Thistle asked. "The way Uncle Warren here ambushed Clove or the way my dad jumped to the conclusion that we would ... freak out?"

"Neither," my dad said in an even tone. "I think emotions are just running a little high. It's a difficult situation."

"Why didn't you tell me sooner?" Clove turned to her dad accusingly.

"I didn't know how to," Warren admitted. "We've only known each other a few months. We just clicked. I didn't feel the need to tell you when we were just dating. I wanted to wait until it was serious. We just got engaged yesterday," he said, glancing at Karen for reassurance. "I was going to wait until dessert to tell you but things just didn't go that way."

Clove looked placated, which caused Thistle to take a step back, both physically and emotionally.

"We all are a little on edge around each other," I said finally. "It's going to take some time to sort this all out. It's not going to happen in a few weeks." Or a few months, I added silently.

Karen looked confused. "I don't understand what the problem is."

"We're just all getting to know each other again," I supplied. "It's a daunting task."

"I understand that," Karen said. "I just don't understand what Ted thought you all were going to do."

Uh-oh.

"Clove is prone to histrionics," Thistle jumped in. "He just didn't want anyone making a scene."

"Hey!" Clove looked like she was about to get histrionic.

"Thistle and I are a little high strung, too," I said helpfully.

Warren shot me a grateful look. "That's an exaggeration. It's just that everyone is ... ."

"On edge?" Karen suggested helpfully.

"Yes," Warren conceded.

"Yes," Thistle agreed.

"I think everyone is just hungry," I said. "We're having dinner, right?"

"Yeah," Teddy said, clearly still nervous. "I ordered Chinese. I hope that's fine with everyone."

"We love Chinese," I said honestly.

"Good," Teddy looked relieved. "We thought about cooking, but we don't have all the supplies out here that we need yet."

"We understand," Clove said and then turned to Karen. "Are you from this area?"

"I grew up in Dowagiac," Karen said, smiling warmly at Clove. "I have a business in Traverse City now. That's where your fathers found me. I jumped at the chance to help decorate an inn over here. Hemlock Cove is famous throughout this region. It was a great opportunity. There are so many great inns here, to be a part of decorating one was an opportunity I couldn't pass up."

"Yeah, there are a lot of great inns around here," I agreed.

"We want this to be the most popular inn in the area," Karen continued. "We want it to be the best decorated inn and the one with the best food."

Thistle and I exchanged wary glances. "I think that title is already taken," Thistle said finally. "I'm sure the Dragonfly will be popular, though."

"Taken?" Karen looked confused. "What title?"

"The best inn," I said briefly, glancing at my father, who was suddenly fixated on something on the wall over my shoulder that didn't exist.

"What do you mean?" Karen looked baffled.

"Our mothers and aunt own an inn," Thistle said guardedly "The Overlook."

"Oh," Karen looked surprised, and then realization dawned on her. "Oh."

"Yeah, oh," Thistle said grimly.

"I didn't realize," Karen said, casting a dark look in Warren's direction. My guess was, he'd been less than truthful with her, too.

"It's fine," I said briefly. "It's not a big deal."

"Of course," Karen said hurriedly, trying to erase her earlier statements. "I'm sure The Overlook is a beautiful inn."

"It is," Thistle said, exchanging a tired look with me. "It's fine, Karen. It's not a big deal. The Overlook's reputation is safe and secure."

"That's right," Teddy said boldly. "It's a great inn."

"You've been there?" Karen turned to him.

"I've eaten there a couple of times. Wonderful food," he turned to me kindly. "With wonderful company."

Oh, good grief. He was so scared of Aunt Tillie he was worried about what I would tell her. "The company is always colorful," I agreed.

Thankfully, for all of us, the uncomfortable conversation was interrupted by the sound of something falling in the laundry room.

"What was that?" Warren asked curiously, moving toward the door.

The minute he had it open, I wasn't surprised to see a familiar figure trying to flee out the back door. Thistle caught sight of her at the same time I did. "Aunt Tillie?"

Aunt Tillie froze when she heard her name and then straightened before she turned around. "What?"

"What are you doing here?"

Warren was regarding Aunt Tillie with cold curiosity and flagrant fear. I couldn't help but wonder if this was the first time he'd seen her since he'd been back in town. This was a great way for them to reconnect, an emotional firestorm.

Aunt Tillie opened her mouth and then shut it. She was trying to think of an acceptable lie. I knew exactly what she was doing here. Spying. "Are you lost?"

Aunt Tillie fixed me with a cold stare. "Are you?"

"No, I know exactly where I am," I replied.

"So do I," Aunt Tillie shot back.

"That doesn't explain what you're doing here," Thistle interjected blandly.

Aunt Tillie pursed her lips. "I was looking for the three of you," she said finally.

"Why?"

"I thought you would be out at the inn for dinner," she said, sliding into her lie comfortably. "When you didn't show up, I got worried."

"Why didn't you call?" Clove asked.

"I didn't think of that," Aunt Tillie said evasively. "You know, when you get old, things like that don't naturally occur to you."

It's funny. Aunt Tillie is only old when it suits her purposes.

My father moved to Aunt Tillie's side warily. "We were about to have dinner. Would you like to join us?"

Aunt Tillie looked surprised at the invitation. Then she looked intrigued at the opportunity for reconnaissance. "That sounds like a great idea, Jack," she said. "Thank you for treating an old woman with such kindness and respect."

Thistle and I rolled our eyes.

"What are we having?"

"We ordered Chinese," Teddy said nervously.

Aunt Tillie turned to him irritably. "I don't like Chinese."

Teddy looked panicked. "We can order something else. What do you want?"

"She'll eat Chinese," Thistle said firmly, grabbing Aunt Tillie's arm and directing her toward the dining room. "Won't you?"

"I don't like Chinese."

"It's meat and vegetables," Thistle said. "You like meat and vegetables."

"In a stew, not a stir fry."

"You'll live," Thistle gritted her teeth. "You weren't supposed to be here and yet you still got invited to dinner. You'll live."

"That's not how you talk to your elders," Aunt Tillie warned her.

"When you invade someone else's personal sanctum, you eat what they're serving," Thistle practically growled, dragging her from the room.

Once they were gone, my dad turned to me. "Well, your Aunt Tillie was always ... entertaining."

I blew out a sigh. "Evil, entertaining, you can look at it both ways."

I glanced over at Karen, who seemed to be amused by the situation more than anything else. "She seems fun," she said brightly.

"Just give it time."

"What?" Karen turned to me, her face blank.

"Nothing," I said finally. "I think you would enjoy sitting next to her at dinner, though. She loves entertaining new people."

Warren looked horrified by the suggestion, but I ignored his fleeting look.

"I would love to."

Once Karen had followed Thistle and Aunt Tillie out of the room, I turned to my dad. "I'm sorry about this."

"That's fine," my dad waved off my apology. "She was just worried about you guys."

Clove and I glanced at each other dubiously. There was no way we were going to tell him what she was really doing here. They'd probably figured it out on their own anyways.

"Yeah, that's Aunt Tillie," I finally agreed. "Always looking out for us."

"When's the food getting here?" Aunt Tillie bellowed from the other room. "Are you trying to starve an old woman?"

This was going to be a really long dinner.

FIVE

"What were you thinking?"

We were standing in front of the guesthouse after what can only be described as a disastrous dinner and Aunt Tillie was doing everything in her power to avoid hard questions.

"I don't think I like your tone," Aunt Tillie placed her hands on her hips and glared at Thistle angrily.

"You don't like my tone?" Thistle looked incredulous. "You were out there spying and you don't like my tone?"

"How come when you were out there spying it was okay?" Aunt Tillie challenged Thistle. "But when I'm out there checking on the wellbeing of my family, it's somehow something terrible?"

"Checking on our wellbeing? You're such a liar," Thistle grumbled. "You probably didn't even know we were out there."

"What were you doing out there?" Aunt Tillie was trying to turn this around. I didn't blame her.

"Having dinner," Thistle shot back. "What were you doing out there?"

"I was at the same meal as the three of you," Aunt Tillie sniffed. "I was having dinner, too."

You really had to give her credit; she wouldn't ever admit her culpability, even when directly caught doing something wrong. "Did you find what you were looking for?" I asked.

"I found the three of you, so I guess so. You're home. You're safe. That's all that really matters."

"Oh, that's rich," Thistle grumbled. "I can't believe you have the audacity to even say that."

"What?" Aunt Tillie was all faux lightness and innocence now.

Thistle walked over to Aunt Tillie, positioning herself so they were face to face. Or, well, more like face to neck. "I want you to know that I know what you were up to."

"Is that supposed to scare me?"

"No," Thistle replied honestly. "It's supposed to make you realize that I'm not stupid."

"Of course you're not stupid," Aunt Tillie scoffed. "You share blood with me. You can't be stupid."

This was the night that would never end, I swear.

"What's going on here?"

I recognized the voice and my heart skipped a beat. I scanned the darkness, smiling when my gaze landed on Landon Michaels. He was standing at the edge of the driveway, all lean muscles and rugged good looks, watching the scene unfold in front of him. He wasn't alone, though. Marcus Wellington, as fair as Landon was dark, was also standing there regarding us nervously.

"Nothing is going on," Aunt Tillie said stiffly. "It's family business."

Landon shook his head and moved to my side, dropping a kiss on my temple but never moving his blue eyes from Aunt Tillie's suddenly bright stare. "Why don't I believe you?"

"Because you're an FBI agent and that makes you naturally suspicious," Aunt Tillie said snottily. "It's an ugly quality."

Landon bit his lower lip. He was constantly waging an inner battle where Aunt Tillie was concerned. On one hand, he found her delightfully batty. On the other, she often got in his way when it came to affairs of the heart – and his job. He had learned – and he had learned quickly – that Aunt Tillie was always up to something and that something always meant bad news for someone.

"Do you need someone to walk you up to the main house?" Landon asked, clearly deciding against a huge fight for the time being.

"Do I look like an invalid to you?"

"No," Landon conceded. "It's dark, though."

"I'm fine. I've been walking myself home since before your parents were born," Aunt Tillie turned and started making her way to the inn. She stopped and turned back, her face set. "No funny business. I'll know if there's funny business going on down here."

Marcus looked appropriately abashed but Landon just looked amused. "Good night."

"Good night," Aunt Tillie huffed.

Once we were all inside the guesthouse, Landon greeted me with a much more enthusiastic kiss. We'd been together a little more than two months, and things still felt new. Whenever he got close, I could almost feel the desire wash over me at the same time a relaxed calmness claimed my heart.

"How was your day?" I asked, once we broke apart.

"Long," Landon admitted.

"I wasn't sure you were going to make it back over here tonight," I said cagily. Landon had an apartment in Traverse City, where his main office was located. He spent weekends in Hemlock Cove – when he wasn't working – but he had taken to making frequent overnight visits during the week when his schedule allowed, as well.

"Yeah?" Landon raised his dark eyebrows and ran a hand through his shoulder-length black hair suggestively. "Maybe I missed you."

"Maybe?"

"Maybe," Landon winked. "Okay, probably." He dropped another kiss on my mouth slyly.

Thistle and Marcus were already snuggled up in a chair by the fire and Clove was pouting on the couch. I glanced at her carefully. "Are you alright?"

"I'm fine," she said dismissively. "Just a really long night."

"You can say that again," Thistle moaned. "What a crappy evening."

"What happened?" Landon asked, sitting in the large chair at the edge of the living room and pulling me into his lap.

I recounted the night's events, including Aunt Tillie's sudden arrival and Uncle Warren's big announcement, and then waited for Landon to respond. When he started laughing, I couldn't help but be surprised. "It's not funny."

"Oh, it's funny," Landon laughed. "Your whole family is batshit crazy."

"She was spying on them," I countered.

"Something all three of you have done," Landon replied pragmatically.

"That was different. We thought Uncle Teddy might be a drug dealer. We had a reason."

"Maybe she has a reason, too," Landon said. "Like protecting you guys."

"She's not protecting us," Thistle retorted. "She's trying to eliminate the competition."

"Is that a bad thing?"

"It's not necessarily a good thing," I said. "She's got some really whacked out ways to get rid of them running through her busy little mind."

"Like what?"

"Magical moles," I said.

Landon raised his eyebrows in surprise. While he had come to accept that we really were magical, he was still uncomfortable with the prospect at times. "Magical moles?"

"She's got all sorts of ideas," Thistle said quickly. "Last week she wanted to create a targeted earthquake to swallow the inn whole – whether anyone was inside of it or not."

"Can she do that?" Landon looked worried.

"Maybe," I shrugged.

"You don't seem too worried about it."

"She won't really do it," I said. I mostly believed that. "She's just venting."

Landon didn't look so sure. "Maybe I should talk to her."

"And say what?"

"Tell her that if anything happens out there, I'll know she's responsible," Landon said.

"And how will you prove that?" Thistle asked pointedly.

"I don't know," Landon shrugged. "I'll figure out something. I've got ways."

"Speaking of," I said suddenly, remembering the little girl I had seen this morning. "There aren't any reports of missing kids in the area, are there?"

Landon furrowed his brow. "No, why?"

"That's right," Thistle teased. "Bay thought she saw a little black girl running around the inn this morning."

"A little black girl?" Landon looked confused.

"I thought I saw her hiding in a clump of trees at the edge of the property," I admitted.

"I haven't heard any missing kid reports," Landon said. "I'll check tomorrow, though."

"Thanks." I snuggled into his lap, resting my head on his broad chest.

"What were you doing down at the edge of the property?" Landon asked suddenly. He was well aware of Aunt Tillie's pot field – and its relative location.

"Our moms are building a greenhouse for Aunt Tillie," Clove said.

"A greenhouse? Isn't that what that little building on the other side of the inn is?"

"I think it was supposed to be, a long time ago," I admitted. "It's falling apart, though. We just use it for storage now."

"So why are they building her a greenhouse?"

"They think it will distract her from plotting against our fathers," Thistle said. "And it's also a way to lure the contractors that are working on the Dragonfly away from that inn so their opening is delayed."

"Really?" Landon looked surprised. "That doesn't sound like something your mothers would do. Your Aunt Tillie? Yes. Your mothers? No."

He obviously didn't know them well enough. "Aunt Tillie would be a lot more overt with her efforts," I explained. "This is subterfuge."

"What's that supposed to mean?" Marcus asked.

"It means it's exactly something they would do," Thistle supplied. "We knew they were up to something. We just didn't know what."

"Well, that doesn't sound fair," Landon said finally. "I thought you said that your fathers opening another inn wouldn't hurt business?"

"It won't," I replied. "It doesn't mean they want them setting up shop here. If it was anyone else, they would be fine with it. Because it's them, though, they're a little out of sorts."

"More out of sorts than we initially realized," Thistle agreed.

Landon glanced from Thistle's drawn face to my worried one. "What aren't you telling me?"

"Nothing," I said hurriedly. "We're just concerned that things are going to get worse."

"They can get worse?" Landon looked doubtful. "That's a terrifying thought if I ever heard one."

"With our family?" Thistle snorted. "Things can always get worse."

That was another terrifying thought.

SIX

"Get up!"

"Who is talking, please?"

I refused to open my eyes. This had to be a nightmare. Given the grunt that the new voice elicited from the lump under the covers next to me, though, I had a feeling this was all too real.

"It's your favorite aunt," the voice said testily.

"That could be anyone," I muttered, pulling my pillow out from under my head and pressing it to my face.

"It better not be." I felt a figure move in close to me and I peeked out from under the pillow and met Marnie's angry brown eyes and pursed lips.

"Why are you in here?"

"We're having a family meeting in the living room," Marnie said, moving away from the bed. "And, last time I checked, you're part of the family."

"How come you only say things like that when it's convenient?"

"Get up!" Marnie screeched again.

I felt Landon's foot nudge me under the covers. "Go out there."

"Whatever they're doing here at ... seven in the morning, can't be good," I replied knowingly.

"You don't know that," Landon said sleepily, his long black hair spread like a fan around his head. "You won't know until you go out there."

"Why do you want me to go out there?" I asked suspiciously.

"So I can get another fifteen minutes of sleep," Landon admitted easily.

I slapped him playfully and then climbed out of bed. I cast a dubious glance at myself in the mirror above the dresser, ran a hand through my sleep-mussed hair, and then walked out into the living room in resignation.

Clove and Thistle, still in their pajamas, were already sitting on the couch – and neither of them looked happy to be there. My mom, Twila and Marnie were standing in the middle of the room waiting for me to join the fray. This couldn't be good.

"We need to change the locks," Thistle grumbled, her short-cropped purple hair standing on end.

"This is our property," my mom reminded her.

"This is still our living space," Thistle shot back. "We should be able to sleep in peace without the three of you sneaking in here during the middle of the night to spy on us."

"Like you're doing anything worth spying on," my mom scoffed.

"I could've been," Thistle shot back. "You scared poor Marcus to death."

"He'll live."

"Actually, that's the opposite of scared to death." Thistle was clearly in a fighting mood.

"So, you're saying that the naked blond in your bed is dead?" My mom was spoiling for a fight, too. "Maybe we should call the police?"

"There's an FBI agent in the other room still sleeping," Marnie offered. "We could just wake him up."

My mom glanced over at me questioningly. "Do you think we should go wake Landon up?"

"What do you guys want?" I groaned, throwing myself into the striped chair adjacent to the couch dramatically.

"We want to talk to you," my mom said carefully. "It's about your Aunt Tillie."

I was suddenly wide-awake, both suspicion and concern warring in my previously sleep-befuddled brain. "What about her?"

"She's not sick is she?" Clove had jumped right to freaking out. "Oh, God, she's dying, isn't she? We're going to lose poor Aunt Tillie. She was such a great aunt. I'm going to miss her so much."

"She's not dying," Thistle challenged. "You can't kill evil. It only grows and grows until it eats us all."

"You're going to feel really bad if Aunt Tillie is dying," Clove sniffed.

"She's not dying," my mom said quickly. "At least not today."

"Tomorrow?" Thistle asked hopefully.

"Your cousin is right," Twila chided. "You're going to feel really bad one day when your Aunt Tillie really does pass to the great beyond and you remember all the horrible things you've said about her."

Thistle looked like she wanted to press the situation, but she wisely decided against it. "Fine. Aunt Tillie is a wonderful human being. She's sunshine and light and blooming flowers. What about her is so important that you had to wake us up at the ass crack of dawn about?"

"As you know," my mom started, like she was giving a formal presentation to a bunch of stockholders. "We have decided to gift your Aunt Tillie with a greenhouse of her own choosing."

"Yeah, we were there when the announcement was made," I replied blandly.

My mom shot me her patented 'shut your mouth' look and continued. "Unfortunately, with spring here, we're just too busy to help her with the minutiae of planning," she said.

Wait a second.

"So," my mom plowed on. "We were thinking that we would put the three of you in charge of the project."

"Over my dead body!" Thistle exploded.

My mom ignored her and turned to me. "Don't you think that's a good idea?"

"Only if I get to use Thistle's dead body as a shield," I replied dryly.

"Why us?" Clove whined.

"We're being punished," Thistle grumbled.

"You're not being punished," Marnie said. "It's just that we're so busy we don't have time to give. We've got a big group of people coming to the inn in several days that we have to get ready for."

"And the grounds still need a lot of work from the winter," Twila added. "They're a mess."

"And we have a lot of spring cleaning that needs to be done," my mom said quickly, averting her gaze from mine. "We're just too busy. We run a business, and that takes a lot of work."

"We run a business, too," Thistle reminded my mom. "Clove and I have a bunch of stuff we have to do ourselves to get ready for the season."

"Yes, but your stuff isn't nearly as monumental as our stuff," my mom replied.

Thistle narrowed her eyes dangerously. "That seems a little presumptuous."

"What about Bay?" Clove interjected hastily. "She only has one edition of the paper to put out a week and she doesn't have any extra work because it's spring."

"Hey!"

"Sorry," Clove shot me an apologetic look – one that said she was sorry for throwing me under the bus, not for what she said.

"We agree that Bay should be the point person," my mom said. "She has more time and a good head for things like this."

"This is crap," I complained. I knew the backhanded compliment was just a way to get me to crumble.

"Bay is a great organizer," Thistle said with faux enthusiasm. "Putting her in charge was a great idea. Good job."

I openly glared at her.

"Bay is in charge," my mom repeated. "You two are helping, though."

"But Bay is in charge," Clove repeated carefully.

"Yes," my mom nodded. "However, if she needs your help, then you two are to help her. No complaints. No whining. Just do it."

"So, what you're really saying, is that Bay is in charge?" Thistle looked like she was about ready to explode again.

"That's exactly what I'm saying," my mom said succinctly and then straightened up. "Now you three get dressed. You get those lumps out of bed in the other rooms. You come up to the inn for breakfast. After that, Bay, the contractor should be here for a discussion and then we can get started."

"You're only doing this to keep Aunt Tillie busy," I said tiredly. "How come it looks like I'm the one that's going to be busy?"

"This is family," Marnie said primly. "We all do our part."

"And what part are you doing?" Thistle challenged her.

"We're paying for it. You want to switch jobs?"

Thistle turned to me and shrugged. "How bad could it be?"

"Why do you keep asking that?" I grumbled. I had a feeling I knew exactly how bad it could be.

FORTY-FIVE MINUTES LATER, the five of us were down at the inn and seated at the dining room table. I had filled Landon in on the big meeting and his response had been a loud bark of laughter and then twenty minutes of urging me to hurry up so we could get breakfast. My mom and aunts had won him over with their cooking – and he wasn't even a little ashamed of it.

"This is delicious," Landon said, enthusiastically dipping his pancakes in a mountain of syrup. "You guys are seriously the best cooks ever."

My mom beamed at Landon. "You're such a sweet boy. I can't think of a sweeter boy. I'm so glad you're dating my daughter."

Thistle leaned across the table and met Landon's sparkling eyes with her decidedly darker ones. "She's offering you candy, Landon. Don't get in the car."

Landon shook his head and ignored Thistle. "So, this greenhouse is going to be a big deal, huh?"

"It's going to be beautiful," Twila agreed. "Aunt Tillie is going to love it."

"Where is Aunt Tillie?" I asked worriedly.

"She already ate her breakfast in the kitchen," my mom said. "She's upstairs gathering her stuff for the contractor. She's very excited."

"What stuff?" I asked around a mouthful of pancake.

"That's attractive," my mom chided me. "Swallow before you speak."

"Yeah, Bay," Thistle said, shoving a huge forkful into her own mouth and then smiling at me widely.

I swallowed exaggeratedly and then turned back to my mom. "What stuff is Aunt Tillie gathering?"

"Her plans," my mom shrugged.

"What plans?"

"I don't know. I haven't seen them."

"Why do I think this greenhouse is going to be bigger than the inn by the time she's done?"

"Because you're a pessimist," my mom said. "The contractor knows the budget. Your Aunt Tillie can't deviate from that."

"Like that will stop her," I muttered.

"You're in charge," my mom reminded me.

"Does Aunt Tillie know that?"

"She does now," my mom replied, glancing down at her plate evasively.

Oh, great. "And how did she take it?"

"She's fine with it."

"Really?"

"Are you calling me a liar?"

"I'm calling you a big fat fibber," I challenged her. "There's no way Aunt Tillie is fine with me being in charge."

"You've got that right," Aunt Tillie charged into the dining room. My mouth dropped open in surprise when I saw her. She was wearing work coveralls and a bright pink hardhat. "I've decided to make the best of the situation, though."

"Where did you get a hardhat?"

"This old thing? I've had it for years," Aunt Tillie said dismissively. "Are you done shoving food in your face? The contractor just pulled up outside."

Even I had to admit that her enthusiasm was kind of cute. "Just a second," I sighed.

Aunt Tillie was halfway back through the kitchen door when she stopped and turned back to me. "If you get all fat and dumpy – and that's what's going to happen if you keep eating like that – then Landon's not going to want to stay with you."

She wasn't so cute anymore. I glanced over at Landon and saw him smiling as he continued to eat. "You think that's funny?"

"I think this whole family is funny."

"Give it time," Thistle grumbled. "By the time this construction project is in full swing, we're going to be downright hilarious."

"I can't wait," Landon replied with an impish grin and a small wink.

I could.

SEVEN

An extremely long two hours later, I found myself happy to be away from Aunt Tillie and at The Whistler. When my mom had said that Aunt Tillie had plans – she wasn't kidding. She had drawn up her own blueprints – which had tickled the contractor to no end. When Aunt Tillie was out of earshot, he said he would take her plans home – work on them – and come up with something that was actually feasible. Since I knew absolutely nothing about construction, I decided to leave him to his work.

Once I got to The Whistler, I was busily working my way through a schedule of spring events that had been provided by area businesses when Edith popped into view.

"He's on the phone again."

I knew whom she was talking about, but I decided to play the game anyway. "Who?"

"Brian."

"Oh, yeah? What's he talking about?"

"He says he's going to expand The Whistler."

"I know," I frowned. "I don't think he realizes that his plan isn't really ... feasible."

"You don't think expanding the paper is a good idea?" Edith seemed surprised. "I would think you would jump at that."

"I don't think that Hemlock Cove can sustain more than a weekly edition," I said. "We're talking about ten thousand people in the immediate area – and most of the locals don't give a fig about the paper. It's mostly for the tourists."

Edith considered what I said. "You're probably right. Still, though, it could be exciting?"

"Not if he overextends himself and runs the paper into bankruptcy," I replied.

"Well, that's definitely true," Edith said. "Why aren't you trying to talk to him?"

"He doesn't want to hear what I have to say," I said. "I figure he'll bring in a professional numbers guy and when that guy tells him it's a bad idea, he'll listen and I won't be the bad guy."

"Well, he's been on the phone since he got here – hours before you, I might add – and he's like a kid on Christmas morning he's so excited."

Come to think of it, Brian hadn't been at breakfast this morning. He was currently the only lodger at The Overlook until the spring guests started making their presence known, so his absence should have jumped out at me. Since he and Landon generally loathed each other on sight – I had just been relieved to have a relatively peaceful meal.

"Well, hopefully he'll come back to Earth soon," I sighed. "I can't deal with anymore grand plans."

"What's that supposed to mean?"

I told Edith – who had known Aunt Tillie when she was still alive – about the big greenhouse construction. When I was done, she shook her ghostly head back and forth. "Your family really coddles her too much."

Let's just say Edith hadn't liked Aunt Tillie in life any more than she did now in death. I had a feeling they had been something like rivals for my late Uncle Calvin's affections – with Aunt Tillie obviously winning – but neither one of them would speak expansively on the subject.

"It's not about coddling," I said. "It's about distracting her. She's obsessed with spying on my dad and uncles at the new inn. We're just trying to keep her out of trouble – or, just keep the trouble localized, I guess."

"How is the new inn?"

"It's nice," I said. "It's still uncomfortable for everyone involved. I'm not sure how to fix the situation."

"Do you want to fix the situation?" Edith asked curiously.

"Sure," I shrugged. "Everyone wants their family to get along. I'm not sure that will ever be totally possible with Aunt Tillie around, though. I don't think there are any grand family picnics in my future."

"Well, she can't live forever," Edith said brightly.

"That's not what Thistle says."

I went back to my work after that, burning a few hours without even realizing it. I looked up when there was a knock on my door. Brian was there – and he wasn't alone. He had another man with him.

"Bay, are you busy?"

"No," I stood up and moved around to the other side of my desk. "What's up?"

"This is Sam Cornell," Brian introduced the stranger.

I plastered a smile on my face and extended my hand to the man. "Nice to meet you."

"Sam is a financial expert from the Detroit area," Brian said excitedly. "He's going to put together a plan for us to expand The Whistler."

Oh, goody. "Well, coming to Hemlock Cove must be a shock for you," I said amiably. "Coming from the big city and all."

"It's definitely different," Sam laughed, running a hand through his brown hair. Up close, he was an attractive man. His face was all high angles and his dark eyes were piercing. I guessed he was in his early thirties, and he was dressed up – at least for Hemlock Cove – in black pants and a blue button down shirt. "I'm not used to all the quiet."

"Yeah," I nodded. "Living in the city, you don't realize all the ambient noise you absorb."

"You lived in the city?"

"I was down in the Detroit area for a few years after college," I replied.

"And you gave it all up for this?" Sam looked dubious.

"My family is here," I replied simply. "Sometimes, you just want to come home."

"Well, this is a beautiful home to come back to," Sam said, although there was a certain edge to his tone that I couldn't quite identify.

"It is."

"I thought we could talk a little," Brian interjected. "Sam wants to get to know you and get your thoughts on the expansion."

"Uh, sure."

I sat back down at my desk and waited until Brian and Sam got situated in the two chairs on the other side of it. I wasn't surprised to see Edith pop back in. She was nosy by nature.

What did surprise me is that I could've sworn that Sam reacted to her arrival by turning in her direction. He focused his eyes back on me, though, after a quick moment and I realized that he must have just been checking out my office. That had to be it, right?

"So, what do you want to know?"

"I was just curious if you thought expanding to three days a week was a good idea?" Sam asked the big question right out of the gate.

"I don't know," I hedged, glancing at Brian. "I think that expanding the paper is going to be a difficult process." I was trying to be diplomatic.

"How so?"

I blew out a sigh. There really was no way around this. "This is a small area, Mr. Cornell."

"Please, call me Sam."

"Sam," I continued. "Even if we had unprecedented growth, which is possible down the road, we still won't get enough people to warrant the expansion of the paper, in my opinion."

"So you don't think that this is a good idea?" Sam was blunt, which I respected.

"That's not what she's saying," Brian interjected hurriedly.

"No offense, Mr. Kelly," Sam turned to him carefully. "But you don't handle the news side of the business and Ms. Winchester does. I really need to hear her thoughts – and I need to hear her honest thoughts. That's going to help me come up with the right plan."

Brian looked properly chastised as Sam turned back to me. "Please continue."

"This is a very small town," I explained. "The people that actually live in town only amount to about seven thousand. Then you have the outlying district. There's about another three thousand in the twenty miles in any direction. I don't see how that translates to a lot of news."

"No," Sam looked serious.

I glanced up at Edith, who was watching the two men closely. I had no idea what she was thinking, and it wasn't like I could ask her.

"There's also not a lot of actual news here," I continued.

"Try none," Edith snorted.

I ignored her. "There's just very little news to fill the editorial hole three times a week. I struggle to fill it – and I mostly use fluff – one day a week."

"There has been an increase in crime in the area," Brian said desperately.

Sam looked interested. "How so?"

"Last fall there were two bodies found in a cornfield. Then, a month later, there was another body found in the middle of town. The man who is believed to have done that murder is still on the loose."

"He's not on the loose," Edith scoffed. "Your Aunt Tillie incinerated him."

Now, this time I'm almost positive, Sam's ears twitched at the sound of Edith's voice. He didn't turn in her direction, though. He kept his gaze focused on Brian.

"And then, just this past winter, there was a crazed drug dealer on the loose," Brian finished up excitedly.

Sam turned to me, his dark eyes unreadable. "That sounds like exciting stuff."

"Yes," I agreed. "It was. However, we can't keep hoping that crime finds a way to Hemlock Cove three times a week. Those were all ... flukes. Sure, there's going to be some level of crime from time to time, but it's been quiet for months."

"Once the tourists get here, though, that will change," Brian said defensively.

"You don't know that," I challenged.

"Ms. Winchester – may I call you Bay – is right," Sam plowed on. "You can't count on anything like that."

I raised my eyebrows in Brian's direction. Of course I was right.

"That doesn't mean that we can't come up with alternative news copy ideas," Sam continued.

"See," Brian said triumphantly.

"What are you working on this week?" Sam asked curiously.

"A list of all the spring activities planned by the area businesses," I replied blandly.

"Really?" Sam looked surprised. "That's it?"

"You have other suggestions?" He was starting to bug me.

"I noticed you have two new businesses in town, why not do stories on those?" Sam didn't seem to notice that I was starting to get aggravated with him.

"We did," I said. "When they first opened. They both got the front page spot on different weeks."

"Oh," Sam looked nonplussed. "How about the new inn that's opening on the edge of town? The Dragonfly, I think it's called."

I narrowed my eyes in his direction. "They're still months away from opening. We'll do a story when it's closer. We already did one announcing the business."

"How do you know that it's not ready to open?" Sam asked.

"I was just out there last night."

"Oh, to see if it was close to opening?"

"No, to have dinner. I got the tour while I was there, though."

"To have dinner? Are you dating the owner or something?" Sam's question was pointed.

Now that was definitely none of his business. "No," I shook my head. I didn't like the keen way Sam was looking at me. He was far too interested in things he had no business being interested in.

"The owner is her father," Brian supplied. I wanted to kick him.

"Oh," Sam said. "I see. Well, that will make getting the interview easy."

Brian laughed jovially, but I was uncomfortable with the way he said it. I had no idea why, but there was something about Sam Cornell that was starting to seriously rub me the wrong way. I decided to refrain from saying anything at this point, though. Maybe they would just go away if I was suddenly rendered mute?

"Well, I'm sure we can think of something," Sam said finally.

"I'm sure," Brian agreed.

"Why don't you let me poke around town and I'll come up with some ideas to help you," Sam offered. "It's got to be hard, mired in this town day in and day out, to come up with fresh ideas. I would love the chance to give you a hand."

I realized, after a second, that both Brian and Sam were watching me – waiting for an answer.

"That sounds great," I said finally, getting to my feet. "Have at it."

"Good," Sam said with a wide smile.

"Is that all? I really need to meet Thistle and Clove for lunch." That was a blatant lie, but I needed to get out of this room before I exploded.

"Oh, sure," Brian said. "Sorry to keep you."

Brian and Sam started to move toward the door. As they did, Edith floated toward me. There was no mistaking anything this time. Sam Cornell tracked Edith's movements as she moved to the center of the room. Edith noticed it, too. She looked to me curiously. I gave an almost imperceptible shake of my head to warn her not to say anything.

With one more final goodbye, Sam and Brian exited into the hallway. I remained standing behind my desk, watching them as they moved down the hallway and finally out of sight.

"He saw me," Edith whispered.

"He did," I agreed.

"Why didn't he say something?"

"I have no idea. I'm going to find out, though. You can count on that."

EIGHT

I needed some air. I had to get out of The Whistler and away from Sam Cornell. Even though Edith was pestering me with an endless stream of questions, I ignored them all, grabbed my coat, and exited the paper through the back door.

I had told Brian I was meeting Thistle and Clove for lunch – which was true – but I had an hour to burn. I decided to burn it with a walk to clear my head.

After strolling by the docks – which were empty – and past the library, which was busy for the middle of the week, I found myself in front of the small cemetery at the south edge of town.

The cemetery was old. The headstones were big and ornate. The foliage – when in bloom – was intricate and rich. As part of the rebranding, the town had refurbished the wrought-iron gate and adorned the surrounding cement fence with several gargoyles in various states of menacing protection. I loved the little cemetery. Yeah, I loved it.

When I was a kid, I would spend hours in the cemetery talking to my "imaginary friends." The townspeople thought I was weird. They had no idea about my gift. As I got older, I learned to hide my ability out of fear. Everything you've heard about small towns is true. They're gossip factories. And, even as I got older, I still heard the whispers. Everyone in town thought the Winchester women were weird but Bay, well, she was weird even by Winchester standards.

Clove and especially Thistle had gotten in many a fight to protect my honor when we were kids. Thistle was still spoiling for a fight whenever someone was mean to me as adults – but I had learned to ignore it, or at least I tried to fool myself that I had.

I let myself into the cemetery through the gate and looked around. It didn't look like the town beautification committee had been by yet – but that wasn't surprising. They had a lot to clean up after the harsh winter and the cemetery wouldn't be a focus for at least another few weeks. The town itself – the streets and gardens – were the main priority right now.

I meandered through the cemetery a few minutes, lost in thought. Could Sam Cornell see ghosts? If he could, why didn't he acknowledge Edith? Maybe he was like me and hid his gift. He probably didn't realize that I could see Edith, too. Or, maybe I was imagining the whole thing. Maybe he had seen a shadow of Edith – which many people were capable of, even if they didn't know it – and he was just reacting to that shadow?

Maybe I was going to drive myself crazy with all of this.

I made my way over to my Uncle Calvin's grave, stopping to clean off some winter debris before moving on to my grandmother's tombstone. We usually came out to clean up the family plots together in the spring. The truth was, I didn't come to the cemetery alone very often anymore – mostly out of fear that someone would see me talking to myself and the whole rumor mill would start up again.

As if on cue, I caught a hint of movement out of the corner of my eye and turned. The cemetery had a few regular visitors – most of whom I remembered from my childhood – but the figure standing to the left of Uncle Calvin's tombstone was one I recognized from earlier this week – not my childhood.

It was the little girl from the inn. The one I had seen hiding amongst the trees.

"Hi." I greeted the child calmly. I didn't want to scare her away again.

The little girl's eyes widened in surprise. She glanced behind her and then back to me. I couldn't figure out what she was doing.

"Are you lost?"

The little girl continued to stare at me. I took a step toward her, causing her to move backwards a step. When I got a closer look, I grimaced. I realized now what I hadn't seen – but should have – from the beginning. She wasn't a lost little girl; she was a dead little girl. She was a ghost.

Crap.

I glanced around the cemetery, hoping no one was in earshot. When I didn't see anyone, I turned back to the little girl. "Are you from around here?"

The little girl still wasn't speaking. She watched me, every move, every gesture, but she didn't open her mouth and try to speak. I figured she was stunned someone had actually been able to see her. I was hopeful, when that wore off, she would try to communicate with me.

I took the chance to look her over. Her skin wasn't just black, it was ebony – which was why I hadn't realized she was a ghost right away. She was dressed in a plain white dress, one that looked like it had seen better days even when it was real. Her black hair was wild – despite the braids – and her dark eyes were bright and inquisitive, although filled with fear.

"Well, you're not a big talker, huh?" I was going for levity.

Still nothing.

"How about we play a game?" I suggested. "Hide and go seek? How about that?"

The little girl continued to stare at me, her hollow dark eyes searching for some answer she wasn't getting.

"I'll hide and you come find me," I suggested, looking toward the larger tombstones a few rows away. "How does that sound?"

When I turned back, she was gone again.

"Or, maybe you can hide," I muttered.

I glanced around the cemetery, giving it a cursory search, but I couldn't find her. I figured, now that she knew I could see her, she would find me again. After about a half an hour of waiting, I gave up and headed toward Hypnotic.

When I entered the store, I found Clove and Thistle bagging herbs at the little craft table in the corner. "I just saw a ghost," I announced.

"Edith?" Thistle didn't bother looking up.

"No, not Edith. It was a little girl. The little girl I saw out at the inn. It turns out she's a ghost."

Clove looked up in surprise. "The little black girl is a ghost?"

"Yep."

"How do you know?"

"I saw her at the cemetery."

"Just because she was at the cemetery, that doesn't mean she's dead," Thistle scoffed.

"She was floating and had no feet."

"Oh," Thistle shrugged. "Then she's a ghost."

"Did she tell you what she wants?" Clove asked.

"No, she didn't speak," I admitted. "I think she's scared."

"I bet," Thistle said. "There's a weird woman talking to ghosts in the cemetery. Who wouldn't be afraid? What were you doing in the cemetery anyway?"

I told them about Sam Cornell – including the fact that I was sure he had seen Edith – and waited for them to respond. I expected histrionics from Clove and a string of curses from Thistle. I got neither.

"That's weird," Thistle said finally. "Does he really think that this area can sustain a paper three times a week?"

"That's what you find surprising? Not the fact that he could see Edith?"

"It was bound to happen eventually," Thistle replied nonchalantly. "You're not the only one with that gift. Odds are that he does what you do and just pretends he doesn't see them when he's around other people."

"It doesn't bother you that he's suddenly in town?"

"Should it?" Thistle looked confused. "He's just a numbers

cruncher from the city. He'll realize soon enough that this isn't going to work and leave. I don't see any reason to freak out."

"I hope so," I grumbled.

"What's he look like?" Clove asked suddenly.

"Why?"

"I don't know. I was just wondering."

"She wants to know if he's hot," Thistle laughed.

"I do not!" Clove looked scandalized, but her cheeks colored all the same.

Thistle was right. Clove was always on the lookout for new men in the area. The pickings in Hemlock Cove were mighty slim – especially in our age group. Unfortunately, the last one she was interested in turned out to be a drug dealer from Canada. The one before him had been Brian Kelly – and no one wanted that – although I had a feeling there was still a little interest there.

"He's attractive," I said finally. "High cheekbones. Brown hair and eyes. Looks like he has a decent body."

"Hmm," Clove looked interested. Great.

"He's also a danger to us," I reminded her. "If he finds out I can see ghosts then he could tell someone."

"Landon knows," Clove pointed out. "That turned out to be fine."

"Yeah, but it could've gone either way," Thistle said sagely.

She had a point.

"Fine," Clove pouted. "I'll stay away from the hot new visitor and remain a lonely spinster while you two are happy with your hot boyfriends."

Thistle smirked, but I felt a small tug of pity for Clove. She had been left to her own devices a lot more lately since Thistle and I were so often engaged with Landon and Marcus.

"I'm sorry," I said. "If you want to meet him, I'm sure that will be fine."

"Pushover," Thistle teased. "So much for protecting the family secret. One look at her crestfallen face and you fold."

Clove shot Thistle a dark look. "I don't have a crestfallen face."

This was getting us nowhere. "So, we're all just ignoring my worry about the new guy in town?"

"Pretty much," Thistle said. "It's not like we can do anything about it."

"I think you're overreacting," Clove said honestly. "It's not like the big family secret is that much of a secret. Everyone in town knows."

"They suspect, they don't know," I countered.

"Oh," Thistle groaned. "Not this argument again. I can't take it. Get over it. You were worried about Landon, and look how well he took it."

"He didn't at first," I bit my lower lip. They were making me feel ridiculous.

"Well, let's just wait to see if this guy actually starts acting all squirrely before we start stalking him," Thistle said. "I think that would be best for everyone. Let's refrain from gathering pitchforks until we have an actual reason to burn him at the stake."

"Fine."

"Fine," Thistle nodded, turning to Clove for affirmation.

Clove, however, was busy staring out the front window of the store. "Who is that?"

I turned to follow her gaze and frowned. "Sam Cornell."

Sam was standing outside of the store and peering in through the window. When he caught sight of me, he waved enthusiastically and moved toward the front door in an obvious effort to enter the store.

"Why is he here?"

"I guess we'll find out," Thistle said. I couldn't help but notice that she didn't look as sure about his harmless nature as before, though.

"It's weird that he just showed up here, right?"

"Really weird," Thistle agreed.

We both watched the front door with trepidation as Sam stepped into our world – bright smile and mysterious intentions completely intact.

NINE

"This is a great store!"

Sam was barely inside Hypnotic before he was dousing both Thistle and Clove with a nonstop litany of compliments.

"The color palette is pleasing and the way you've set up the shelves makes the eyes of your customers dance. They literally dance."

Thistle shot a wary glance in my direction. She may have thought I'd been overreacting before, but anyone that immediately tried to blow sunshine up her ass was suspicious in her book.

"Wow! Look at these great candles. Do you guys have a supplier or do you make them yourselves?"

Sam had made his way over to one of the display shelves -- his back was to the three of us. Thistle was frowning, but Clove was smiling.

I watched as Clove smoothed her long black hair down, checked her teeth quickly in the mirror behind the counter and then made her way over to Sam. "You must be Sam Cornell," she said by way of introduction. "Bay was just telling us all about you."

Sam fixed Clove with a wide and curious smile. "Was she now?" He slid an unreadable look in my direction and then turned back to Clove. "What was she saying?"

"Oh, nothing major," Clove said dismissively. "Just about how Brian hired you to decide if The Whistler should be expanded to three days a week."

"Is that all she was saying?"

Sam obviously sensed that Clove would tell him just about anything. He clearly had a sense for reading people.

Thistle sensed trouble, so she stepped in. "What else would she tell us?"

Sam glanced at Thistle and frowned when he saw the challenging look on her face. "I don't know what you mean."

Thistle narrowed her eyes, challenging Sam to defy her. Anyone that knew her would be running and screaming in fear under her stern countenance, but Sam was either too stupid – or just stupid enough – to ignore it. "What do you think Bay said about it?"

Sam chuckled. "I think she told you that it's a bad idea and Brian and I are crazy for even considering it." He slid another sly look in Clove's direction and winked at her. "Is that what she said?"

Clove giggled. "Kind of," she admitted.

Thistle looked murderous, while I suddenly wished one of Aunt Tillie's magic moles would open a sinkhole directly underneath me.

"That's okay," Sam held up his hands in a placating manner. "I'm used to people doubting my talents."

"I don't see how anyone could," Clove said. "I'm Clove, by the way. And that grumpy one over there is Thistle. We're Bay's cousins."

"Brian filled me in on the family dynamic," Sam said.

"I just bet he did," Thistle replied coldly. "And what did Brian say?"

"He said that your family ran the best inn in the area, with the best food in the entire state," Sam beamed at Thistle. When she refused to alter her expression, though, he fixed his attention back on Clove. "He said that you're all witty and a lot of fun. Oh, and that you're all unbelievably beautiful."

Clove visibly melted under the compliment.

"Really?" Thistle looked doubtful. "What did he say about Aunt Tillie?"

Sam furrowed his brow at Thistle's antagonistic nature. "Is she the elderly aunt that lives with you?"

Thistle nodded mutely.

"He said that the sense of family that you all share is amazing," Sam looked uncomfortable. "That you all keep your aunt living with you, even though she's suffering from dementia, it just proves what wonderful people you all really are."

Thistle laughed hollowly. "Really? That's what he said?"

"Did I say something wrong?" Sam looked to Clove, concern etched all over his handsome face.

"No," Clove said hurriedly. "It's not that. Brian is just sort of scared of our Aunt Tillie."

"Well, sometimes mental illness makes people uncomfortable," Sam replied sagely. "It doesn't mean that person is a bad person, just that he or she might not understand the situation fully."

The only one who didn't understand the situation was Sam Cornell. I couldn't wait until Aunt Tillie found out that Brian was telling people she had dementia. That would go over about as well as his newspaper expansion plan would.

"Our Aunt Tillie doesn't have dementia," I said, finally speaking for the first time since Sam entered Hypnotic. "She's not crazy."

Thistle raised her eyebrows. "Well, she doesn't have dementia," I corrected myself quickly. "She's just set in her ways."

"Then why does Brian think she has dementia?" Sam looked embarrassed. I didn't blame him.

"Because she terrorizes him," I admitted. "She thinks it's fun."

Sam broke into a wide grin. "Well, I can't wait to meet her then."

"Yeah, it will be fun," Thistle agreed. "I'd open with that whole bit about her having dementia and see how it goes from there. She's going to love spending time with you."

Sam frowned at Thistle. "Have I done something to offend you?"

"No," Clove said hurriedly. "She's just grumpy by nature."

"I am not."

"You are, too," Clove argued.

Thistle turned to me angrily. "Bay, am I grumpy by nature?"

I shrugged. Really, what did she want me to say to that? Thankfully, I didn't have to vocally answer Thistle's query because the wind chimes over the door were clanging to announce the arrival of someone new. I glanced at the door and saw Landon standing in the entryway watching everyone curiously. "Hey," I said in surprise. "I didn't know you were in town today."

"I don't have anything going on," Landon said, his eyes never leaving Sam Cornell's face as he made his way over to me. "I thought I would join the three of you for lunch."

"How did you know I would be here?"

Landon finally turned his full attention to me and smiled as he tipped my chin up and gave me a quick kiss of greeting. "Where else would you be?"

"I guess I'm predictable," I said.

"That's not the word I would use," Landon said, slinging an arm over my shoulders and then turning back to Sam. "And who is this?"

"This is Sam Cornell," Clove said, a hint of wistful whimsy in her tone. "He's in town to see about expanding The Whistler to three days of publication a week. Brian Kelly hired him."

Landon's lips tightened. He wasn't exactly a fan of Brian. "Really? That seems like a waste of time."

Sam met Landon's gaze curiously. "Why do you say that?"

"Because Bay has trouble filling one paper a week," Landon replied smoothly. "How is she going to fill three?"

"That's one of the things we're here to discuss," Sam said, refusing to rise to Landon's bait. "I won't know exactly what is feasible until I spend some time in Hemlock Cove and get a feel for the area."

"Well, this is pretty much it," Landon said snidely. "If you've walked down Main Street, you have a feel for the town."

"For someone that obviously spends a lot of time here, you have a low opinion of the area," Sam challenged him.

"I don't have a low opinion of the area," Landon replied easily. "I happen to love the area. I like the people. I like the peace. I'm rather fond of the newspaper," Landon winked at me. "I don't think it needs to be changed."

"What? The paper or the town?" Sam asked curiously.

"Either," Landon said.

I glanced over at Thistle. She was watching the verbal exchange between the two men with as much interest as I was. Clove only appeared interested in looking Sam up and down, paying particular interest to his rear. I had a feeling that she wasn't even aware of the fact that Landon and Sam were trying to slap each other down with words.

"Anyone hungry?" I broke in suddenly. I didn't want this exchange to devolve anymore that it already had.

"I am," Thistle said, catching on to my intentions immediately. "You want Thai?"

"Sounds good," I agreed, tugging on Landon's arm to draw him over to the counter and away from Sam. "What do you want?"

Landon glanced down at the menu Thistle was spreading out and pointed to the Pad Thai. I ordered the same, while Thistle tried to cajole Clove over to the counter to place her order. Clove wasn't about to be deterred, though. "You want to have lunch with us, Sam?" Clove offered.

Sam shifted his gaze between the four of us at the counter and then smiled widely. "That sounds delicious. I'll have whatever ... I'm sorry, I didn't catch your name?" He turned to Landon expectantly.

"Landon Michaels."

"I'll have whatever he's having."

"You don't even know what he pointed to," Thistle grumbled.

"I'm not picky."

Sam sauntered over to a chair and sat down, linking his fingers together and placing them on his stomach as he watched the rest of us uncomfortably order lunch and then join him in the little den area.

"So, how long are you going to be in town?" Clove asked, slipping into the chair next to Sam.

"It depends," Sam replied. "Probably a few weeks. I have to earn my money, after all."

Landon sat on end of the couch farthest away from Sam. I thought it was an unconscious attempt to put distance between the two of them, but then I realized it was actually so Landon would have a better view of Sam in all of his smug glory. I joined Landon on the couch, making room for Thistle to sit on the other side of me. Once everyone was situated, the room lapsed into uncomfortable silence.

Sam was the first to break. "So, tell me about your family?"

"Why?" Thistle asked derisively.

"I don't know, I'm just fascinated, that's all," Sam said. "Especially now that I know your Aunt Tillie really isn't mentally ill."

Landon barked out a laugh. "Who told you that?"

"Brian told him she had dementia," I explained.

"Oh, I can't wait until she hears that," Landon smirked. "That's going to send her on a tear."

"You know her?" Sam looked surprised.

"I've spent some time with her," Landon said cagily. "She's Bay's aunt, after all, and there are a lot of family dinners."

"So, you're Bay's boyfriend?" The question was pointed.

I watched Landon curiously to see how he would answer. We'd never really defined our relationship. We were just suddenly together.

"I am," Landon replied easily.

"For how long?"

"What?"

"How long have you been together?" Sam kept pushing.

"A few months," Landon said. "Is there a reason why you care?"

"Just curious," Sam replied. "I wasn't aware Bay had a boyfriend. Brian never mentioned it."

"Well, Brian is a douche," Landon wrinkled his nose distastefully.

"You don't like him?"

"Let's just say we're not going to set a golf date anytime soon," Landon said.

"And what do you do for a living?"

"I'm with the FBI," Landon said pointedly.

"Really?" Sam looked genuinely surprised.

"Really," Landon nodded his head.

"And how did you and Bay meet?"

"Oh, that's a fun story," Clove clapped. I figured she was trying to draw Sam's attention back to her.

"Why don't you tell it, Clove," Thistle interjected dryly.

Clove didn't need another opening. She launched into the story with gusto. By the time she got to the end, I was relieved she had left any magical bits out – because she had gone into great detail on just about everything else. At least she hadn't completely lost her mind in the shade of Sam Cornell's brown eyes. When she was done, she turned to Sam expectantly. "It's that romantic?"

Landon snorted. "I don't remember thinking it was that romantic when I had a bullet in me."

"Well, it all worked out," Clove sniffed.

Landon cast a sidelong glance at me. "Yeah, it definitely worked out."

"I'm just fascinated with your family," Sam said suddenly. "You have roots to this area that stretch back centuries, right?"

"We do," Clove agreed. "We've been here for years."

"How did you know that?" Thistle was on edge again.

"I've just done some light reading on the area," Sam said smoothly – although I sensed an evasive quality to his words. "I'm a history buff."

"Me, too," Clove smiled.

"Since when?" Thistle challenged her. "Your idea of history is watching *Downton Abbey*."

"That is history," Clove grumbled.

"Not really," Thistle shot back.

"What do you know about the history in this area?" Sam broke in quickly.

"It was mostly uninhabited until the early 1930s," I replied. "There were small homesteads and families, but no real town so to speak."

"That's interesting," Sam mused. "From some of the stuff I read, even though there wasn't an actual town here, there was a real sense of community."

"In what way?"

"Well, the homesteaders in this immediate area were believed to be performing witchcraft," Sam said, suggestively waggling his eyebrows in Clove's direction. "Real black magic and stuff. That's why they thrived when others were failing. Or that's how the legend goes, anyway."

I felt Landon stiffen next to me. "You don't believe in that stuff, do you?"

"Of course not," Sam shook his head. "It's still fascinating to think about. The people in this area did so well that the people in the outlying area thought they were using magic to grow their crops and thrive. That just makes a great story, doesn't it?"

"I guess it depends on who you're asking," Landon replied carefully.

"Well, I think it makes a great story," Sam said, his attention turning to the front door as the delivery boy arrived with our food. "I'd like to buy everyone lunch as a thank you for the warm welcome." He got to his feet and moved toward the delivery boy – Clove right on his heels.

"That is so nice," she cooed as she followed him.

Once he was out of earshot, Landon turned to me. "Well, he's up to something."

"See," I shot my tongue out at Thistle. "I told you."

"I'll never doubt you again," Thistle mumbled. "What do we do?"

"Let me run a background check on him," Landon said. "I'll know more tonight. Just be careful around him."

The sound of Clove giggling filled the air. Landon scowled. "And pull Clove away from him somehow."

"Any suggestions on that?" I asked.

Landon looked dubious. "Can't you put a spell on her or something?"

"What? A He Stinks spell?" Thistle looked agitated.

"I don't know," Landon shrugged. "Like maybe make her think she's smelling garbage whenever he's near her or something. Or maybe make her want to throw up when he looks at her. Or, can't you give her like a month-long period so she's crabby and wants to stay in bed with a heating pad all day until he leaves?"

Thistle and I exchanged surprised glances.

"You're more devious than I initially gave you credit for," Thistle said finally. "I like it. We'll talk to Aunt Tillie and see what she can do."

"We're going to go to Aunt Tillie and ask her to curse Clove?" I bit my lower lip. I didn't like that idea.

"Do we have a lot of other options?"

"No," I shook my head. "Fine. We'll go to Aunt Tillie."

"She's going to hold this over our heads forever," Thistle complained.

"There are worse things," Landon interjected, never moving his eyes from Sam as he and Clove moved back toward us with the bags of food. "Trust me, there are worse things."

TEN

After lunch, I made an excuse so I wouldn't have to go back to The Whistler with Sam. Instead, I returned to the guesthouse and worked from home for the rest of the afternoon. Landon said he was going to check on a few things and then meet me up at the inn for family dinner. Once he'd decided that Sam was up to something, that idea was all he could focus on.

I had been working at home for a few hours when I heard Thistle and Clove return. It's not like I could've missed them, they were squabbling like a couple of cats in a bathtub.

"You don't even know him," Clove complained bitterly. "You just don't like him on general principle."

"That's not true," Thistle shot back. "I don't like him because I've met him and he's shady."

"How is he shady?"

"Were you even listening to the conversation? He practically asked us if we were witches."

"He did not," Clove looked horrified. "He's a history lover. That's not a bad thing. You're just looking for a reason to dislike him."

"He sees ghosts and he's a history lover?" Thistle challenged her.

"We don't know that he sees ghosts, Bay just suspects that," Clove whined. "Bay, back me up here."

I glanced between the two of them. "We don't know that he sees ghosts," I said finally. "Maybe I'm just projecting."

Thistle opened her mouth to argue, but I silenced her with a wave of my hand. "We also don't know that he's not up to something. We're just asking you to think about it and stay away – at least until we know more."

Clove didn't look happy with the suggestion. "Fine," she said. "I just think you guys are suspicious of everyone, though."

"With good reason," Thistle grumbled.

"We'll have to wait and see, won't we?" Clove countered angrily. "And, when I'm right, I'm going to make you both do a little song and dance number telling me I'm right."

"We'll be happy to," Thistle said boldly. I could tell she didn't believe, even for a second, that she would ever have to make good on that promise.

TWO HOURS LATER, the three of us let ourselves into the back door of the inn – the one that led into the family living quarters – and we were still fighting. For a change, none of us were fighting aloud, though. Instead, we were fighting with our silence. That was something that wasn't lost on Aunt Tillie – who was parked in front of the television watching *Jeopardy*.

"What are you three fighting about?"

"Who says we're fighting?" Thistle asked in surprise.

"Usually you're all gossiping like a bunch of clucking hens when you come in here," Aunt Tillie replied, her eyes never moving from the television. "I usually have to tell you to quiet down so I can watch my show. Not today, though."

"That doesn't mean we're fighting," I said wearily. "Maybe we're just tired."

"That never stopped you before," Aunt Tillie pointed out. "Sometimes you even fight in your sleep."

She had a point. Not about the fighting in our sleep thing – that was a gross exaggeration – but about the other stuff.

"I met a new man today and Bay and Thistle don't like him," Clove announced boldly, shooting daggers in our direction as she did.

"We didn't say we don't like him," I protested weakly.

"We just said we're suspicious of him," Thistle added.

"Why don't you like him?" Aunt Tillie was suddenly interested.

"He's just a little off," I replied.

"I am not going to sit here and listen to the two of you malign his character," Clove sniffed angrily. "You don't need me for that." With those words, she flounced through the door that led to the kitchen, leaving Thistle and me to tell Aunt Tillie our problems.

Not surprisingly, Thistle was the one to launch the verbal offensive. When she was done, Aunt Tillie was flabbergasted. "Brian told him I have dementia?"

"That's what you're worried about?" Thistle asked. "Not that this guy just might see ghosts and that he's questioning us about the witchy history of this area? The real witchy history?"

"I don't have dementia," Aunt Tillie replied angrily. "That Brian Kelly is going to wish I did have dementia by the time I'm done with him."

I thought about trying to talk her out of whatever revenge was boiling in her brain at the moment, but I couldn't muster the energy. Besides, I wasn't thrilled with Brian myself, at this point. Maybe cursing him would make him see reason – and send Sam Cornell out of town. Hey, a girl can hope.

We left Aunt Tillie to plot her revenge. I realized we hadn't asked her for a curse to thwart Clove's romantic aspirations toward Sam. I was hoping it wouldn't ultimately be necessary, I guess. Plus, teaming up with Aunt Tillie against Clove seemed like a step backwards. We had always been a three-pronged united front against her. Breaking up into a smaller faction and working with her just seemed wrong.

Once I stepped in the kitchen, I heard Clove complaining to her mother that Thistle and I were being mean to her.

"They treat me like I'm a child. I'm not even the youngest one. Thistle is the youngest one. She should be the one treated like a child."

Marnie didn't look impressed with Clove's complaints. "Can't you three just get along? You don't see your aunts and me squabbling like this."

Thistle rolled her eyes. "Not today. Give it time, though."

"Thanks for your input, fresh mouth," my mom smacked Thistle on the back of the head lightly as she moved behind her. "You guys just seem to enjoy fighting with one another."

"I wonder where we learned that from," I teased my mother.

"We don't fight," my mother disagreed.

"Really? Maybe I should invite Chief Terry for dinner so you guys can play musical chairs to see who gets to sit next to him?"

"That's not a fight," Twila chimed in from her place by the sink.

"Of course it's not," my mom agreed. "I've already won."

"You have not, Winnie," Marnie said snidely. "As long as I have these," she grabbed her heaving – and yes, impressive – bosom with both hands. "You're not even in the running."

My mom glanced down at her much smaller chest ruefully. "Terry is a man of substance," she said finally. "He's not mesmerized by your boobs like everyone else in town."

"I guess that's why you spent an entire year doing exercises to grow yours when we were kids," Marnie replied snottily. "I must, I must, I must increase my bust," she sang.

Twila laughed heartily. "That was so absurd."

"You did it for two years," Marnie reminded her.

Since Twila had the smallest amount of cleavage to boast about, I was starting to think that chant had an adverse effect.

"What's for dinner?" I decided to change the subject.

"Lasagna," my mom said. "We wanted something simple tonight. When that travel group gets here, we're going to have to go fancy. We wanted an easy night."

That was fine with me. I loved lasagna.

Everyone grabbed dishes of food, including salad, two sides of vegetables and fresh-baked bread – hey, this was simple for our family

– and headed into the kitchen. Marnie paused by my mom as she cracked the door open. "I must, I must, I must increase my bust," she chanted again, just one further dig to infuriate my mother, before practically skipping into the dining room.

She didn't respond, but I had a feeling Marnie was going to have some cold, hard comeuppance coming her way once we had all cleared out tonight.

When I made my way into the dining room, I saw Landon first. I shot him a welcoming smile, but the one he sent me back wasn't as warm. I frowned until I got a better look at the two other people sitting at the table with him. One was Brian Kelly – and Aunt Tillie had zeroed in on him the minute she saw him. The other was Sam Cornell. No way.

"What are you doing here?" I blurted out.

"Eating dinner?" Sam raised his eyebrows in surprise. "Is that not allowed? I thought meals were for the guests."

"You're staying here?"

"Isn't that a fun coincidence?" Landon grumbled from a few chairs away.

Not really.

"You know Sam?" My mom asked curiously, sliding the lasagna pan onto two trivets in the center of the table.

"He's working with Brian and me at The Whistler," I said carefully, moving to the other side of the table and taking the open seat next to Landon. We traded tight smiles.

"Oh, really," my mom didn't catch on to the sudden tension. "Doing what?"

"We're hoping to expand the distribution of The Whistler and print three days a week," Brian responded excitedly. "Sam is up from Detroit to run some numbers and see if it's a good way to go or not."

"Sounds like a stupid idea to me," Aunt Tillie huffed, climbing on to her chair at the head of the table – which was conveniently located between Landon and my mother.

Brian frowned. "You don't think Hemlock Cove deserves a real paper?"

"It already has a real paper," Aunt Tillie fixed her angry eyes on him. "Unless I'm mistaken, that's where Bay goes to work every day. Of course, I might be mistaken, what with my dementia and all."

Sam, who had been watching Aunt Tillie with a mixture of awe and amusement, suddenly shifted his attention to the plate in front of him.

"Dementia?" Marnie asked, confusion written on her face. "Who said you have dementia?"

"I've been saying it for years," Thistle offered cheerfully. Everyone ignored her, though.

"Brian told his little friend, Sam, that I had dementia and that you guys were taking care of me out of the goodness of your hearts – yeah, right -- so you didn't have to put me in a home," Aunt Tillie explained snottily.

"Oh, that's not true," Twila said dismissively. "Brian would never say anything like that. He loves our food. Why would he? Where do you even come up with this stuff, I swear?"

"Bay and Thistle told me."

"Thanks," Thistle chimed in from her spot in the middle of the table.

"Well, you did," Aunt Tillie grumbled.

"Sam told us," I exclaimed worriedly. "It's not like we made it up."

"I didn't tell you to tell her, though," Sam said through gritted teeth.

"We're family, we don't have any secrets," Thistle said with faux earnestness.

"Really?" My mom raised her eyebrows doubtfully. "Did you ever tell your Aunt Tillie that you once wore one of her dresses to a high school costume contest?"

"What's so bad about that?" Aunt Tillie asked suspiciously.

"She was dressed up as a clown," my mom replied. "The one from *It*, if I remember right."

Landon was shaking with silent laughter next to me. He couldn't help himself.

"A clown?" Aunt Tillie glared at Thistle. "If you were dressing as a clown, why wouldn't you raid your mother's closet?"

"Hey," Twila looked hurt. "I don't dress like a clown."

I glanced at her flame red hair – more Ronald McDonald than anything else – and grimaced. That was actually a good question.

"Mom dresses with a bohemian flair," Thistle countered. "You wear those ugly big prints and those other dresses with the big color blocks."

"They're not ugly," Aunt Tillie argued. "They're age appropriate."

"If you're dressing age appropriate these days, maybe you should start wearing underwear," my mom suggested.

Brian and Sam looked like they wanted to be anywhere but at this particular dinner table. There was no gracious way for them to exit, though, so they started shoveling food into their mouths instead.

"This is delicious," Sam finally said, trying to ease the tension.

No one acknowledged the compliment.

"I don't like underwear," Aunt Tillie said. "It's too constricting. My parts like to breathe."

"I didn't need to know that," Landon sighed.

"I wear a bra," Aunt Tillie continued. "Isn't that enough?"

"If you didn't wear a bra, one of those things could break free and kill someone," Marnie said. Since Marnie had the same build as Aunt Tillie, she would know. Plus, since my mother and aunts had a propensity for naked dancing under the moon in the summer – I'd seen the horrifying truth of that statement myself from time to time.

"I think we're getting off point," I started.

"The point is, I don't have dementia," Aunt Tillie announced, jumping to her feet. "And anyone that says that, well, I think they're going to wish they never had." Her eyes landed on Brian, who gulped hard when they made eye contact.

Aunt Tillie turned on her heel and stalked out of the room. Once she was gone, my mom blew out a frustrated sigh. "And why did you tell her?"

I couldn't really admit that the dementia portion of the conversation had only come up because of a larger conversation regarding

Sam Cornell's possibly nefarious intentions – especially since Sam was sitting at the other end of the table. "We were just making small talk," I said finally.

"And that's your idea of small talk?" My mother looked incensed.

"You were the one that brought up her lack of underwear," I reminded her.

"That was a public service endeavor," my mom said primly.

"Whatever." I glanced over at Landon, who could've swallowed an entire plate if he was smiling any wider. "You still think family dinners are fun?"

"Absolutely."

ELEVEN

"Why are you up so early?"

I glanced back at Landon, who I had thought was still asleep in my bed when I crawled out – an hour earlier than I had initially wanted – in an effort not to wake him.

"I have to go down to the inn this morning," I said. "I was trying not to wake you."

"Why do you have to go down to the inn?"

"They're breaking ground on the greenhouse today, I have to be there to look over the new plans."

"They're breaking ground before the plans are complete? That sounds like a bad idea," Landon grumbled sleepily. "Why don't you come back over here and I'll make your morning a little brighter – no construction required."

That sounded like a heavenly idea – one I actually considered, for about two seconds, until I realized that the one sure route to a bad morning would be for my mom to come looking for me. "I have to go down there," I replied ruefully. "You don't want my mom to come and interrupt us, do you?"

Landon considered the question. "I can be quick."

"How romantic."

Landon sighed. "Do you want me to come down with you?"

"No," I shook my head. "Just come down to the inn after you're ready. I'm sure my mom and aunts will ply you with food before you start your day."

Landon's face brightened. "Sounds good."

I showered quickly, slipping into simple jeans and a T-shirt, and then headed off to the inn. When I got down to the spot where the construction crew had gathered, I wasn't surprised to see Aunt Tillie already there.

"Why can't we just go with my plans?" Aunt Tillie was facing off with a man in a hard hat – she was wearing her own, I might add – and she had her hands on her hips, when she wasn't aggressively gesturing.

"Your plans were good," the contractor said carefully. "I think these are just a little bit better. Just look at them."

"I don't want to look at them," Aunt Tillie said stubbornly. "This is my greenhouse. I want it done my way."

"Yes, ma'am, I understand that," the contractor said. "I just don't think turrets on a greenhouse are going to work."

Turrets? Good grief. I picked up my pace and was between Aunt Tillie and the contractor within seconds. "Hi, I'm Bay Winchester," I said hurriedly. "I'm here to make the hard decisions with you."

The contractor looked relieved. "I'm Dirk Langstrom," he replied. "I'm with Langstrom and Sons contracting out of Traverse City. Your family hired us for this project."

"There was a different guy here the other day," I started.

"That would be my brother," Dirk said. "He brought your aunt's plans back and we worked on them to polish them up. We think you're really going to like them. Your aunt won't even look at them, though."

No big surprise there. "Why don't you let me see them?"

Dirk spread the plans out on the hood of a nearby truck. Unfortunately, I had no idea what I was looking at. Dirk seemed to guess that, so he started pointing out specific things in the design. Once he did, the plan started to take shape in my mind. "It looks really nice," I said.

"We even made room for the dark room over here," he pointed. "Although I don't know why you need a dark room in a greenhouse. Is someone a photographer?"

"It's not that kind of dark room," I admitted. "That's where Aunt Tillie makes her wine. She needs a dry and dark place to do it."

"She makes wine?" Dirk looked like he wanted to laugh.

"I make the best wine in three states," Aunt Tillie announced as she moved over to look at the plans. "In the world really."

Dirk took the opportunity to launch into his spiel again and, this time, Aunt Tillie paid attention. When he was done, she met his gaze evenly. "That's exactly what I had in my plans."

Dirk opened his mouth to argue with her, but I shook my head to stop him. It just wasn't worth it. Dirk caught on quickly and smiled at Aunt Tillie. "Then we're on the same page, then?"

"Of course," Aunt Tillie said. "Why would you think we weren't?"

I left Aunt Tillie with Dirk and moved around to watch the other workers. I wasn't sure what they were doing, but it looked like they were driving wooden stakes into the ground and winding colorful tape around the stakes to outline the edges of the greenhouse so they would have a visual reference.

I caught a hint of movement out of the corner of my eye and turned swiftly. The prickling sensation between my shoulder blades was warning me, but I looked anyway. There she was. The little girl from the cemetery. She was back by the group of trees again – where I had seen her the first time – and she was watching me.

I glanced around at the construction workers, but I wasn't even a blip on their radar. I carefully made my way over to the girl, making sure that it looked like I was just wandering around the grounds and not heading to a specific point, and then I moved right past her until I was on the other side of the trees and hidden from the view of the workers.

"You're back."

The little girl followed me until we were both out of sight. She was still silent, but she didn't seem quite as jumpy – *can ghosts seem jumpy?* – as before.

"I wondered where you had gone to," I tried again.

"I'm always here."

I jumped a little when the girl finally spoke. Her voice was small, timid, like she hadn't had occasion to use it in a long time.

"You're always at the inn?"

"I'm always here," the girl repeated.

"What are you doing here?"

"I live here."

"Here? Here in Hemlock Cove?"

"Why can you see me? No one else can."

I considered how to answer the question. I didn't want to scare her away again. I didn't think telling her I was a witch would be the best way to earn her trust. I decided to go with a watered-down version of the truth. "I have a special ability that lets me see people, people like you, who other people can't see."

"You mean ghosts?" The girl asked bluntly.

Well, at least she knew she was dead. That was one conversation I hadn't been looking forward to having with her. "Yes, ghosts."

"And you can really see me?"

"I can really see you," I smiled as I carefully lowered myself to the ground a few feet from her. I didn't want to make any sudden moves that might scare her off again.

"And you live here?"

"I live in the smaller house," I explained. "The one right through those trees over there. If you ever need to see me, that's where I'll be."

"But not in the big house?"

"That's where my family lives," I replied. "You can go in there, too, if you want."

"They won't be mad?"

"No. In fact, my Aunt Tillie will be able to see you, too," I said. "She'd probably love to talk to you." Once I told her not to be mean, that is.

"Okay," the little girl said finally. "Maybe I will."

"What's your name?" I asked.

"Erika."

"What's your last name?"

The little girl furrowed her brow. "I don't know."

"Okay, that's fine," I said hurriedly. I was hoping that she would remember the longer we talked. "How did you get here, Erika?"

"I've been here for a long time."

"How long?"

The girl shrugged. "It feels like forever."

"I bet. Did you ... did you die around here?"

"I don't know," the girl said. "I wasn't here all the time."

"What do you mean?"

"I was out by the water for a long time. There was a big building by it. I got bored there, though, so I decided to come here. Only a few people ever went out to the building by the water. I didn't like it, especially at night."

"Well, that was a good idea," I said warmly.

"I was tired of being alone."

My heart clenched a little in my chest. "Well, you're not alone now."

"No," Erika agreed.

"Erika, do you know how you died?"

Erika thought about it for a second. "No."

"What do you remember, from being alive, I mean?" I prodded.

"I remember that there were a lot of other kids," Erika said. "We were all on a boat together."

"A boat?"

"A big boat," Erika said. "I had never been on a boat before, so I thought it was really fun at first. Then, we were on the boat so long, that I started to get tired of it."

I let the little girl tell her story at her own pace.

"I remember getting sick," Erika said, brow furrowed. "I kept crying for someone to help me, but no one came. I was so hot and I kept throwing up and then I just went to sleep."

"Were there only kids there? No adults?"

"There were big people, but they didn't stay in the basement with us."

"The basement?"

"Below the top of the boat."

"Okay, I got you," I said. "Where were the big people?"

"They stayed upstairs mostly," Erika said. "They would come down to feed us, but they never really talked to us."

Something about this story was really starting to bug me – and it wasn't just because I was talking to a ghost. "How many kids were with you?"

"I don't know how to count," Erika said. "There were loads of us, though."

I swallowed hard. "And why didn't the big people help you when you got sick?"

"I don't know," Erika shrugged. "They weren't nice people. They told us we were going to new homes and to stop crying. All I wanted was to get off the boat. I'm not sure I ever did, though."

"And then what happened?"

Erika's face went blank. "I don't know," she said finally. "I just woke up dead."

I hadn't had breakfast yet, but if I had, I would have lost it. A bunch of kids in the bottom of a boat couldn't add up to anything good. "Erika, I need you to think really hard," I said. "Did you hear any of the names of the big people?"

"No," Erika shook her head. "I told you. We didn't really see them very much. They just kept coming down to tell us to be quiet and if we didn't keep quiet, we would be hurt."

If I could've pulled the little girl to me and offered her any sense of solace, I would have. The only think I could offer her now, though, were words. "We're going to figure this out," I said. "We're going to figure this out and get you ... to a happier place."

"Home?"

"Where is home?"

"I don't know," Erika said. "It's not here, though. Where I come from, there are different kinds of trees and it's warmer. It's warmer all the time. We don't get the white stuff."

The white stuff? "You mean snow?"

"Is that what it's called? Then, no, we don't get any snow."

"Well, I don't know if I can get you home," I said finally. "I can try to get you some place better, though."

"How?" Erika looked genuinely curious.

"I don't know yet," I forced a smile for her benefit. "I'll figure it out, though. That I promise you."

TWELVE

I spent another hour with Erika. It was only after leaving her – with a promise to come back as soon as I could – that I realized I'd missed breakfast at the inn. I thought about calling Landon, he was probably wondering why I didn't show up, but there was something else I wanted to do first.

Instead of heading toward The Whistler, though, I went to Hypnotic. I wanted to tell Thistle and Clove what I had learned. When I got there, though, I found that I wasn't the only visitor at the shop.

"Hi, Chief Terry," I greeted him warmly.

"Bay, what are you doing here?" Chief Terry asked in surprise. "Aren't you supposed to be at work?"

"I'll get there eventually," I said, finally noticing that Chief Terry wasn't alone. He had another man with him.

"This is Dean Browning," Chief Terry said, suddenly realizing he hadn't introduced us. "He's the new dock operator."

"We have a dock operator?" Hemlock Cove didn't exactly have a busy port. In fact, the only boats that usually came in – or launched – were small fishing boats owned by local denizens. In the summer, tourists rented boats for quick excursions, but it's not like any commercial boats ever made a stop in Hemlock Cove. If they ever had in the past, they certainly weren't doing so now.

"Well, he's not just going to be working on the dock," Chief Terry conceded. "He's also going to be working on restoring the Dandridge. The dock job is more of a part-time thing."

I blanked out for a second. I couldn't figure out what he was talking about.

"The Dandridge," Thistle furrowed her brow. "That old lighthouse?"

"Yeah," Chief Terry nodded. "The building has been falling apart for ages."

An old building by the lake. Erika's words chimed in my head, chilling me from within. "What's the deal with the Dandridge?"

"What do you mean?" Chief Terry looked confused. He was used to the scattered chaos that often masqueraded as my brain, but this time, even he couldn't keep up.

"I mean, what's the history behind it?"

"I don't know," Chief Terry said. "Do I look like a history professor? I would have to look it up."

I turned to Dean expectantly. "Do you know the history of it?"

Dean looked surprised by the question, but happy to converse. "It was initially built in 1847 and was in general use up until the 1960s."

"Why did they build it here?"

"There are some dangerous rock formations out a little further in the bay," Dean explained. "I wasn't on the original planning committee but, back then, lighthouses were usually built as a safety precaution."

"So, why would people just let it fall by the wayside?"

"Older lighthouses are a lot of money to keep up," Dean shrugged. "They probably thought it was cheaper to let it go. And with modern updates, lighthouses can be tricky to refurbish."

"But you want to refurbish it? Why?"

"I like lighthouses," Dean shrugged. "I like the history behind them. Plus, given this town's little niche, I thought I could turn it into a tourist destination. You know, a haunted lighthouse"

I ignored the haunted comment. What could I tell him? It was really haunted? That probably wasn't the best tactic. "So, you bought it?"

"Not exactly," Dean hedged. "It's more like I leased it."

"You can lease a lighthouse?" Clove looked surprised.

"The state owns the land," Dean explained. "I have come to an agreement with them. If I refurbish the lighthouse, I can have operating rights over it for ten years. After that time, they're willing to work out an extended deal. We'll see where it goes. There's a lot of work to be done out there. The building itself is sound, but it needs some cosmetic work and the grounds are a mess."

"It sounds like a great project," I said honestly, an idea forming. "How would you feel about me doing a story on it for the paper?"

"Really?" Dean looked tickled, running a hand through his brown hair excitedly. "That would be great."

"I would want to go out there, you know, get a feel for the property," I said.

"Sure, we can set something up for next week, if that works for you?" Dean said.

"Sounds great," I agreed, taking his business card from him and shoving it in my back pocket. "I'll call you."

I made small talk with Chief Terry and Dean for a few more minutes and then waited until they were safely on the other side of the door before I spoke again.

"The ghost is back."

"The little black girl?" Clove asked curiously.

"Her name is Erika."

"She talked to you?" Thistle said. "Well, that's a step in the right direction."

"Not after what I tell you," I said grimly. When I was finished with the story, Clove looked ashen and Thistle looked enraged.

"I want to hit somebody," Thistle said. "A bunch of kids in a boat? Not allowed out? You know what that means, right?"

"It's not a three-hour tour, that's for sure," I agreed.

"That's why you want to go out to the Dandridge," Clove said suddenly. "The little girl said she was by a building that was falling down, by the water."

"Exactly," I agreed.

"You're not going to be able to talk to Erika out by the lighthouse with Dean there," Thistle pointed out.

"No," I agreed.

"So we're going, all three of us," Thistle said, she looked excited at the prospect. "We'll go out there and explore."

"You doing anything this afternoon?"

"Yeah," Thistle said. "We're going to check out a haunted lighthouse."

"I don't know," Clove hedged. "It could be all gross out there. Maybe there's a body. I might just stay here."

"Fine," Thistle said irritably. "But when Bay and I solve a child trafficking ring, you're going to be the one that stayed at the store – and we're not letting you have any of the glory."

I frowned. I didn't like the way she put it, but it was an effective argument.

"Fine," Clove blew out a sigh. "And, just FYI, for all we know, that little girl died decades ago. We don't know that she died recently. She told Bay she had been here a long time. There might not be any children to save anymore. Why do I think this is going to lead us to nothing but trouble?"

"Because you're a pessimist?" I suggested.

"No, because this has trouble written all over it," Clove countered. "I can feel it."

"Are you getting a vision?" I asked hopefully. "Maybe one that says this is all going to turn out fine?"

"I don't get visions, remember?"

"Well, I thought maybe you suddenly could."

"No, you hoped," Thistle replied. "We're going out to a lighthouse in the middle of the day. There's nothing dangerous about that."

"Maybe Bay should call Landon, just to tell him where we'll be," Clove suggested. "Just in case we go missing or something."

"That won't make Landon happy," Thistle pointed out.

She had a point. "Let's just keep it between the three of us for now," I said finally. "We don't even know if the lighthouse has anything to do with this. There could be lots of abandoned buildings by the water."

"It's seems like too much of a coincidence," Thistle said. "Like the powers are driving us there. I mean, what are the odds that we would find out the lighthouse is being refurbished right after your little ghost decides to start talking?"

I didn't say it out loud, but I agreed with her.

"Let's take it one step at a time," I said. "First, we go to the lighthouse. After that? We'll figure it out."

"To the lighthouse it is," Thistle agreed.

"I just know this is a bad idea," Clove grumbled. "At least we're not sneaking around in the snow this time."

"See, you *can* see the bright side," Thistle said.

THIRTEEN

"You didn't tell me we would have to hike."

Clove hadn't stopped whining since we left Hypnotic and the sound of her voice was starting to mentally chafe.

"This isn't hiking," Thistle grumbled. "This is walking from the car to the lighthouse. It's like a half a mile."

"That's hiking," Clove complained.

"Hiking is climbing up a mountain or traversing the wild terrain of Alaska," Thistle countered. "A half a mile is not hiking."

"Traversing the wild terrain?" I raised an eyebrow as I glanced at her.

"I was watching *Finding Bigfoot* the other night," Thistle replied absently. "They're a little dramatic."

"That's something we should do," I said. "Look for Bigfoot."

"We would be awesome at that," Thistle agreed.

"Camping in the great outdoors, following tracks, it sounds like fun," I laughed. "We would need to bring Aunt Tillie, though. Even Bigfoot would be scared of her."

"We would definitely bring Aunt Tillie," Thistle agreed. "If she didn't scare off Bigfoot, at least she'd be slow enough to distract him while we got away."

"Bigfoot isn't real," Clove interjected knowingly.

"That's what people say about witches," Thistle replied.

"Bay, you don't think Bigfoot is real, do you?" Clove was now scanning the tree line worriedly, despite her oral bravado.

"I don't know," I replied truthfully. "Most of those old legends have some basis in fact. Bigfoot was sighted in this area for more than a century, if you believe the old stories."

"And that song," Thistle added. "What was it called? The *Legend of the Dogman?*"

"I remember that," Clove said suddenly. "It was a big deal when we were kids."

"It was just a radio gimmick," Thistle scoffed. "Every seven years or so they bring it back around. Every group of kids thinks they're the first one to hear it."

"But it's not true," Clove said, her eyes skittering warily around the dense foliage that surrounded us. "Right? It's not true?"

I glanced over at Thistle, who wasn't even trying to hide the evil expression gracing her face. I had a feeling a plan was forming and the next solstice celebration was going to be a full on Bigfoot extravaganza – just to torture Clove.

"I think you're safe," I replied. "If Bigfoot is real, he's probably more scared of us than we are of him."

"I doubt that," Clove said nervously.

"Don't worry, we'll protect you," Thistle teased.

"I won't," I said. "If I see Bigfoot, I'm running like hell. I'm not worrying about you two."

Clove seemed to consider the statement. "Okay. If Bigfoot attacks, then it's every witch for herself."

"This is easily the silliest conversation we've ever had," Thistle muttered, rounding a bend in the trail we were following and pulling up short. "There it is."

The three of us picked our way through the overgrown trail and found ourselves in front of the Dandridge. It had probably been beautiful when it was built – even majestic. Tall white walls, a red cap on the spire, and octagonal windows at various points across the structure.

Time had marred all of that, though. The white paint was peeling. The red cap was now a muddy brown. And most of the windows were either shrouded in fallen ivy or missing altogether.

"I bet it was pretty, back in the day," Thistle said finally.

"Yeah," I agreed. I glanced around the area for a second. "How are they going to use this as a tourist destination, though? Do you think people are going to be willing to hike up here to see it?"

"I told you it was a hike," Clove said triumphantly.

Thistle ignored her. "I think there's a road over there," Thistle pointed through a line of trees. "Isn't that Wetzel Road?"

I wasn't sure, but I followed Thistle to the area she was pointing. Once we moved through the trees, I realized she was right. Wetzel Road was two lanes of rural highway that cut a swath through the forest and ended at a small Lake Michigan inlet two miles away. The road could use some repairs – especially after this snowy winter – but it wasn't in terrible disarray.

"All they have to do is rip this line of trees out," Thistle said thoughtfully. "There's enough room here to build a small parking lot."

I nodded, letting my eyes wander through the landscape. "This actually could be pretty cool," I said finally. "There could be a picnic area over there," I pointed. "And the building is big enough for the haunted lighthouse tour and a gift shop."

"I'm surprised someone hasn't thought of this before," Thistle mused.

"Well, someone has thought of it now," I said. "The truth is, this could be really good for the town. It's another draw that sets us apart from the rest of the touristy towns in the area. Plus, it's something that could draw people back to the area – people that haven't seen the lighthouse yet."

"Then what's wrong?" Thistle asked knowingly.

"Nothing is wrong," I countered. "I just feel ... uneasy out here. I can't really explain it."

"Maybe it's Bigfoot," Thistle suggested.

"Or maybe it's a ghost," Clove said ominously.

"Erika?" I glanced around again, hoping the little girl with the sad eyes would return, but the area around the lighthouse was empty. "I don't see her."

"Are you sure?" Clove asked, a little miffed. "Maybe she's here and you're just not looking hard enough."

I glanced at Clove curiously. "Why would you say that?"

Clove started nervously wringing her hands. "If I tell you, you'll think I'm crazy."

"We already think you're crazy," Thistle replied.

"You'll think I'm being a baby," Clove added.

"We already think you're a baby," Thistle replied with a bright smile.

I shot a glare in Thistle's direction. "Why don't you tell us what you're getting at and then we'll decide if you're a baby or crazy," I said wearily.

"Okay," Clove said, glancing at me for reassurance. "Well, you see that window up there?"

Thistle and I followed the line of her finger midway up the building, to a lone window in the peeling paint. "Yeah," I prodded her.

"I swear, when we were coming back through the trees – after looking at the road – I swear that I saw someone watching us."

Thistle and I exchanged dubious glances. "And why wouldn't you tell us then?" Thistle asked.

"Because I thought it might be Bigfoot and you guys would laugh at me," Clove lifted her chin defiantly.

"Maybe it was just a reflection of the sun," I offered lamely.

"Or maybe it was a ghost," Thistle said grimly.

"Clove can't see ghosts," I reminded her.

"Clove can't see ghosts like you," Thistle agreed. "But everyone has the capacity to see sometimes. Aunt Tillie taught us that. She came to this place expecting to see a ghost – or Bigfoot – and maybe she really did see a ghost."

"You're saying it was a self-fulfilling prophecy?"

"Maybe," Thistle shrugged noncommittally.

"There's only one way to find out," I replied grimly.

"What way?" Clove looked confused and then, when realization washed over her, terrified. "I am not going in that building."

"It will be fine," Thistle waved off her concerns. "Ghosts can't hurt us."

"And if Bigfoot is in there, we'll run right out, I swear," I added.

"What if it's dangerous?" Clove tried a different tactic. "What if the building is about to cave in?"

"Dean said the problems with the building were all cosmetic," I reminded her.

"Well, Dean said," Clove complained. "Dean, a guy we've never met before and who could be crazy – or stupid, for all we know – said that building was safe so we automatically take him at his word."

"If you don't want to go in, don't go in," Thistle said irritably, climbing the steps to the main door of the lighthouse. "Wait here. Bay and I will go in and check out things and then we'll come back out and get you."

"You want me to stay out here alone?" Clove squeaked.

I couldn't take much more of this, so I pushed past Thistle and tugged on the door of the lighthouse. It didn't open at first, but with a little magical push, the lock tumbled and the door sprang open.

I entered the lighthouse first, pausing in the doorway to let my eyes get accustomed to the sudden gloom. Inside, the building was surprisingly clean. There was a musty odor permeating the premises, but that was from abandonment. If there was a body in here, it was so old that it couldn't decay anymore. That was, at the very least, a small sense of comfort.

Thistle must have been thinking the same thing. "It doesn't smell like death," she said.

"What does death smell like?" Clove asked curiously.

"Rotting flesh, in a lot of instances," Thistle replied dryly.

"Thanks for the visual."

"You're welcome."

"We should've brought a flashlight," I lamented. "It's too dark in here to do a proper search."

Thistle thought about it a second and then rubbed her hands together, causing a spark to emanate from between them. I heard her mutter a spell under her breath. When she opened her hands again, she had conjured a handful of small fireflies – magical fireflies that would dissipate on their own in an hour or so – that she tossed into the air. The fireflies dispersed through the room, emitting enough of a glow to make the lighthouse visible – if not quite cheery.

"That was neat."

I jumped when I heard the new voice, glancing around quickly until my eyes fell on Erika. She was standing on the spiral staircase in the center of the room, watching the three of us curiously.

"Erika," I breathed, trying to calm my heart rate. "You surprised me."

"She's here?" Clove looked around nervously. "Where is she?"

"She's on the stairwell."

"They can't see me?" Erika looked disappointed.

"No," I replied. "In a few minutes, though, they should be able to hear you."

"Really? Why?"

"I have no idea," I admitted. "It's just that, when a ghost is around and I'm talking to it, they can start to hear it after a while. I think it's our family bond, but I can't be sure."

"Are they your sisters?" Erika asked.

"No," I shook my head. "They're my cousins."

"That's nice," Erika said. "I wish I had cousins."

"Did you have sisters?" I asked.

"I have two brothers," Erika brightened considerably. "I haven't seen them in a long time, though."

"Were they on the boat with you?"

"I'm not sure," Erika said. "I don't know where they went. I can't remember the last time I saw them."

"I can hear her," Clove said suddenly.

"Me, too," Thistle nodded.

"See," I smiled warmly at Erika. "I told you they would be able to hear you."

"But they can only hear me when you're around?"

"Actually, now that they've heard you, they should be able to hear you again even when I'm not with them," I replied.

"Don't tell her that," Clove hissed.

I ignored her. "Why did you come back out here?" I asked Erika.

"I was following you."

"Is this where you were? The place you were alone for so long?"

"Yes," Erika nodded. "It's not as scary now. Especially since I saw the other children."

I felt my heart go cold. "What other children?"

"The ones on the boat?"

"What boat?" Thistle asked sharply.

"The one outside," Erika replied simply.

Thistle moved to a ground floor window, one that faced the lake, and glanced out. "I don't see a boat out there."

"It's not out there now," Erika said. "It was out there a while ago, though."

"Where did it go?" Thistle asked.

"It floated away," Erika replied.

I glanced at Thistle worriedly. "You just saw this boat?"

"Yes," Erika said.

"Just now – or in the time since I saw you out at the inn?"

Erika nodded, her eyes widening. "Did I do something wrong?"

"No," I shook my head quickly. "You didn't do anything wrong, honey. We're just wondering where the boat went."

"It's going away," Erika said. "It will be back, though."

"It will?"

"Yes."

"How do you know that?"

"The other little girl told me."

"What other little girl?" I was starting to get exasperated. The wisdom of a child – even a dead child – is hard to focus on a specific task.

"The one that talked to me."

"She saw you?"

"Yes."

"On the boat?"

"Yes."

"And where is she now?"

"She's still on the boat," Erika said testily. "I told you that."

Thistle put her hand on my arm to still me. "She doesn't understand," she said in a low tone. "You can't make her understand. Getting frustrated with her isn't going to help."

"Since when are you the voice of reason?"

"It happens. Rarely, but it happens."

Thistle turned back to the staircase, fixing her gaze on the area I had been staring at while conversing with Erika. She couldn't see Erika, but she wanted to speak directly to her. "Erika, we need you to try and find the boat again."

"Why?"

"Because we want to know where it went," Thistle said calmly. "We want to see if we can find those children."

"Okay," Erika shrugged and then popped out of view.

"And when you find out, come and find us at the inn and tell us," Thistle continued, unaware that Erika had disappeared. "Can you do that?"

"She's gone," I informed Thistle.

"Do you think she understands?"

"No," I shook my head ruefully.

"Then we're going to have to try and figure this out ourselves," Thistle said grimly. "Where do we start?"

That was a really good question.

FOURTEEN

We headed back to town a few minutes later. I wasn't expecting Erika to pop back in and magically solve this quandary for us any time soon. That would be way too easy – and that's not how the Winchester witches roll.

Thistle parked in front of Hypnotic, killing the engine of her car, and then turning to me in the passenger seat. "Do you think there is really a boat out there with little kids on it?"

"I don't know," I answered honestly. "The problem is, there are a lot of options here."

"What options?" Clove asked curiously from the backseat.

"Well, there could be a boat out there with kids on it," I said. "It could also be a memory from when she was on the boat and she's getting it confused with the present day."

"Or," Thistle added. "Maybe there's a ghost ship out there with a bunch of dead little kids on it and that's what she saw."

Huh, I hadn't thought of that one.

"She said one of the kids saw her and talked to her," Clove said. "If they were all ghosts, wouldn't they all be able to see each other."

She had a point.

"I don't know what to think," I admitted.

"Shouldn't we tell someone?" Clove asked.

And that was the question that was truly gnawing at me.

"What are we going to say? And who are we going to call?" Thistle asked.

"What about Chief Terry?"

"And what do we tell him?" Thistle pressed again. "Bay saw a little black ghost and she told us that there's a boat full of kids out on Lake Michigan and they may or may not be in trouble? He'll lock us in a loony bin."

"He knows that we're witches," Clove was insistent. "He might believe us."

"And he might not," Thistle replied.

"Then what about Landon? He knows," Clove said stubbornly.

Yeah, what about Landon? "I'm going to talk to Landon tonight," I said finally.

"Are you sure that's a good idea?" Thistle asked.

"No," I admitted reluctantly. "I just know if I don't tell him he's going to freak out. I promised I wouldn't lie to him anymore."

"Omission isn't technically a lie," Thistle pointed out. Aunt Tillie taught us that when we were kids. It was one of few lessons she imparted us with that stuck.

"I bet Landon wouldn't see it that way," Clove said sagely.

"I'm going to tell him," I said firmly. "We need him. I don't know how to move on this without him."

"Do you think he'll be mad?" Clove asked worriedly.

"I don't think he'll be happy."

"He'll be fine," Thistle scoffed. "Just wait until you're in the middle of sex and then tell him. He can't be mad them."

"That sounds like a great idea," I agreed.

"Really?" Thistle looked surprised.

"No."

We climbed out of the car and moved toward Hypnotic. We had been so involved in our conversation, we hadn't noticed the woman sitting on the bench just outside. It was Karen.

"Oh, hi," Clove said awkwardly when she finally caught sight of her.

"Hi," Karen greeted us warmly. "I wasn't sure if you were coming back today. I decided to take a chance and wait for you here."

"Have you been waiting long?" Clove asked. I could tell she was nervous.

"No," Karen shook her head hurriedly. "I've only been here about twenty minutes. It's a nice day. I enjoyed the wait."

"Well, that's good," Clove said, reaching around Karen to unlock the door of Hypnotic.

Thistle and I followed the two of them into the store, exchanging wary glances. Karen was a minefield of trouble where Clove was concerned. It would be easy to hate her if she weren't so nice.

"Oh, this is a beautiful store," Karen said when we got inside. "Your father told me that it was nice, but I had no idea."

"Thank you," Clove said stiffly.

"Is everything here handmade?" Karen asked, walking up to Thistle's candle display.

"Thistle made those," I offered.

"They're very cool," Karen said, picking up one of the leftover skull candles Thistle had been hawking around Halloween.

"The trick is to use a softer wax," Thistle said, trying to fill the uncomfortable silence that was threatening to engulf the room. "It makes the candle easier to mold."

"I've always wanted to learn how to make candles," Karen said wistfully. "You should offer a class."

Despite myself, I laughed out loud. Karen turned to me in surprise. "Thistle doesn't have the patience to teach a class," I choked out.

Clove joined in. "She'd kill the first person that asked her a dumb question."

Thistle looked like she was going to argue but decided against it at the last second. Instead, she just shrugged. "They're right. I don't have the patience for anything like that."

"Where did you learn to do it?"

Thistle cocked her head to the side, considering. "All of our moms and aunts are pretty crafty," she said. "They can all do certain things. My mom can sew and paint. They're all great cooks. Aunt Tillie can make stained glass, although she hasn't done it in years. And Marnie, well, Marnie can make some really awesome candles."

"And Marnie is your mother?" Karen turned to Clove. She didn't look uncomfortable, merely curious.

"Yes," Clove said. "She's definitely my mother. There were times I wanted a DNA test as a child, but that would have been a waste of money."

"What?" Karen looked confused.

"They look like clones," I supplied.

"Oh," Karen nodded, understanding washing over her face.

"We all look like our moms unfortunately," Thistle said.

"Your mom has purple hair?" Karen asked, covering her mouth the instant she realized how rude the question was.

"Ronald McDonald red," I replied before Thistle could. "Thistle changes it up every few months. It's mostly just to irritate her mother."

"That is a vicious lie," Thistle countered. "And it's neither here nor there. I like the purple."

"I miss the blue."

"I kind of miss the blue, too," admitted Thistle. "Maybe I'll revisit it this summer."

"I can't wait."

Karen watched us interact for a second and then smiled. "You're all very close."

"We were raised together," Clove explained. "We all lived in the same house as kids. I guess we're more like sisters than cousins."

"You fight like sisters," Karen said. "I like it."

"You have sisters?" Clove asked.

"I do."

"I don't really know anything about you," Clove admitted. "You're going to be my stepmother, I guess I probably should."

"I was hoping we could get to know each other a little better

AMANDA M. LEE

today," Karen said. "That's why I was here. I was going to invite you to lunch."

"We were going to order lunch in here," Clove said. "We took off for more than an hour to ... run an errand," she glanced at me guiltily. "We really shouldn't leave again."

Karen's face fell. "Oh, well maybe some other time."

"Or you could eat here with us," I offered.

"Really?" Karen's face brightened.

"Sure," Thistle said. "What do you like? We were just going to order some sandwiches and fries from the deli."

"That sounds good," Karen said.

Twenty minutes later, we were all sitting around the little den area in the store conversing – and eating. Karen really was pleasant – and she'd led an interesting life.

"You were really in the Peace Corps?" Thistle was impressed.

"Yes," Karen said. "I spent some time in Africa. I would have liked to stay longer, but I had to come back home because my mother was sick."

"That's terrible," Clove said.

"She got better," Karen said. "But, I had to take care of her for a while. So, when I was back, I enrolled in college and decided to focus on interior design."

"Any reason why?" I asked.

"I don't know, I just always liked decorating," Karen admitted. "I'm kind of a hoarder – or I have hoarding tendencies. I love to pick out knick-knacks and paintings. So, I figured the best thing for me to do was to pick them out for other people. That way, I get to shop and I don't have a house overflowing with too many things."

"That sounds like a good idea," Thistle said.

"What made you guys decide to open the store?" Karen said.

Clove shrugged. "It just seemed like a natural progression. We knew how to do a lot of things and we thought the best thing to do, especially in this town, was to play to our strengths."

"You never thought of leaving Hemlock Cove?" Karen asked.

"No," Thistle said. "I mean, sure, when we were kids, we all dreamed of running away to a big city, one where Aunt Tillie couldn't find us. Bay went to Detroit for a couple of years. This is just home, though. We don't want to leave."

"It's a beautiful area."

"I think we're suited for wide open spaces," I said. "I felt smothered down state."

"It is definitely easier to breathe here," Karen laughed. "There's no smog."

"There's also no good shopping," Clove lamented. "When we want to actually shop, we have to drive to Traverse City."

"That's only an hour away," Karen said. "That's not really so bad. And you have so much to love here that going to Traverse City once in a while probably isn't a big hardship."

"No," Clove agreed.

"So, are you dating anyone?" Karen asked, her eyes twinkling.

Clove flushed. "I'm not, but Bay and Thistle both have boyfriends."

"Why don't you?" Karen pressed.

"I just haven't found the right guy yet," Clove said. "I'm not in a hurry. I'm only twenty-five."

"You still have plenty of time," Karen agreed.

"So, how did you end up in Traverse City?" Clove asked curiously, turning the conversation back on Karen.

"I went to college at Western Michigan University," Karen said. "When I decided to set up shop, I did so down in the Grand Rapids area first. I was doing okay, but I just felt a little restless. I went to a seminar – one of those networking deals – and it was held at that big resort in Traverse City. I just fell in love with the area. About six months later, I just decided to move here. I've been here almost ten years now."

"And you've never been married?" Thistle asked.

"No," Karen shook her head. "This will be the first time."

"Well, that's convenient, I guess," Thistle laughed – although it sounded hollow.

After a few more minutes, Karen finished up her lunch and stood.

She impulsively reached for Clove, pulling her forward into a friendly hug. Clove looked uncomfortable with the gesture.

"I'm so glad we had this time together," Karen said. "I'm looking forward to really getting to know you. We're going to be family, after all."

"Yeah," Clove said. "I had fun."

Once Karen was gone, Clove turned to Thistle and me. "What do you think? She's nice, right?"

"She seems nice," I said cautiously.

"Her story is a little too ... neat," Thistle said. Sometimes I think she just wants to be contrary for the sake of being contrary.

"What do you mean?" Clove asked.

"I don't know, it was like it was designed to draw us in, to weave a spell over us, so we wouldn't question it," Thistle said. "There was nothing really messy about it and real life is messy."

"So, you're saying that, because nothing bad really happened to her – which we don't actually know for a fact – that you think something is wrong with her?" Clove asked incredulously. "Maybe she just didn't tell us anything really private. Did you ever consider that?"

"I didn't say there was something wrong with her, just that I wasn't sure if I trusted her," Thistle said.

Clove turned to me. "Do you agree with her?"

"I'm not sure," I hedged.

"What do you think is wrong with her?"

"Let's just say I think she's trying a little too hard," I said finally. "It doesn't seem natural."

"Or, maybe, that's just how people that don't share our gene pool are," Clove huffed. "Why is it, the minute anyone shows any interest in me, whether it is Karen or Sam, you two immediately think there's something wrong with them?"

"We're just trying to protect you," Thistle said in a low voice.

"Well, maybe I don't need your protection," Clove said. "Maybe I'm sick of you guys always acting like you're right and I'm wrong."

"No one said that," I protested.

"Well, guess what?" Clove said. "From now on, I'm going to be the one that's right and you two are going to be the ones that are wrong. Get it?"

Thistle and I exchanged a wary glance.

"Got it?"

"Yeah, we got it," Thistle replied.

Clove turned and stalked to the storeroom, pulling the curtain shut behind her as she did.

"Well, she's in a snit," Thistle said.

"She has a point," I said. "We do kind of tell her what to do."

"She needs direction," Thistle countered.

"Maybe we should try being, I don't know, nicer to her," I suggested. "She seems a little frazzled lately."

"Fine," Thistle blew out a sigh. "When this blows up, though, and she gets crushed – again – I'm blaming you."

"I would have it no other way."

FIFTEEN

I was happy to leave a pouting Clove and a wallowing Thistle to their own devices and head to The Whistler for the rest of the afternoon. Unfortunately for me, when I got there, both Brian and Sam were wandering around the building and talking about their "grand" plans.

"Bay," Brian greeted me when I walked in. "I was starting to wonder if you still worked here or not."

Jerk.

"I'm sorry," I apologized, although I put absolutely no truth behind my words. "I was actually out scouting a story for next week."

"And what story would that be?" Sam asked curiously.

"A man named Dean Browning is moving to town," I explained. "In addition to taking a part-time position at the docks, he's also going to be refurbishing the Dandridge."

"What's the Dandridge?"

"It's an old lighthouse that's been abandoned for years," I said. "He's going to turn it into a haunted lighthouse attraction."

"That's cool," Brian brightened. "That's a whole other advertiser."

"Yeah," I agreed. "He seems really enthusiastic. He's going to give me a tour next week. Clove, Thistle and I just ran out there to take a look around. I hadn't been there in a long time, I had kind of forgotten about it. It's going to be really nice when he gets it done."

"You found a story all on your own," Sam said enthusiastically. "That's great."

Could he be any more condescending?

"Yeah, Chief Terry brought him by Hypnotic," I said. "The story just kind of fell into my lap."

"Hey, a source is a source," Sam said.

"I have to make a quick call from my office," Brian said suddenly, glancing at his watch. "Bay, will you keep Sam company while I'm on the phone? It shouldn't take more that fifteen minutes."

"Sure," I smiled thinly. "It sounds like fun."

It sounded like hell.

Once Brian was gone, Sam turned to me, plastering a friendly smile on his face. "So, you had a busy morning, I guess."

He had no idea. "Not really. You never really have busy mornings in Hemlock Cove." I was going for levity, but it came out a bit whiny.

"Well, hopefully that will change," Sam said. "I think Hemlock Cove could be a tourist Mecca."

"I don't think you can use Mecca in the same sentence with Hemlock Cove and be realistic," I admitted.

"I just don't think you're looking at the big picture," Sam said. "That's okay, you're from a small town. You don't see things the same way I see things."

I was really starting to dislike him. "What is the big picture? And please use small words so my small-town brain doesn't implode under the effort of understanding them."

"This is a tourist destination and it keeps growing," Sam said, ignoring my snarky comment. "We could really have something special here."

"We?"

"Well, the town."

"The town is run by a commission," I reminded him. "You're not the town." The statement had come out a little harsher than I had meant for it to.

"You don't like me, do you?" Sam asked the question bluntly, his gaze focused on me. There was a certain coldness to it.

Well, if we were telling truths ....

"I don't trust you," I said honestly. "You swoop in here, with your condescending nature and these big proclamations, but you have no way to make any of it work. You're feeding Brian's big dreams, even though you know they're not even remotely feasible. I just haven't figured out why."

Sam looked like I had just hit him with a truck instead of verbally unloading on him. "Well, at least you're honest," he said finally. "Now, let me tell you what I know. I know that this town has a unique niche. There's a lot of growth that can happen here, even if you don't want to see the bigger picture."

I opened my mouth to argue, but Sam didn't give me the chance.

"Since the moment I met you, you've had attitude with me," Sam continued. "At first, I just thought you were leery around new people. That's a weird trait for a journalist, but it's been known to happen. Then I realized it's just me you have a problem with. Me specifically. I want to know why?"

"I think you might be a little paranoid," I said evasively.

"Okay, let me ask you something else then," Sam said. "Why did you tell your Aunt Tillie what I said about the dementia?"

I smirked. "She deserved to know."

"No, you told her to be vindictive," Sam corrected me. "You told her to be mean."

"See, that's where you're wrong, Sam," I said. "You see my Aunt Tillie is the vindictive one. She's been fixated on causing trouble for my father and uncles at their new inn. She wants them out of town and she doesn't care how she does it. And, yes, I have a complicated relationship with the man, but he is my family and I'd like him to stay around a little longer. I told her what you said because I wanted to distract her from spying on the Dragonfly and I thought fixing her attention on Brian – *Brian*, not you – would be a good way to do it."

Sam looked properly abashed. "I'm sorry, I thought ... ."

"I don't care what you thought," I snapped. "You need to realize that not everything is about you."

"I said I was sorry."

"What are you really doing here, Sam?" I asked suddenly.

"Excuse me?"

"What are you really doing here?"

"My job," Sam narrowed his eyes in my direction. "I don't have some big plan of Hemlock Cove domination, no matter what you think."

"Then why don't you focus on doing your job and leave my Aunt Tillie out of things," I suggested. "Just stay away from her."

"From what I've seen, your Aunt Tillie can take care of herself," Sam said stiffly.

"I wasn't warning you away from her because I was worried about her," I replied. "If you want to take her on, you'll deserve what you get."

"What makes you think I want to have anything to do with your Aunt Tillie?"

"I don't," I said. "I do think you have more on your mind than just expanding The Whistler, though," I said.

"And what would that be?" Sam was trying to pretend he was nonchalant, but my words had thrown him.

"I have no idea," I admitted. "Just know that I know that you're up to something. That's enough for me for right now."

"I'll keep that in mind," Sam said dryly.

"You do that."

SIXTEEN

I headed straight for The Overlook when I left work that evening. Landon had texted me to tell me he would be there for dinner. I had no idea if he was mad about breakfast, but I figured I would find out the minute I saw him.

Thankfully, for me, Sam had wisely given me a wide berth the rest of the afternoon. If Brian sensed the tension, he didn't say anything.

I let myself into the family quarters, finding only Aunt Tillie present. She was watching a *Modern Family* rerun. "Why aren't you watching *Jeopardy*?"

"It's a rerun."

"Does that matter?"

"I already know all the answers from that episode, there's no need to watch it," Aunt Tillie said from her new easy chair. My mom and aunts had bought it for her a few weeks ago, when she had finally agreed to let them throw away the old one she had been practically living in for two months in the kitchen. It had picked up a weird smell. Maybe the scorpion had died in it or something?

"You know all the answers?" I had my doubts.

"All the ones I care about."

"Well, that's good, I guess," I sighed wearily and dropped onto the couch.

"What's wrong with you?"

I was about to say nothing when, instead, I shifted gears. I unloaded three days of anger, frustration and worry into a three-minute diatribe and then sat back and watched Aunt Tillie process everything.

"I knew that Sam Cornell was bad news," Aunt Tillie said.

"He's the least of my worries," I admitted. "What do I do about Erika?"

"What can you do?"

"What?"

"With the information you have, what can you do?" Aunt Tillie wasn't being mean, she was genuinely curious.

"I'm going to tell Landon, after dinner tonight," I said. "I need help."

"Well, at least you admit it."

"Admit what?"

"Everyone needs help, Bay," Aunt Tillie said. "It took you a long time to be able to admit that. You and your cousins tend to close ranks around each other and try to solve every crisis yourselves. That's not always possible."

"So you think I should tell Landon?" I was surprised. Aunt Tillie's usual mantra was that the only good law enforcement official was an absent one. Okay, she actually usually said the only good law enforcement official was a dead one – but I was cleaning it up for her so she didn't look so bad.

"Yes, you should tell Landon," Aunt Tillie said. "The boy has more gumption than I initially gave him credit for. He took our secret and he kept it and he's still around. He doesn't look like he's going anywhere. He might actually be able to help."

"He's going to be mad."

"He'll be fine," Aunt Tillie said. "I don't think you're giving him enough credit. It's not like the three of you have done anything especially dangerous."

Not yet.

"I hope you're right," I said, glancing up at the wall clock. "We should probably get to dinner. We're late."

"They'll live," Aunt Tillie said. "I was really good today. I've built up some good will."

"How were you really good?"

"I didn't terrorize the contractors and I didn't terrorize the guests. That's a good day in my book," Aunt Tillie said.

That was a good day.

We entered the dining room together, and I was relieved to find Landon already sitting at the table. I was surprised to see Chief Terry was also there, and he'd brought Dean Browning with him.

"There you are," my mother chided. "What have the two of you been up to?"

"Nothing," I protested.

"None of your business," Aunt Tillie challenged her. "We were just talking. Is that a crime?"

"It depends on what you were talking about," Landon said suspiciously, his eyes trained on my face.

"Family stuff," Aunt Tillie shot back, slipping into her chair at the head of the table.

"What kind of family stuff?" My mom asked curiously. I couldn't help but notice that Chief Terry was sandwiched between her and Marnie, both of whom were continuously patting his arm to get his attention fixed on them.

"What is this? The Spanish Inquisition?" Aunt Tillie barked. "Mind your own business."

"See, now I know you're up to something," my mom frowned.

"We're not up to anything," I said, slipping into the seat next to Landon and fixing him with small smile. He didn't return the gesture.

"I'm glad you showed up," he said. "After breakfast, I wasn't sure you were even still alive."

I knew his words were meant to be facetious, but they cut to the quick. "I'm sorry," I said honestly. "Something came up."

"What?"

Chief Terry was watching our exchange with a mix of consternation and curiosity. My mom dragged his attention back to her, though, by sliding two huge slabs of meatloaf onto his plate.

I glanced down to the end of the table, where Sam and Brian were also watching me with a certain level of interest and shook my head. "You know, work stuff," I said evasively.

Landon saw where my gaze had traveled and eased up. "Sorry," he said stiffly. "I was just worried."

"She's a big girl, she can take care of herself," Aunt Tillie said.

"I didn't say she couldn't," Landon protested. "I was just worried."

"Well, I'm sure Bay will tell you all about it later," Aunt Tillie said evasively. "Now, where's my food?"

"It's right in front of you," my mom said blandly.

"Well, good then," Aunt Tillie sniffed. "Where's my wine?"

"You don't need any wine," Marnie said.

"I want some wine."

"Oh, just give her some wine," Thistle groaned. "I like her better when she's drunk."

"You keep out of this," Aunt Tillie pointed her gnarled finger at Thistle. "I'm not in the mood for any of your nonsense."

"You tell her, Aunt Tillie," Clove chimed in.

"You stay out of this, too," Aunt Tillie said, but then she turned to Clove. "Why are you mad at her?"

Every set of eyes at the table turned to Clove, waiting for an answer. "She was just mean to me this afternoon."

"She's always mean to you. What happened today that was so different?"

"Nothing," Clove muttered.

Aunt Tillie turned to me. "Why is Clove upset?"

I pinched the bridge of my nose tiredly. "How should I know?"

"The three of you were together this afternoon, checking out the lighthouse, something must have happened?"

"You went to the lighthouse?" Dean looked surprised.

"We just wanted to check it out," I explained quickly. "We hadn't seen it in so long. We think you've got a great idea for out there. There's a lot of potential."

Dean smiled. "Yeah, I think so, too."

"He's fixing up the Dandridge?" My mom asked.

"Yeah," Dean replied. "I'm going to turn it into a haunted lighthouse."

"That's a great idea," Twila enthused.

"It's a great idea," Chief Terry agreed. "I don't think the three of you should've been traipsing around up there, though. What if one of you had fallen and gotten hurt? That place needs to be fixed up."

"We're obviously fine," Thistle said.

"Clove's not fine," Aunt Tillie said. "She's upset."

Crap on toast. This was spiraling out of control. "We just teased her about Bigfoot a little bit and scared her and she's mad," I lied.

"Why would you do that?" My mom asked.

"It seemed like a good idea at the time," I said lamely.

Aunt Tillie didn't look like she believed me. She wisely let it go, though. "So, Brian, tell anyone else I have dementia today?"

Chief Terry sucked in a breath and glanced down at Brian. His face had gone red under Aunt Tillie's sudden scrutiny. "I didn't say you have dementia."

"So Sam is lying?" Aunt Tillie turned her attention to Sam.

"No," Sam said hurriedly. "I probably just misheard him."

"Yeah," Thistle said around a mouthful of potatoes. "He really said you're demented. That's different."

"You're full of yourself this evening, aren't you?" Aunt Tillie turned back to Thistle.

Thistle swallowed, leveling her gaze on Aunt Tillie. "No. Just trying to lighten the mood."

"It's not working," I said.

"I noticed."

"This is an excellent meal, ladies," Chief Terry said. "I do love your meatloaf."

"Thank you, Terry," my mom said warmly. "I made it just for you."

"I made it," Marnie countered.

"I made it," Twila complained from her spot next to Dean.

"No, I made it," Aunt Tillie said.

"You didn't make it," my mom turned on her.

"It's my recipe."

"But you didn't make it."

"So, Landon, what do you have going on at work?" Clove decided to change the subject again.

"Not much," Landon said. "It's been really slow these last couple of weeks, not that I'm complaining. I've just been working on a few cold cases."

"Nothing big?"

"No."

"Well, that gives you more time to focus on Bay," Aunt Tillie said. "She better than any cold case any time of the week."

"Okay," Landon said uncomfortably.

I rubbed my forehead, trying to ward off the headache that was building. "Landon has a job, Aunt Tillie. There's nothing wrong with doing it."

"You're his job, too."

"Yeah," Thistle chimed in again. "He should just do Bay."

Landon's face colored while Chief Terry coughed uncomfortably. Aunt Tillie fixed Thistle with a hard stare. "That did it!"

"What?" Thistle looked confused.

"It's lesson time."

The color drained from Thistle's face. "No, it's not."

"Yes, it is."

"What's lesson time?" Sam asked curiously.

"You don't want to know," Clove said, smiling flirtatiously at him. "Trust me."

"Stop that," Aunt Tillie ordered.

"Stop what?" Clove asked, dumbfounded.

"Flirting with that man. I don't like it."

"I wasn't flirting." Clove blushed furiously.

"It looked like it to me," Aunt Tillie said.

"Well, you're old, your eyesight isn't great," Clove shot back, although I could tell she almost immediately regretted the words.

"I see you need a lesson, too."

"No," Clove said, panic wracking her voice. "You're the one who said you have glaucoma. That's why you need the weed."

"What weed?" Sam asked.

"Let's not talk about the weed," Landon said.

"I agree," Chief Terry added.

"Why not?" Aunt Tillie complained. "It's medicinal."

"You have a cop and an FBI agent sitting at the table and you don't have a prescription for medical marijuana, let alone a license to grow it," Landon reminded her. "You probably shouldn't be talking about it."

"So?"

"So, that's illegal."

"Oh, it's not illegal," Aunt Tillie scoffed.

"No, it's illegal," Chief Terry affirmed.

"It's just a little illegal," Aunt Tillie said.

"There's no such thing as a little illegal," Landon replied.

"Let's talk about something else," my mom suggested.

"Yes," Marnie agreed. "Let's talk about Sam's work at the paper," she suggested.

"That sounds like a great subject," my mom agreed, turning to me. "What do you think of it Bay?"

I glanced down at Sam and Brian at the end of the table. "Let's go back to talking about the pot."

SEVENTEEN

"There are no words."

I glanced over at Landon and smirked. "Dinner wasn't so funny tonight, huh?"

"Oh, it was funny," Landon countered. "Just not funny ha-ha. More like you should all be in straightjackets funny."

We were behind The Overlook, on the back patio, after declining dessert. I knew Landon was at his limit where family shenanigans were concerned and I didn't want him to explode all over my family and the other guests and make things any worse – if that was even possible.

"I can't argue with the necessity for straightjackets," I said calmly. I was still waiting for the storm.

Landon turned his luminous eyes to me; the bright moon – only a few days from being full – illuminated his handsome features as he considered me under the unearthly glow of the spring night. "You have something you want to tell me?"

"I do," I agreed.

"And what would that be?"

I glanced behind us, making sure that everyone else was still safely inside, and then turned back to him. "I'm sorry I missed breakfast this morning. Trust me, it wasn't planned."

"So, what happened that made you miss it?"

I sucked my top lip into my mouth worriedly.

Landon recognized the gesture for what it was – fear. "If you tell me, it will be over with. Just rip off the Band-Aid."

"I saw a ghost."

Landon blew out a sigh. "I figured it was something like that when you didn't want to talk in front of strangers. What kind of ghost?"

"A little girl," I replied.

Landon furrowed his brow – something I would have found adorable under different circumstances – and met my gaze evenly. "A little girl? How did she die?"

"That's the thing," I said. "She said she was on a boat with other kids and that she got sick and fell asleep. Then she woke up by a building by the water."

Landon shook his head, considering. "A boat with other kids? I don't get it."

"A boat where a bunch of kids were kept together, under the deck, and barely fed and not really taken care of. The adults, or big people, as she puts it, were mean to them."

"Mean how?"

"She doesn't go into a lot of detail," I replied. "She kind of jumps around. I'm trying not to scare her away so I don't press her too much."

"And you saw her where?"

"Down by a clump of trees by where they're going to build the greenhouse."

"And she just walked up to you and started talking?"

"No," I said shortly. "I went to her to make sure I didn't talk to her until we were in a place where the construction workers couldn't see us."

"Don't get testy with me, I don't know how this works," Landon said irritably. "I'm trying here."

"I know," I adjusted my tone. "It's just ... I'm scared."

Landon searched my face for an answer to the question but decided to ask the question anyway. "What are you scared of?"

"I know you don't like this stuff," I admitted, turning my face so I wouldn't have to look into his soulful eyes and see the doubt reflected there. "I don't want to freak you out."

"You think I'm going to be freaked out by a ghost after I saw that big wind monster you guys conjured? I think, if I was going to have a meltdown that would have been the point."

I continued staring out at the night, letting the twinkling stars calm me like they had when I was a child. "I know," I said finally. "But there's only so much one person can take and, I guess, I'm scared that the more you learn the more you're going to realize that we're just too much work."

Landon laughed, a reaction I wasn't expecting. I turned to him in surprise. Landon reached over and grabbed my wrist, wrapping his hand around it tightly. "These crazy people made you who you are, and I'm fairly happy with the person you are. No one is perfect. This isn't going to work, though, if you don't feel you can open up to me."

"I know."

"So, we'll take this a step at a time," Landon said patiently. "Tell me about the little girl. Tell me everything you know about her. Just tell me what's going on."

So, I did just that. I told him about Erika, about the lighthouse and about Sam. When I was done, I watched his face for signs that he would walk away – or explode. Instead, he seemed more intrigued than anything else.

"So, what do you think?"

"What do you mean?"

"Is she telling the truth?"

"Why would she lie?"

"Okay, maybe telling the truth isn't the right way to put it," Landon ceded. "Do you think she is talking about something that happened recently?"

"That is the question," I agreed.

"So, you don't know?"

"I honestly don't."

Landon sighed and pulled me toward him, wrapping me in his arms and resting his chin on top of my head. "I don't know what to do with this," he admitted. "So, we're going to go about this the smart way – instead of whatever way you and your cousins usually approach a problem."

I raised an eyebrow as I looked up at him. "I wouldn't put it that way when we're around Thistle."

"I'm not scared of her," Landon smiled down at me, pressing his lips to my forehead. "She's going to be distracted the next few days anyway."

"How so?"

"She pissed off your Aunt Tillie; she's not going to just let that slide."

He had a point.

"So, what are you going to do?"

"I'm going to try and get a patrol out on the lake to look around and I'm going to see if I can find a missing little girl named Erika. I'm sure there's going to be a lot of them. When I do, I'm going to show you some pictures, and we're going to go from there."

"That sounds very practical," I said, an idea forming in my mind.

"Well, that's how real investigators do things," Landon said. "I honestly don't know another way to approach it. So that's what I'm going to do."

"Thank you," I murmured, pressing my face into his neck.

"You're welcome."

"So, you're not mad?"

"I'm not mad," Landon said. "If I'm telling the truth, the things I was imagining the three of you to be up to were a lot worse than what you were really up to."

"That sounds a little insulting."

"You'll live."

The patio door opened behind us and we both swung around to find Clove and Thistle standing there, looking frustrated and exhausted. "Way to start World War III and then run and hide," Thistle said sarcastically.

"We had a few things to talk about, and they weren't really dinner conversation," I reminded Thistle.

"I know," she sighed. "I just know Aunt Tillie is going to do something really mean to me."

"Not just you," I said, glancing over at Clove. "For once, you might not be number one on her list."

Clove scowled. "I blame you two."

"You always do," Thistle said.

"Well, I happen to agree with them," Landon said, shooting a stern look in Clove's direction. "For once, they're being the voices of reason and you're being the irresponsible one."

Clove's mouth dropped open in surprise. "How can you agree with them?"

"We don't know anything about this guy," Landon said. "If I've learned one thing about this family, it's that you should probably trust your guts. If Bay and Thistle think this guy is acting strange, then he's probably acting strange."

"Bay and Thistle are suspicious of everyone," Clove pouted. "You should've heard the things they said about you the day we met you."

I internally cringed but Landon only tightened his arm around my shoulder. "I was undercover with a group of rude meth heads by a cornfield where a girl was found with her heart ripped out," Landon replied pragmatically. "You should've all had a bad feeling about me."

"But that wasn't who you really were," Clove said triumphantly. "You were really a heroic FBI agent who saved our lives."

"And you give her a lot of orgasms, so we have to like you for that," Thistle interjected pointedly.

Landon flashed a wry smile in Thistle's direction. "So should Bay and Clove say the same thing to Marcus?"

"No," Thistle said hurriedly. "Forget I said anything."

"That's what I thought," Landon replied smugly.

"See, Landon knows I'm right," Clove said.

"You're not right." Thistle reached over and pinched Clove viciously.

"Ow!"

"You feel that? Whatever Sam does to you is going to feel a lot worse than that. Don't forget it."

Landon rolled his eyes as Clove smacked Thistle angrily. "Stop pinching me."

"Stop acting like an idiot."

"Both of you stop it," Landon said irritably. "If you don't, I'm going to slap cuffs on both of you."

"Bay says that you won't do that," Clove replied honestly. "She says you told her those cuffs aren't for fun."

"Yeah, they're professional tools of the trade and can't be used for anything but official purposes," Thistle said snidely.

Landon colored. "Do you three tell each other everything?"

"Pretty much," Thistle said grimly.

"I need to find some guy friends," Landon said. "All this female stuff is starting to emasculate me. I need someone to go have a beer with and talk about manly things."

"Like what?" Thistle asked curiously. "Shaving? Flexing? Zipping up your pants without clipping anything accidentally?"

Landon shrugged. "I don't know. Sports. Politics. Not the nonsense you three are always chatting about. Is that what you think guys really talk about?" Landon rounded on Thistle. "That's a little stereotypical. That's like thinking you guys sit around talking about tampons."

"We do sit around talking about tampons," Thistle said dryly. "And cramps. And bloating."

Landon looked uncomfortable with the turn in the conversation.

"Speaking of which, we're almost out," Clove said.

"Yeah," Thistle agreed. "We're going to need them by the end of the week."

Landon frowned. "All of you?"

"Yup."

"I thought that was one of those myths."

"What?"

"That women that live together all sync up together."

Thistle patted Landon's arm, moving past him to the trail that led down to the guesthouse. "Sorry, dude," she said. "It's definitely true."

Landon's eyes connected with mine. "Okay, the mere thought of the three of you having PMS together freaks me out more than any ghost ever could."

"Be afraid," I teased him. "Be very afraid."

"Oh, trust me. I'm terrified."

EIGHTEEN

Marcus was waiting on the front porch when we got to the guesthouse. He looked relieved when the four of us appeared on the top of the hill.

"Why didn't you come up to dinner?" Thistle asked him curiously, greeting him with a kiss.

"Because I was running late," Marcus said. "I knew your Aunt Tillie wouldn't like that."

"She wouldn't have noticed," Landon said grimly. "She was too busy fighting with every single other person at the table."

Marcus didn't look convinced. "I decided to play it safe."

"I don't blame you," Landon said, patting Marcus on the shoulder. "You should be happy you missed it. I wish I had."

"You and Marcus are friends," I said suddenly.

Landon turned to me in surprise. "What?"

"You said you needed male friends to go have a beer with," I reminded him. "Marcus hasn't had dinner. Go to a bar and get dinner and beers with him."

"Now?" Landon didn't look thrilled with the idea. "I had other plans for tonight."

"We can do that when you get back," I brushed off the suggestion. "I need a bath first."

Thistle regarded me curiously for a few seconds. I was worried she would argue, but she apparently decided against it. "Actually, I think that's a really good idea."

"You do?" Marcus looked her up and down dubiously.

"I'm not cooking for you," Thistle said.

"I can just make a sandwich or something," Marcus suggested.

"We're out of bread."

"Oh." Marcus looked a little confused. He exchanged a wary glance with Landon. "I can have a bowl of cereal or something."

"We're out of milk," Clove interjected.

Landon looked down on me, suspicion etched on his perfect face. "What are you three up to?"

"Nothing," I lied. "I just want to take a bath."

"And then we're going to talk about tampons," Thistle added.

Marcus coughed loudly, his face reddening at the mere thought of being present for a conversation like that. "I could use a burger," he said finally.

Landon shifted his gaze between the three of us. "I could use a beer," he agreed. "But somehow, I think that something else is going on here."

"What?" Clove asked innocently.

"I have no idea," Landon admitted. "That's what's scary."

"I promise, we will be here when you get back," I said calmly.

"Is this like when you said you'd see me at breakfast?" Landon asked pointedly.

"No," I frowned. "I thought I was doing you a favor."

"Let it go, dude," Thistle said angrily. "She told you what was going on and you said you weren't mad so don't be a pain now. You just earned a bunch of points in our book; don't lose them now."

Landon pursed his lips as he met Thistle's challenging gaze. "I'm going to go," Landon said finally. "Just know, I know that you guys are up to something. If you're not here when I get back, I'm going to arrest you all."

"On what charge?"

"Lying to law enforcement."

"Is that a real thing?" Thistle asked me suspiciously.

"I think so," I admitted.

Thistle considered the threat. "Well, since we're not up to something, I guess we don't have to worry about it."

"I guess not," Landon agreed. He turned to Marcus. "Let's go. I could really use that beer after that dinner."

"I'll drive," Marcus offered.

"Good, I might want more than one beer."

"Hey," Thistle stopped the two of them before they got into Marcus' truck. "Stop at the store on your way back."

"To get what?" Landon looked tired.

"Lunch meat, bread and milk," Thistle said.

"Fine," Landon grumbled.

"Get a box of Tampax while you're at it," Thistle shot back.

Landon froze. "Over my dead body."

Thistle raised her eyebrows at Marcus expectantly, but he shook his head furiously. "Absolutely not."

"Fine," Thistle blew out a sigh. "We'll buy our own tampons."

"Awesome," Landon said, pausing at the passenger door and fixing his gaze on me. "Be good."

"We're always good," I said.

Landon shook his head. "Be better than that."

"Have fun," Thistle said brightly.

Once they were gone Thistle turned to me. "So, what are we really doing?"

"Having a quick séance."

"Why?" Clove whined.

"I need to check in with Erika and since I can't exactly call her on my cell, we have to try and call her to us."

"You want to see if she found the boat?" Thistle asked.

"Yeah," I nodded. "I'm also hoping, if we anchor her and join together, maybe we can boost her memory."

"Sounds like a good idea," Thistle said. "Even if it's a waste of time, we'll at least know it's a waste of time."

"It's dark out," Clove said.

"So?" Thistle challenged her. "We're not even leaving the property."

"Fine," Clove said. "I'm doing this under duress, though."

"Fine," Thistle said, opening the door to the cottage and walking in.

"I thought we were going to the clearing for a séance?" Clove complained.

"We need candles," Thistle reminded her.

"Oh, yeah."

We knew the property well enough that finding our way to the clearing wasn't difficult. Even though we hadn't cleaned up all the branches that had fallen during the winter yet, the path to the clearing was relatively free of debris.

Once there, Thistle set up the candles and lit them, arranging them in a small circle. We each sat on the ground, clasping each other's hands before looking to the sky. Since there were only three of us, we did a simple summoning chant.

Nothing happened.

"Well, that was a waste of time," Clove said, moving to get up.

"Try another spell," Thistle suggested.

Clove sighed and plopped back down on the ground. "I knew it wouldn't be that easy."

"Like what?" I ignored Clove's constant stream of complaints.

Thistle shrugged. "We really should've paid more attention when our mothers tried to teach us this stuff."

"That doesn't really help us now," Clove complained.

"Maybe we should just call her," I suggested.

"Isn't that what we just did?" Thistle asked.

"I mean, just call her name."

"Oh. Okay. Erika!"

"Erika!" I joined in.

Clove rolled her eyes but added her voice to the chorus. After a second, Erika flickered and then appeared in the illuminated circle. "What are you doing?"

"Looking for you," I said, relief washing over me when I saw her.

"I'm here," Erika said. "I'm always here. I told you that."

"I know," I said. "It's just that ... never mind. Did you find the boat again?"

Erika shook her head. "It wasn't there. It went away."

"Where do you think it went?"

"How should I know?"

Okay, that was a stupid question. "Erika, I know you've had it rough," I said sympathetically. "But I need you to do something for me."

"What?" Erika's eyes widened.

"I need you to try to remember."

"Remember what?"

"What happened to you?"

"I told you," Erika said. "I was sick and then I went to sleep."

"Okay," I said calmly. "Tell me about the boat."

"It was big."

"How big?"

"Big."

"Okay," I tried a different tactic. "Was it like fifty feet long big or bigger?"

"I told you, I don't know how to count."

"This isn't going to get us anywhere," Thistle muttered under her breath. "Erika, were you always on the boat?"

"I don't know what you mean?"

"You said that your home was a warmer place," Thistle said. "Did you get on the boat by your home? Was your home by water, too?"

"Oh," Erika mused. "No, I never saw the water by my home."

"So, how did you get to the boat?"

Erika cocked her head to the side. "I don't remember."

"Did you go in a car?"

"I don't remember."

Thistle looked at me, frustration slashing across her face. "When was the last time you saw your mom?"

I was surprised at the question, but the complexity of it was simple and yet multi-layered at the same time.

Erika smiled brightly. "She was sewing my dress," Erika gestured at the white frock she was wearing. "I had a small rip in the hem. She was fixing it for me."

"And what did she say?" Thistle prodded.

"She said to go and get my brother, Solomon, and tell him it was time for dinner."

"Did you get him?"

"I don't remember."

"Did you have dinner?"

"I don't remember."

Thistle rubbed her head tiredly. "Did your mom say goodbye to you? Before you got on the boat? Was your mom on the boat?"

"My mom wasn't on the boat," Erika said. "I don't remember saying goodbye to her." Erika jerked her head up, scanning the woods behind us fearfully.

"What is it?" I started to get to my feet.

"Someone is out there."

"Run," I whispered. "Hide. We'll find you again tomorrow."

Erika was gone before I finished speaking. Thistle, Clove and I climbed to our feet and turned to the dark tree line that had been at our backs. At first, I didn't hear anything. Then, the snap of a twig told me that she had been right – someone was out there.

"We should go back to the house," Clove whispered.

"How do you suggest we do that?" Thistle asked. "Wave our magic wands, click our ruby red shoes together and wish for it?"

"Sarcasm isn't going to help us."

"I wish Aunt Tillie was here," Clove lamented.

I would never have said it out loud, but I was mentally agreeing with her.

Another twig cracked and then the bushes to our left rustled.

"Alright, that did it," Thistle snapped. "This is our property. I refuse to be scared on our property." She strode to the bushes and peered behind them boldly. My fear told me to stay here, but my loyalty to Thistle urged me to back her up. Loyalty won out.

When I got to the bushes and looked behind them, relief washed over me – quickly followed by anger. "What the hell?"

Landon and Marcus were both crouched down behind the bushes. Landon seemed to be considering what to say when Marcus solved that particular problem for him. "We weren't spying!"

Landon sighed and stood up. "We were spying."

"Really?" Thistle asked sarcastically.

"Why?"

Landon looked at me, shame and anger warring for dominance on his face. "Because I knew you were lying."

"I wasn't lying," I countered. "Technically, I wasn't lying," I corrected.

"How do you figure that?"

"We didn't leave the property," I said.

"You're not taking a bath."

"I was going to do that when we were done," I said.

"Done doing what?"

Oh, screw it. "Holding a séance."

Landon looked around the clearing in confusion. "A séance?"

"We called Erika."

"Did she come?"

"She did," I said.

"And what did she say?"

"Who is Erika?" Marcus asked.

"A ghost," Thistle said. "She died on a boat and we're trying to figure out exactly when it happened."

"Oh," Marcus said. "Did she tell you?"

"No," Thistle shook her head. "She's all over the place. Then she heard you guys and ran away."

"That's too bad," Marcus said. "Call her back. We promise to be quiet."

I glanced at Thistle. Marcus was clearly curious about ghosts – which was better than fearful, I guess.

"You wouldn't be able to see her," Thistle said.

"Can you see her?"

"No," Thistle admitted. "If Bay is around, we can hear her, though."

"Why?"

"I have no idea."

"Oh, it's cool, though," Marcus said.

"How is that cool?" Landon looked irritated.

"It's like stuff you see in movies," Marcus said easily. "I think that's cool."

"I think I'm getting a headache," Landon lamented.

Another twig snapped. This time, it was on the far side of the clearing. Landon went from agitated to FBI agent in one second flat. His body tensed and then he strode over to the other side of the clearing to investigate.

The four of us stood where we were, watching.

Landon growled as he searched through the bushes. "What are you doing out here?"

I watched with wide-eyed wonder as Landon reached down and dragged Aunt Tillie into the clearing. She didn't look happy about being discovered.

"This is undignified."

"What are you doing out here?" Landon repeated the question.

"Taking a walk."

I looked her up and down, my eyes lingering on the bag she was carrying. "What's in the bag?"

"Nothing."

"Why don't I believe her?" Landon asked, pulling the bag from Aunt Tillie, who only put up a token fight before she relinquished it.

"Because you're not stupid," Thistle replied.

Landon unzipped the bag and looked inside of it. Disbelief registered across his face before he held it out toward me. "What is that?"

Uh-oh.

I moved to his side, taking the bag from him and peering into it. I frowned when I saw its contents. "What are those?" I questioned Aunt Tillie.

"I'm sure I don't know what you mean."

"You're lying."

"That's an ugly thing to say."

"Just tell me what's in the bag."

"I have no idea," Aunt Tillie said.

"You packed it," I reminded her.

"I'm old, I forget things. It must be the dementia."

"Oh, just let that go," Thistle sighed, picking her way over to us and taking the bag from me. She looked inside and then turned to Aunt Tillie incredulously. "Is this what I think it is?"

"That depends, what do you think it is?"

"It's some kind of larvae."

"Like for bugs?" I took a step away from Thistle and the bag.

"Yeah."

"That's gross."

"Where were you taking this? And what kind of bugs?" I asked.

"And where did you get them?" Thistle added.

"I ordered them off the Internet."

We had to find out where she was shopping, I swear.

"What are they?"

"Butterflies," Aunt Tillie responded coldly. "They're butterflies."

"Why would you be sneaking around at night with a bag full of butterfly larvae?" Clove asked suspiciously.

"I am not sneaking," Aunt Tillie countered. "This is my property. You can't sneak around on your own property."

"You can if you're hiding something from your nieces and grand-nieces," I shot back. "So, I ask again, why are you sneaking around with a bag full of butterfly larvae?"

"They're not ready to swarm yet," Aunt Tillie admitted. "I couldn't risk your mothers finding them and destroying them."

"Why would they kill butterflies?" Clove asked.

"Because they're not just butterflies," Thistle interjected. "She's done something to them."

"Why?" Landon asked.

"My guess? Because she's enchanted them so they'll do something evil and she plans on releasing them at the Dragonfly," I replied.

"You're on my list now, too," Aunt Tillie threatened.

"It sounds like a pretty long list," Landon sighed.

"It's getting longer every minute," Aunt Tillie agreed, narrowing her eyes at him suggestively.

"Well, I'm going to take the ... larvae, and you're going to go back to the inn, and we're going to go back to the guesthouse and I'm going to try and pretend like this entire night never happened."

"Good for you, Sparky," Aunt Tillie scoffed.

"Marcus," Landon barked. "I want you to walk Aunt Tillie back to the inn, make sure she goes inside and then join us at the guesthouse."

Marcus didn't even attempt to argue with Landon. He moved to Aunt Tillie's side quickly and directed her out of the clearing. She complained bitterly the whole time.

"I'm not going to forget this," Aunt Tillie warned. "You're all on my list."

"Fine," Landon waved her off.

Once they were gone, Landon fixed me with an angry glare. "We're going back to your place and we're going to bed. I can't even ... I don't even ... I just want some sleep right now."

"Okay," I replied worriedly.

"You people ... you give me a headache."

Landon stalked out of the clearing, but not before snatching Aunt Tillie's bag from Thistle and slinging it over his shoulder. I heard him mutter something, but I only caught three words: crazy and loony bin.

Thistle turned to me. "I think we might have broken him."

"He'll be fine," I said. "He just needs some sleep."

"You better give him a little treat when we get back. You know, take his mind off things."

"Yeah," Clove agreed. "He looks like he's about ready to flip out."

"He said he wouldn't flip out."

"We make people crazy," Thistle said. "That's our family's true gift."

All three of us jumped when we heard another twig snap, this one was back in the direction Marcus and Aunt Tillie had fled.

Thistle sighed. "It's probably just Aunt Tillie being ... well, Aunt Tillie."

"Yeah," I agreed. I stopped to stare at the area one last time, though. A chill ran through me.

"Bay!"

I pulled my gaze from the spot I had been staring and hurried after Landon and my cousins. I was actually looking forward to this night ending, too. Sometimes my family made me tired, as well.

Just don't tell Aunt Tillie.

NINETEEN

"What is that smell?"

"What smell?" Landon mumbled from his spot under the covers next to me.

"I don't know, breakfast or something," I replied, snuggling in closer to him. I felt his arms come around me, pulling me closer, and I exhaled a sigh of relief that he didn't pull away. He'd been fairly angry when we returned to the guesthouse the previous evening. While he hadn't been overtly cold when we went to bed, he wasn't his flirtatious self either.

Landon paused, his face buried in my hair for a second, and then he sat up straight. "It does smell good. Like bacon."

"I don't think we have bacon," I said. "We really need to go grocery shopping."

"Obviously someone is cooking something." Landon climbed out of bed and I took a second to enjoy the view. Lean muscles, toned skin, narrow hips, cute butt. He really did have the whole package. When you added his dimples and soulful eyes, he looked just good enough to eat.

Landon pulled on his jeans and shirt and, when he turned around, caught me checking him out. He smirked when I reddened. "I can have these pants off in less than ten seconds."

I considered the offer. "Let's see if something is really being cooked out there first," I said.

"You don't want to work up an appetite first?"

The truth was, I was already pretty hungry. When my stomach growled, Landon extended his hand to pull me out of bed. "I don't think I'm what you're hungry for right now."

I padded out to the living room, expecting to find Thistle and Clove toiling in the kitchen, but instead found them standing in the living room staring at each other accusingly.

"What's going on?"

"You don't know yet?" Thistle looked infuriated.

"Don't know what?"

"You don't smell that?"

I glanced at the two of them warily. "I thought you two were cooking breakfast."

"Really?" Thistle asked sarcastically. "When have I ever cooked you breakfast?"

"Well, then, what's that smell?"

"It's bacon," Clove said grimly.

"Yeah, I figured that out," I replied irritably. "That's why I thought you were cooking breakfast."

"No," Thistle shook her head. "We're not cooking anything."

"Then where is it coming from?"

Landon, who had been standing behind me, leaned in and sniffed my hair curiously. "It's coming from you."

"It's coming from them, too," Marcus said helpfully from his spot in the kitchen where he was sipping from a cup of coffee. "They all smell like cooking bacon."

"I don't get it," I said, furrowing my brow. Then, suddenly, I realized. "Aunt Tillie."

"You think?" Thistle shot back. "I'm going to find that old lady and kill her."

"Why would she do this?" Clove whined.

I was surprised when I felt Landon move in closer behind me and nuzzle his face against my hair. "Really? This turns you on?" I asked him blandly.

"You smell really good," Landon admitted. "I can't help it. Who doesn't love the smell of bacon?"

"And what do you think people are going to say when they smell us out in public?" I asked him.

"Well, they better not get close enough to get a good whiff," Landon said pragmatically. "You're going to be beating men off with a stick if they smell you."

"Yeah, a hot dog on a stick," Thistle spat out.

"She's making me stay over here," Marcus lamented. "I had the same reaction you did."

"Let's go back to bed," Landon suggested.

"I thought we were having breakfast?" I reminded him.

"That's exactly what I have planned."

"I'm a little freaked out that you're more interested in me now than you've ever been before – and all because I smell like bacon."

"Do you think you taste like bacon?"

I rolled my eyes. "We're not going to find out ... hey, did you just lick my face?"

"You do taste like bacon," Landon said excitedly.

Marcus' eyes brightened from across the room as he focused on Thistle.

"Let's just go back to bed for a little while," Landon pleaded. "I promise I'll buy you breakfast afterwards."

"It better be a big breakfast," I complained, but I let him drag me back to the bedroom. What? I was kind of interested to see what would happen.

TWO INCREDIBLY ENTHUSIASTIC HOURS LATER, Landon and I were leaving one of the small diners downtown after he had delivered on my promised breakfast.

"Best morning ever," Landon announced once we were outside.

"I'm glad you're happy," I replied, although the glow I had seen emanating from my own skin when we left home a half hour before had been proof that I couldn't really argue with his assertion. "I still don't know how I'm going to explain this to anyone else who smells it."

"How long do you think it will last?" Landon asked.

I shrugged. "I have no idea. It depends on how mad she was when she conjured her curse."

"I'm hoping it's a while," Landon said honestly. "A good long while."

"I smell like bacon," I reminded him.

"And taste, don't forget taste," Landon added.

"I just know this is going to become a thing," I grumbled. "Brian is going to start questioning me about it."

"Tell him it's perfume oil or something," Landon suggested. "And he better not find out you taste like bacon, too," he warned me.

"They don't have perfume oil that smells like bacon," I countered.

"I bet they do," Landon said. "Bacon is everywhere."

"Awesome."

"You don't have to worry about it today," Landon said. "It's Thursday. You don't have to go in, right?"

"Right," I agreed warily. "What did you have in mind? And, no, spending the entire day in bed isn't an option."

"Not even if I bring lettuce and tomato?" Landon teased.

"Especially if you bring lettuce and tomato."

"Actually, that wasn't what I had in mind," Landon said.

"Really?" I arched an eyebrow. I was having trouble believing him.

"Not right now at least," Landon ceded. "I was thinking you could take me out to the Dandridge instead."

"Really?"

"Yeah, I want to see it."

"Okay," I shrugged. "Let's go."

"We're going to revisit the lettuce and tomato thing later, though. Just be ready."

Good grief.

I directed Landon out to the Dandridge, having him park at Wetzel Road so we wouldn't have to walk as far. Once we were in front of the lighthouse, Landon whistled lowly in surprise.

"This is actually pretty cool."

"It's run down," I said.

"Not as bad as you would think, though," Landon said, climbing up the front steps of the lighthouse and tugging on the door in an attempt to open it. "It's locked. How did you guys get in here?"

I glanced up at him. "Do you really want to know?"

Landon grinned. "Impress me."

I shook my head ruefully but climbed the steps to give him the performance he wanted. I placed my hand on the doorknob, whispered a quick spell, and then turned the knob when I heard the lock tumble.

Landon looked truly impressed. "That must have come in handy when you were a kid. No one could lock you out of your Aunt Tillie's wine closet. My brothers and I would have loved a way to get into my dad's beer shed."

I cast a curious glance in Landon's direction. "You don't talk about your family much."

"Yes, I do," Landon countered.

"No," I shook my head, wandering into the lighthouse in front of Landon. "You don't. You put up with my family constantly, and yet you never really talk about your family. I don't know anything about them."

Landon pressed a kiss to my neck – which I'm sure was just another gambit to get a taste of my bacon skin – and then moved away to get a better look at the interior of the Dandridge.

"What do you want to know?"

"I don't know," I said. "Are your parents both alive?"

"They are," Landon said. "They live in the Bay City area."

"Close to your brother, the Baptist minister in Saginaw?"

"See, I *have* told you about my family." Landon looked pleased that I remembered what he had told me.

"Not really," I pressed.

"What are you getting at, Bay?" Landon asked seriously. "Do you want to meet my family?"

I felt my face color and was glad it was dim enough that he couldn't see me blush from several feet away. "I wasn't fishing for an invitation to meet your family. I was just curious."

"Okay," Landon said easily. "Well, let's see. I'm the oldest of three boys. My parents were fairly strict when we were growing up. My mom was a homemaker and my dad was a police officer."

"Really? Is that why you became an FBI agent?"

"Probably," Landon said. "I think my parents were worried there for a while, when we were teenagers, that we were all going to end up on the wrong side of the bars in jail."

"Really?" I was amused at the thought. "You were rowdy?"

"We got in our fair share of trouble."

"But you said that your parents were strict."

"They were," Landon nodded. "Kids will be kids, though. I think, maybe, because they were so strict, that's why we all rebelled so hard."

"And yet you have a brother that decided to be a minister," I mused.

"Yeah, and he was the wildest one," Landon said with a small laugh. "I guess he was making amends for all the beer he drank and all the bras he tried to undo without anyone noticing."

"Do you see them much?"

"I see them every couple of months, when I get time to go down there," Landon replied.

"When was the last time you went down there?"

Landon met my gaze evenly. "Right before I came back to Hemlock Cove."

I swallowed inadvertently. "Oh."

Landon stilled his wandering. "I can't quite figure out what you're worried about," he admitted. "Is it that you think I told them about you? About you and your family?"

"No," I said hurriedly. "That's not what I was thinking."

"Then what were you thinking?"

"I was thinking that they're probably a nice, normal family," I said honestly. "They're not going to like me. They're not going to like us. They're probably going to wonder why you're with me."

Landon's face broke into a wry grin. "They'll like you," Landon said. "Trust me. There's a lot to like – and that was before the whole bacon thing. If that's still around when you meet them, they'll love you."

My heart was warmed by his answer, but I was still bothered. "How are you going to explain my family?"

"Everyone's family has ... quirks, Bay," Landon replied calmly. "I don't have to explain anything about your family. You're all tight. You all love each other. You all fight. If you eliminate that whole witch thing – which I'm starting to get used to, by the way – you're all extremely normal, too. There's nothing wrong with your family."

"Aunt Tillie is normal?"

"Well, Aunt Tillie is Aunt Tillie," Landon said. "I've got my own Aunt Tillie. We don't call her Aunt Tillie, but trust me, I've got my own Aunt Tillie."

"Really?" I had my doubts.

"Oh, yeah, Aunt Blanche is pretty much Aunt Tillie's clone – only she can't curse anyone," Landon said. "If she could've cursed my brothers and me, though, you can be very sure she would have."

I smiled softly, relief warming my heart. "I just ... ."

Landon crossed the room and pulled me toward him, planting a soft and reassuring kiss on my lips. I sank into it; relishing his strength and that soft hum I felt whenever he was near.

The sound of someone clearing his throat caused us to pull apart swiftly.

Dean was standing in the door watching us, a smile playing at the corner of his lips. "I was going to call the police when I saw the door open. Since there's an FBI agent already here, though, I guess that would have been a wasted call."

"I'm sorry," I apologized profusely.

"The door was open," Landon said hurriedly. "I just wanted to see the building. After you were talking about it last night, I just thought it sounded cool."

"It's fine," Dean said, waving off Landon's explanation. "I don't blame you. It's not like you were doing anything. Well, at least not yet." Dean winked at me.

"I'm surprised at what good shape the building is in," Landon said, changing the subject. "I would have thought it would be more run-down. It looks pretty sound, though."

"They built to last back in those days," Dean said.

"What year was this built?"

"Um, 1847," Dean said. "Right when the Underground Railroad started picking up steam."

Something clicked in my head.

"The Underground Railroad? You mean, like during the Civil War?"

"Well, actually the Underground Railroad started early in the 1800s," Dean said. He was clearly a history buff. "It hit its peak around 1850, so a lot of safe houses were set up along routes people were traversing in an attempt to get from the U.S. to Canada – including along Lake Michigan."

"I didn't think the Underground Railroad went this far north," Landon said.

"Well, it did," Dean replied. "There weren't a lot of routes along the lake at that time, but they were building more and more as time went on. The Dandridge was built during that time. And, while the official reason given for its construction was that there were dangerous rocks out there – which was true – the real reason was to help people escape up into Canada."

"That's kind of cool," Landon said, smiling at me. He frowned, though, when he saw the contemplative look on my face.

"How did they get the slaves this far north?"

"A variety of ways," Dean said. "Wagons and boats mostly, though. The fleeing slaves would run away on foot and be picked up by caravans and then driven further and further northward."

"Would it always be families?"

Dean looked confused. "What do you mean?"

"Would families flee together, I mean? Or would there ever have been a reason for an entire boatload of children to be shipped separate from adults?"

Realization dawned on Landon's face. He turned to Dean expectantly, waiting for him to answer.

Dean stroked his chin thoughtfully. "That's a really interesting question," he said. "There were reports of children being smuggled together, away from the fighting," he said. "I don't think that was an experiment that lasted too long, though."

"Why?"

"Well, think about it," Dean said. "You would have these big boats, with only one or two adults – so as not to draw attention – and then you would have like fifty kids in squalid conditions underneath. That's a breeding ground for sickness – and no way to treat the kids."

"So, a lot of them died," I mused, more to myself than anyone else. Dean answered anyway.

"Yeah, a lot of them died."

"Well," Landon broke in. "We've taken up enough of your time. Thanks for the history lesson."

He moved over to my side, linking his fingers with mine, and started to lead me out of the Dandridge.

"Hey, stop by any time," Dean said. "I love it when people are as enthusiastic about history as I am."

"We definitely will," Landon said.

"Did you guys have a picnic or something?" Dean glanced around the empty room.

"No, why?" I asked.

"Oh, nothing," Dean shrugged. "I could just swear I smell bacon."

TWENTY

"She was a slave," I said as soon as Landon and I were safely in his vehicle.

"How can you be sure?"

"It fits," I said. "I couldn't figure out why a little black girl would be running around this area."

"That's a little racist," Landon said, surprise on his face.

"Not like that," I said, brushing off his statement. "I mean that there aren't any black families in the area. How could a little girl without a coat end up here?"

"I guess that's a good point," Landon ceded. "Are you sure, though?"

"Not one hundred percent, no," I said. "I'm fairly sure, though. It fills in a lot of the gaps."

"What gaps?"

"Erika said she came from a warm climate and she wasn't always on the boat," I explained. "She's wearing a simple white dress, but it's not a modern white dress. It's just a cotton dress. No labels. No nothing."

"Maybe her family is just poor," Landon pointed out. "You didn't mention that about the dress earlier," he added.

"Maybe," I agreed. "I didn't really think about the dress until now. If she's been dead for a hundred and fifty years, though, it would also explain the big holes in her memory."

"How?"

"She's been alone for a really long time," I said, pity welling in my chest. "With nothing but the stars to keep her company."

"What?" Landon looked confused.

"Nothing," I shook my head. "Just something she said about the stars. Anyway, if you're alone that long, you start to create your own reality."

"How do you know?"

"Let's just say I've met a lot of ghosts," I said grimly.

"Okay," he said. "What are you going to do to prove your theory?"

"Talk to a ghost," I said simply

"And where are you going to find her?"

"She's always around," I said simply. "I'm going to call her."

"Well, while you're doing that, I'm going to run a missing minors check – just to be on the safe side," Landon said. "I'm not going to be able to let it go until we're sure."

I understood that feeling completely.

I had Landon drop me off at Hypnotic with a promise that I wouldn't do anything crazy – or shower. He was worried that the bacon flavor would rub off before he got a chance to sample it again.

Thistle and Clove were plotting when I entered the store.

"What's going on?"

"What's the worst smell you can think of?" Thistle asked, not looking up from the book she was poring over.

"A decomposing body."

"Not that gross," Thistle said.

"Why? What are we doing?"

"I'm going to curse Aunt Tillie with a smell as retribution," Thistle said grimly. "I'm trying to find a really gross one."

"Do you think that's a good idea?"

"We smell like frying pig," Thistle said disgustedly. "I think it's a bloody brilliant idea."

"Well, I have something else for us to focus on right now," I said. "That will have to wait for later."

"Why aren't you more upset about the bacon smell?" Clove asked earnestly.

"Landon likes it," I shrugged. "If we just let it go, it will be gone in a week. I can live with his ... enthusiasm for a week. Heck, I'll probably enjoy it. It's not that much of a hardship."

"Wait until someone else smells it," Thistle said. "We've had five different customers ask us if we had a kitchen in back. It's revolting."

"You like bacon," I reminded her.

"I don't like to smell like bacon."

"Marcus likes the bacon smell," I pointed out.

Thistle blushed furiously. "That's neither here nor there."

"Don't you want to know where I've been?" I decided to change the subject. There was no way I was going to risk pissing off Aunt Tillie any more than she already was.

"Where have you been?" Clove asked brightly.

I told the two of them about my trip to the Dandridge and what I'd found out. Thistle looked decidedly relieved by the time I reached the end of the story. "She was a slave."

"That's what I think."

"That's terrible," Clove said sadly.

"It is," I agreed. "It's also good news for us."

"How?"

"It means there's not really a boat filled with kids out there being mistreated," I said.

"Oh," Clove said quietly. "I guess that is better."

"Better for us," Thistle agreed. "Not so good for Erika. How are you going to get her to move on?"

"I don't know," I admitted. "Right now, though, we've got to make sure that we're right."

"It makes sense," Thistle said. "This idea makes a lot more sense than the idea that people are trafficking kids on Lake Michigan right under the nose of local law enforcement."

"That's still a possibility," I reminded her. "But, if I'm right, then the only thing we have to worry about is figuring out a way for Erika to let go."

"Which is better than trying to find a boat of real children on a really big lake," Clove said knowingly. "So, what do we do first?"

"We call Erika," I said simply.

"Another séance?" Clove didn't look thrilled.

"No," Thistle shook her head. "We didn't call her with the séance last night. We just called her and she showed up. We should just do that again."

"Right," I said. I moved to the front window of the store, glancing up and down the street, and then flipped the sign on the door to 'closed.'

"What are you doing?"

"I just don't want to be interrupted."

"So you're costing us business?" Thistle arched an eyebrow.

"They'll come back," I replied. "This won't take long."

"Fine," Thistle agreed. "Just make it quick."

"Erika!"

I looked around the store expectantly. The little girl didn't appear, though. I turned to Thistle and Clove expectantly. Clove sighed, but she joined in. "Erika!"

Still nothing.

"Erika," I tried one more time. "We need to talk to you."

"I heard you the first time," Erika grumbled, popping into view. "Wow, what is this place?"

"This is our store," Thistle said.

"What kind of store?" Erika looked around. "Are you doctors?"

"No, why would you think we're doctors?" Clove asked curiously.

"You have a lot of medicines in bags."

I glanced over at the herb rack, understanding washing over me. "We're not doctors. Did doctors use herbs a lot when you were alive?"

"Yes," Erika said. "Don't they now?"

"Not herbs like you think," I said finally. "Erika, the reason we called you, is I think I figured out what happened to you."

"Really?" She looked excited. "What happened to me?"

"I have some questions first. Were you ... were you a slave?" There's a question I never thought – or maybe I just hoped – I would ever ask.

"No," Erika shook her head defiantly. I felt my heart drop. "We weren't slaves, but my mama was worried that someone would mistake us for slaves. She was always saying that there were bad people that thought we should all be sold."

"So, you were free," I said carefully. "But there were slaves by you?"

"Not really by us," Erika said. I could tell she was fighting to remember. "They were other places. We lived in a small cabin. My papa worked at a local plantation, but he wasn't a slave. He worked in the house, not in the fields."

"Did your parents decide to send you away?"

"Yes," Erika said excitedly. "I remember now. They sent me and Solomon with the people."

"Solomon," I said. "Your brother?"

"Yes, we were too little, my mama said," Erika explained. "She was worried that someone would just take us. So they sent us with the people. We were supposed to stay up there with some other people until they could come be with us. My mama said it would only be a little while until we were all together again."

"So, how did you leave?"

"We were put on a wagon," Erika said. "It seemed like we were on it forever. Every day, though, it got colder and colder. Then, one day we stopped. I thought we were where we were supposed to be. They put us on a boat then, though, and we were on the boat even longer than we were on the wagons."

"Was Solomon with you on the boat?"

"Yes."

"Did Solomon get sick, too?"

"No," Erika replied quietly. "He was there with me, but he wasn't sick. When I got sick, he used to sing to me – like my mama would – and he would try to make me better. He would put a cloth on my head and sing. He would tell me that it wouldn't be long before we were off the boat and we would be safe. He told me to wish on a star, like we did at home, even though we couldn't see the stars. He told me to wish and I would get better."

"Did you wish?" Thistle asked sadly.

"I wished really hard," Erika said. "I don't think it works without the stars, though."

"And then what happened?" I asked around the lump in my throat.

"Then I went to sleep," Erika said, her voice barely a whisper. "And when I woke up, Solomon was gone."

"It's going to be okay, Erika," I promised. "We're going to find a way to get you to ... we're going to find a way to get you to a better place."

"Will my mama be there? And Solomon?"

"I really hope so," I said honestly. "I'm just glad that the boat you were talking about is gone now. That other little kids aren't getting sick on it."

"It's not gone," Erika said. "The boat I was on is gone but the other one is back."

I froze, fear tingling in my fingertips. "What do you mean? What other boat?"

"The other boat that's out there now," Erika said simply. "I found it again. You have to help those children."

"What children?" Clove asked worriedly.

"The ones that want their mommies and daddies," Erika said. "They keep crying for them."

"What do the children look like?" I asked desperately. "Do they look like you?" I was desperately hoping that she was just getting the present confused with the past.

"No," Erika shook her head. "They're lighter, like you. They just want to go home. You have to save them so they can go home, like I never did."

TWENTY-ONE

I strode out of Hypnotic and headed straight for the police department across the street. Landon had said he wanted to check things out and I had a feeling he hadn't gone too far to do it.

I went in through the back entrance, greeting Chief Terry's secretary and adjusting my trajectory for the hallway that led to Chief Terry's office. I could hear voices inside the office, so I slowed my approach. I paused outside to listen. Okay, I was technically eavesdropping.

"What do you think?" The voice belonged to Chief Terry.

"I don't know what to think. I'm still new to all of this. My brain tells me it's not rational and yet ... ." Landon looked unsure.

"You've actually seen some of the things they can do," Chief Terry filled in for him. "I know. It's an adjustment."

"How long have you known?"

"A long time," Chief Terry said. "The family has always been off – and I'm not just talking about Tillie. I was a few years ahead of Winnie, Marnie and Twila in school, and yet even then people were talking about them, and it wasn't just because they were all cute."

"Cute?" Landon laughed.

"Look at the younger girls and you'll see what the older ones looked like when they were their age," Chief Terry said. "It's not like they're clones – well, except for Clove, she and Marnie could've been twins – but Thistle and Bay both resemble their mothers, in more ways than one."

"When did you first know there was something different about them?"

"There were always whispers that they could do things," Chief Terry admitted. "It started with the aunts. They kept saying that the Winchesters were hexing all the boys in class to only pay attention to them. I always thought that was jealousy. You know how girls that age are. Although, I wouldn't put it past Marnie to do something like that just for some afternoon amusement."

"When did you know for sure?" Landon sounded curious.

"My first year on the job as a police officer, there was a fire at the high school gym," Chief Terry said. "The call we got is that there were a lot of kids trapped inside and that there was no way to get them out. We all went to the gym expecting mass casualties and ... well, you can imagine, burned bodies."

"What happened?"

"When we got there all the kids were outside and safe," Chief Terry said. "Every single one of them was accounted for. We didn't understand how. All the kids would say is that Winnie and Marnie managed to open the door and walk through the fire to get them out. Literally walked through the fire."

"And what did you think?"

"I thought they were suffering from smoke inhalation," Chief Terry responded honestly. "That they were seeing things. That in the confusion of what was happening, they just didn't realize what they really saw and that there was a path through there and they just couldn't see it because of the smoke."

"So you still didn't believe?"

"I don't know," Chief Terry said. "I pushed it out of my mind for years. Sure, people still talked. You know, people were convinced that Tillie was evil incarnate."

"She might be," Landon said.

"And then you'd hear whisperings about certain things going on up on the property, séances and stuff," Chief Terry continued. "Old Lenny Franz said that he saw them dancing naked under the full moon."

"Yeah, I think that one is true," Landon said grimly.

"You've seen it?" Chief Terry asked interestedly.

"Maybe," Landon hedged. "I really don't want to talk about it."

"I bet," Chief Terry chuckled. "Anyway, I wasn't sure – really sure – until the girls started growing up. I got a call from Winnie one day. She was panicked. Bay had gotten in a fight with Thistle and ran away from home. I figured she hadn't gone far, so I had everyone out looking for her."

Landon remained silent.

"I was out looking for her myself – this was before she started going to the tree house when she was upset – so I wasn't sure where to look for her," Chief Terry went on. "I happened to be driving by the cemetery – and that's when I saw her."

A memory jogged in my mind, one I had long since forgotten.

"She couldn't have been more than eight years old," Chief Terry said. "She was all wild blonde hair and sad blue eyes and the minute I saw her I wanted to just ... I don't know ... hug her or something. She looked so sad. She wasn't alone, though. Well, actually, I thought she was alone. She was talking out loud and I thought she was talking to herself. When I approached her, though, it was like she was having a conversation with someone, only I couldn't see who she was talking to."

"She was talking to a ghost?" Landon asked. "She could do it way back then?"

"I think she could probably always do it," Chief Terry said. "The family covered by saying Bay had an active imagination and an imaginary friend for a long time. Although, if I'm being honest, any kid in the neighborhood that hassled Bay either got beat up by Clove and Thistle or had something else unfortunate happen to them."

"Like they died?" Landon sound horrified.

"No," Chief Terry said quickly. "More like they had certain inconveniences happen to them. Chicken pox for little Bobby Briggs. A wart right on the end of the nose for little Clementine Baker. And, for little Lila Stevens – a particularly nasty little thing – her hair all fell out for no apparent reason."

"Tillie," Landon breathed.

"I can't prove that," Chief Terry said. "But, yeah. After a while, everyone in town seemed to put two and two together so no one picked on Bay anymore. At least most people didn't. Lila Stevens never seemed to learn her lesson and there were a few more problems when the girls hit their teens."

"How did you know that Bay wasn't talking to herself in the cemetery?" Landon asked curiously.

"Because, when I asked her who she was talking to, she told me she was talking to my mother," Chief Terry said. "My mom had died a decade before. A car accident. It had been really sudden."

"What did she say she was talking about with your mom?"

"Nothing big really," Chief Terry said. "Mostly just inane chatter. It was just this one thing that she said that made me know she wasn't making it up."

"What?" Landon asked curiously.

"I told him his mother knew he kept the locket," I said, stepping in the doorway to reveal myself.

Landon jumped up in surprise, but Chief Terry merely smiled when he saw me. "That's exactly what you told me."

Landon looked embarrassed to have been caught talking about me, but he asked the obvious question anyway. "And what was the deal with the locket?"

"It was my mom's favorite piece of jewelry, a necklace her mother had given her when she died," Chief Terry said. "My mom always said she wanted to be buried with it, but I couldn't bear to do that. I wanted to hold on to it because it reminded me of her. So, right before they closed the casket, I took the necklace and kept it. No one knew that. No one could know that. And yet Bay knew it."

I smiled at Chief Terry. "She was glad you took it."

"I hope so," Chief Terry said, his voice cracking slightly.

"I had forgotten about that," I admitted. "I had forgotten until I heard you telling Landon."

"We weren't gossiping about you," Landon said hurriedly, sitting back down in his chair nervously. "We were just talking."

"It's fine," I said, waving him off. "It's not a big deal. It's human nature."

Landon looked like he wanted to say something else, but he changed his mind instead. "Did you find Erika?"

"I did," I said, turning back to him. "You told Chief Terry?"

"Yeah, I needed his help," Landon said. "I wanted to run a search on missing girls, but I didn't want to go all the way to Traverse City to do it."

"What does your office think you're doing anyway?" I asked.

"Working on cold cases, which I have been," Landon replied. "Just not necessarily the cold cases they think I am."

"Is that wise?"

"It will be fine," Landon said distractedly. "So, what did she say?"

"She confirmed what we thought, that she was on a ship that was supposed to be taking her to a better place – which I assume was some place in Canada – and that she died en route. Her family was supposed to meet her there and one of her brothers was with her."

"Well, that's a relief," Chief Terry said. "We've been through the missing children in Michigan and the surrounding states and there were no files that matched her description."

"So, what happens now?" Landon asked.

"Can't you help her move on, like you did my mother?" Chief Terry asked.

"Your mom was easy to help move on," I said quietly. "Her unfinished business was fairly simple. She just wanted you to know that everything was okay. That you were going to be okay."

Chief Terry smiled. "And once she told you that, she passed on?"

"She did," I nodded.

"Passed on where?" Landon asked curiously.

"To whatever is waiting for us all when we're gone," I shrugged. "I don't know. I think Heaven is too simplistic. It's a whole other world, though. I know that."

"Why don't you look happier?" Landon asked.

"That's not all she told us," I hedged, biting my lower lip and glancing between Landon and Chief Terry.

"What else did she tell you?" Chief Terry leaned forward in his desk chair.

"She said there's another boat out there," I said carefully. "A boat that has different children on it. Children that are crying for their mommies and daddies."

Chief Terry's face drained of color. "Do you think she's telling the truth?"

"I don't think she knows how to lie," I admitted.

"But you said yourself that she was confusing time periods," Landon said. "Maybe she's still doing that."

"Maybe," I nodded. "And maybe there really are two boats. The one she died on and another one with a whole different group of children on it."

"How are we supposed to explain to the Coast Guard that a ghost told us there's a boat out there with a bunch of kids on it?" Landon asked irritably.

"I don't know," I shrugged. "Can't you just say you got an anonymous tip or something?"

"We can," Chief Terry said. "That's just going to get them to do a cursory search, though. We're going to need more to get a full search."

"How much more?"

"A lot more than the ramblings of a ghost that has been dead for a hundred and sixty years," Landon grumbled.

"Well, I'm sorry I don't have all the evidence lined up for you in a neat little row," I snapped. "I don't know how to give you any more than I've already given you. Give me a flipping break!"

Chief Terry looked surprised by my outburst. Landon's face switched from hurt to astonished anger in mere seconds.

"Well, there's only so much we can do, too," he said firmly. "Acting like a child and stomping your foot and pouting isn't going to help."

"Is that what you think I'm doing?"

"That's exactly what I think you're doing," Landon said bitterly. "I'm trying to help you here. Why don't you try helping instead of sitting there and just expecting everything to magically fall into place? You regress to this childish little foot-stomping thing whenever things get even slightly hard and it's ... well, it's annoying. Grow up."

I felt my mouth drop open and there was a nasty retort on the tip of my tongue. Instead of letting it loose, though, I whirled on my heel and stormed out of the office. I was fighting to hold back the tears as I stalked down the hallway.

I heard a chair slide on the floor in Chief Terry's office.

"Let her go, son. She just needs to blow off some steam. You're just going to make things worse if you go after her now. Trust me. They're complicated women. Did you guys have BLT's for lunch or something? It smells like bacon."

I didn't look back to see if Landon had followed me into the hallway.

Once I was outside of the police station, I found myself at a loss. I wanted to drive somewhere – anywhere, really -- but my car was still out at the inn. I could've asked Clove or Thistle to drive me back home – but I didn't really want to talk to either one of them – so I decided to walk. It took me about fifteen minutes to get back home. Once I was in my car, I took off without a clear destination in mind. Instead, I rolled the window down and just let the chilly spring air wash over me. I needed to think.

Landon's accusations had hurt me – more than I was willing to admit, even to myself. The truth was, I had been waiting for him to get sick of everything and walk away – so it wasn't a big shock. Sure, I was the one that had fed the fight, but everything I had been worrying about was starting to come into fruition – and I couldn't help but feel somewhat vindicated by it.

For the next hour, I just rode up and down area roads until I found myself on Wetzel Road and not far from the Dandridge. On a whim, I parked my car and climbed out. I wandered to the Dandridge, glancing around to make sure Dean wasn't present, and then walked past the building until I was on the end of the old dock and could see the expanse of the water beyond it.

Then I just stood there and stared.

The water was empty. Open tableaus of rolling waves kept moving, but there was nothing else. There was no other boat in sight and yet, still, Erika's words haunted me. I took in a long, shaky breath. Landon was right. I had to figure this out. Being a baby wasn't going to solve this problem.

I turned to move back toward my car but froze when I heard a door shut. Instinctively, I dropped to my knees on the dock and waited. I wasn't sure if I had heard the door of the Dandridge or of a car. After a second, I realized it had to be the door of the Dandridge – because there was a no way a car could get into this immediate area until some of the trees were cleared out.

After a few seconds of not being able to see – or hear – anything, I stood up. I figured it was probably Dean, and he wouldn't mind if I was looking around. The figure I saw moving away from the Dandridge, though – the one that didn't bother to turn around and scan the area to make sure no one else was present – was not Dean.

It was Karen.

TWENTY-TWO

I thought about following Karen, but decided against it. I really didn't have a reason to think she was up to anything nefarious. For all I knew, she was merely meeting with Dean to discuss the renovations that would be starting soon on the Dandridge. Actually, that was probably exactly what she was doing out here.

I let out a shaky breath, internally lambasting myself for acting like an idiot. There wasn't always some evil plot brewing in Hemlock Cove, I reminded myself. I headed back toward my car. There was no reason to make things harder than they already were.

I returned to the guesthouse and pulled out my laptop. I decided to work for the rest of the afternoon. The Whistler's weekly edition would come out tomorrow, but I had already done all the work for that edition and turned it over to the paginator. Basically I was just doing busywork for the next week – but it was something to take my mind off my fight with Landon.

I expected him to show up at the guesthouse that night. When he didn't, I felt my heart drop to my shoes. Could he really be that angry? I thought about texting him, but that sounded too needy. So I did what anyone else would do under the same circumstances – I took a long bath and went to bed early. Sure, some may call it pouting – but

I thought it was a perfectly acceptable way to deal with my inner strife.

The next morning I was woken up by the sound of my cellphone dinging on the nightstand next to me. I reached over to grab it, instinctively hoping it was Landon and hating myself for the need to hear his voice at the same time. I had to push down the feeling of bitter disappointment that threatened to engulf me when I saw the number of the inn pop up.

"What's up?"

"That's not how you answer the phone," Aunt Tillie said irritably.

"Do you want me to hang up so you can call again?"

"Well, you're in a mood," Aunt Tillie grumbled.

"What do you want?"

"The contractors are down here and they want to talk to whoever is in charge," Aunt Tillie sniffed. "I told them I was in charge, but they said that you had to sign off on everything."

"Fine," I blew out a sigh. "I'll be down in a half hour. Give them some food and coffee and I'll be quick."

"What's wrong with you?" Aunt Tillie actually sounded concerned.

"Nothing," I said evasively. "You just woke me up. I'll be down soon. I promise."

I showered, dressed and headed toward the inn in record time. I spent very little time on my makeup or my hair. I really didn't care how bad I looked.

When I got to the construction site, I found Aunt Tillie holding court. "I'm giving you all fresh donuts and fresh coffee, but don't expect me to do it every day. You're here to work, not eat for free."

"Thanks for the donuts," Dirk Langstrom said with a small smile. "They're very good. I promise we'll still work."

"Of course you will," Aunt Tillie said knowingly. "I'll be watching."

"Okay," Dirk laughed.

I plastered a welcoming smile on my face and walked over to Dirk. "Good morning. She's not getting in the way, is she?"

"No," Dirk shook his head. "I wish all of our clients were this ... enthusiastic."

"Is that the word we're using?" I glanced over at Aunt Tillie briefly. "We'll go with that."

Dirk tried to hide his smile when Aunt Tillie frowned at me. "Do you want a donut? Although," he sniffed. "It smells like you already had breakfast."

Aunt Tillie's evil smile told me she was enjoying this too much. "I'm fine," I said. "Thank you, though. Aunt Tillie said you needed something?"

"Yeah," Dirk said. "I just wanted to make sure that you want electricity on both the inside and the outside of the building."

"Why is that important?" I asked.

"Well, inside is obvious," he said. "There might be instances where you need to plug things in like grow lights or even a radio."

"Right."

"Outside, though, it's just a convenience," Dirk said. "You might want to plug in decorative lights or even lawn care equipment."

"And is there a big difference in price?"

"No, not really," Dirk said. "It's just a preference really."

"Let's go for inside and outside."

"Okay," Dirk nodded.

"Is that what she wanted?" I angled my jaw in Aunt Tillie's direction.

"Yep."

"Well," I sighed. "Let's do it anyway."

Dirk narrowed his eyes, amusement flirting with his features. "Okay."

"Dirk," I stopped him quickly. "You know, you're doing a lot of work out here – and you're putting up with a lot of distractions you probably wouldn't necessarily have to on another job."

"It's fine," he said quickly. "I've been hearing about this inn for years. It's just a pleasure to be able to see it up close."

"It's not fine," I said. "She's just ... she's just her. I can't explain it. Why don't you bring your family out for dinner tonight," I suggested. "The inn has very few guests right now and my mom and aunts love to cook for people. I promise it will be a good meal."

"It's no problem? You're sure."

"Absolutely," I said.

"Well, thanks," he smiled. "That sounds really nice."

"I'll see you tonight then."

"Yeah, tonight."

I watched Dirk head back to his crew and found myself amazed at how much they had already managed to get done. Most of the walls were already up. Sure, it was just a frame, but it was still quick work. Once he was gone, Aunt Tillie moved over to me.

"What's wrong with you?"

"Nothing," I said. "Why do you think something is wrong with me?"

"You don't look like you've slept in a month," Aunt Tillie said honestly.

"Well, I have," I said briefly.

"Is Landon keeping you up too late at night?"

I turned on Aunt Tillie tiredly. "Landon wasn't here last night."

Aunt Tillie nodded knowingly. "That's what's wrong. You're in a fight."

"We're not in a fight," I lied.

"You can't lie to your Aunt Tillie," she said.

"Well, if that's the case, do you think you can get rid of the bacon smell? It's starting to become a real distraction."

Aunt Tillie pursed her lips. "I have no idea what you're talking about."

Apparently that lying mandate was one-sided. I decided to change the subject. "How do I get a ghost to move on when she's been hanging around for a really long time?"

Aunt Tillie considered the question. "We're talking about the little girl?"

"Erika," I corrected her.

"Erika," Aunt Tillie said. "We're talking about her?"

"Yeah," I sighed. "Most ghosts just need closure. Chief Terry reminded me yesterday of when his mother moved on. All she wanted was for him to know that everything was going to be okay and not to feel guilty for taking the locket. It's not that easy in this case."

"No, it's not," Aunt Tillie agreed. "What do you think her unfinished business is? Why didn't she cross over when she died?"

"She says she just went to sleep on the boat and woke up by the Dandridge," I said. "We found out that she was on a ship that was transporting her to Canada to make sure she wouldn't be swept up in any slavery sweeps in the south. That was a hundred and sixty years ago. Her family is gone."

"Thistle and Clove told us what you found out at dinner last night," Aunt Tillie said. "A dinner you weren't present for, by the way."

"I had other things going on," I replied briefly.

"Fighting with Landon," Aunt Tillie said.

"No, I did that earlier in the afternoon. I just needed to think."

"And pout."

"I wasn't pouting."

"Don't lie," Aunt Tillie admonished me. "There's no harm in pouting. I've done it from time to time myself."

That wasn't exactly a surprise.

"You just can't dwell on it," Aunt Tillie said. "If you were in the wrong, call him and apologize."

"I don't think I was in the wrong," I said stubbornly.

"Then wait him out," Aunt Tillie said. "He'll come back."

"How can you be sure?" I asked her curiously.

"I told you, I know all and see all."

"Right, I forgot."

"I don't know how you could."

"I really don't have the energy for this today," I sighed. "I need you to help me find a way to get Erika to move on."

"Why is this so important to you?" Aunt Tillie asked pointedly.

"I don't know."

"That's not an answer."

"I just ... I just don't want her to be out there wandering around alone anymore," I said. "She has no one. She was on the boat with her brother, Solomon. He told her to wish on a star and she would be fine. She wasn't fine, though."

"I used to tell you to wish on a star when you were little," Aunt Tillie mused.

"I remember."

"Did your wishes come true?"

"Some of them," I said, a smile playing at the corner of my lips.

"Is that what Landon is? A wish come true?"

I frowned. That made me sound a little pathetic. Aunt Tillie seemed to read my mind. "I can see wishing for him. He's worth a wish or two – even though he needs a haircut."

I glanced at her in surprise. "Really? You don't think that makes me weak?"

"Nope."

"You like him," I laughed hollowly.

"He reminds me of your Uncle Calvin."

Uncle Calvin had died before I was born, but I had seen pictures. Landon and Uncle Calvin didn't look anything alike.

"Not that way," Aunt Tillie said knowingly. "They don't resemble each other. They just have the same spirit. They're both good men drawn to ... difficult women."

"I'm not difficult," I sniffed.

"Oh, please," Aunt Tillie scoffed. "We're all difficult."

In truth, Aunt Tillie idled at difficult.

"That's not a bad thing," Aunt Tillie continued. "It keeps men interested. They all think they want some meek homemaker that dotes on them. They want a challenge, though."

"And I'm a challenge?"

Aunt Tillie met my gaze kindly. "You're the most difficult of us all," she said. "You're probably the one most worth the effort, too."

I was flabbergasted. "That's the nicest thing you've ever said to me."

Aunt Tillie sobered. "Well, don't get used to it."

"Of course," I said primly, hiding the smile playing at the corner of my lips.

"So, are you going to call him and apologize?"

"Probably not," I admitted.

"You're going to wait him out?"

"Yeah," I sighed. "I guess I'm more like you than I want to admit."

"Good girl."

"That still doesn't solve the Erika problem," I reminded her.

"You worry too much," Aunt Tillie waved off my concerns. "That's always been your problem. Ghosts hang around for a reason. You can't figure out why. You have to give Erika the chance to let you know why."

I opened my mouth to protest, but Aunt Tillie silenced me with a look.

"The rules are simple," she said. "Erika has something she has to do before she can go. You have to help her, to be sure, but it's up to Erika in the end."

"She's just a little girl," I said.

"She's a little girl with big help," Aunt Tillie corrected me.

"Me? I don't know how much help I am."

"Alone? Not much at all," Aunt Tillie said honestly. "You're never alone, though, Bay. You need to remember that. We're all here with you, whether you want it or not."

I don't know why, but her words warmed me. The minute the wind picked up and I smelled myself again, though, the feeling faded. This bacon thing had to end soon. Right?

TWENTY-THREE

I stopped in at the inn for breakfast, ignoring the concerned look on my mother's face when she caught sight of the shadows under my eyes.

"I invited the Langstroms to dinner," I informed her.

"Who are the Langstroms?"

"The contractor and his family."

"Why?" My mom looked surprised.

"Because Aunt Tillie is out there hounding them," I replied simply.

"Oh," my mom replied thoughtfully. "That's probably a good idea. We'll make something good. He's earned it, I'm sure."

"You always do," I said, moving toward the door to leave. "Make something good to eat, I mean."

"Bay, are you alright?"

"I'm fine," I blew off her concerns. "I just didn't sleep very well last night."

"Ghosts?"

"Yeah, ghosts," I sighed. "It will be fine. I just have to find a way to get Erika to move on."

My mom patted my arm sympathetically. "You will. I have faith."

"That makes one of us," I smiled wanly.

I went to The Whistler after leaving the inn. Conveniently – or rather pathetically, I'm not oblivious to my actions – the route I picked to get to the paper took me past the police department. Landon's car wasn't there, though, and I was both frustrated and relieved by that fact.

When I got to The Whistler, I stopped in the entryway to peruse today's issue to make sure that everything had been produced correctly, and then made my way to my office. I wasn't surprised to find Edith waiting for me.

"Where have you been?"

"Around," I said briefly. "What's going on?"

"You've been gone for days," Edith chided me. "That's not a very good work ethic."

"I've been working from home," I replied. "There's been some other stuff going on, too."

"Like what?" Edith asked, genuinely curious.

"Is Brian here?"

"No, it's just us."

"Good. I can't deal with him or Sam right now."

Sam. He was a whole other problem I had been ignoring.

"What's wrong?"

The thing about Edith is that she's extremely self-absorbed – which I'm sure is a facet of her personality that's a holdover from life – but she's also randomly sympathetic, as well.

So I told her. I told her everything. There's something cathartic about unburdening yourself to someone – especially someone that can't tell anyone else what you've said.

When I was done, Edith seemed surprised by all she had missed. "That's a lot of information," she said finally.

"I know."

"Well, let's take it point by point," she started, ever the organized personality. "We can't be sure that Sam Cornell actually saw me. We'll just have to be really careful when he's around. I'll make sure that I hide when he's in the office. He can't stay forever, right?"

"Right," I sighed.

"That's one problem solved."

"What about the paper?"

"We both know that making the paper three days a week is going to be a colossal failure," Edith said. "Brian will figure that out. This isn't a great living, but it's better than nothing at all."

That was pragmatic. I would expect nothing less from Edith.

"As for the bacon smell," Edith wrinkled her nose. "You're going to have to take that up with your aunt. I have no way to fix that."

"And what about Erika? Can you solve that one for me?"

"It's a difficult situation," Edith admitted. "If her parents hadn't broken the law and sent her away she probably would have lived and it wouldn't be your problem."

I was aghast. "What? You can't be serious?"

"What?" Edith looked miffed. "It's the truth. They sent the children away to hide them. That's against the law."

"They weren't slaves."

"Well, we really don't know that, do we?" Edith said. "We just know what the little girl said and you know those people lie."

"What people?"

Edith glanced around and lowered her voice. "Black people."

I felt sick. "What are you saying?"

"Well, the little girl is probably lying," Edith said. "She died because her parents didn't take care of her."

"She died because her parents thought they were sending her to a better place," I corrected Edith. "You're not telling me that you think slavery is a good thing? You're not saying that, right?"

"Slavery was a practical necessity for the times," Edith said carefully. "This country was built on slavery. It was an institution, not a minor thing."

"That doesn't make it right," I countered angrily.

"Slavery is present in the Bible, too," Edith said. "Are you saying the Bible is wrong?"

"Don't get me started on the Bible," I grumbled.

"Times were different," Edith said evenly. "Slavery wasn't a bad thing. Not really, when you think about it. What were those people going to do if they weren't working? It's not like they could get regular jobs."

"That is just sickening," I said, my anger starting to build. "No one has the right to own another person. No one."

"That's a narrow view," Edith replied. "This country wouldn't have become as great as it is if it hadn't been for slaves."

"That's because they did all the work," I countered. "How would you feel if you were born into slavery?"

"I wouldn't have been a slave," Edith said.

"Why not?"

"I'm not black."

"And black people are so different than white people?"

"Obviously."

I was infuriated now. "Obviously how?"

"We were created in the image of God," Edith said. "God wasn't black."

"How do you know?" I challenged. "Have you met God?"

"No," Edith shook her head. "Everyone knows, though."

"I don't know that," I shot back.

"Well, you're a witch," Edith said simply. "You're not going to Heaven anyway."

"Oh, really? Why aren't you in Heaven, Edith?"

Edith looked shocked by the question. "Well, obviously I have unfinished business. When I finish it, I'll go to Heaven. God has a plan for me."

"What is your unfinished business? What is God's plan?"

"I don't know," Edith sniffed. "Why are you being so aggressive?"

"Because what you're saying is just so wrong," I replied.

"It's wrong to you," Edith said pointedly. "A lot of people think the way I do."

"Backwards people," I grumbled.

"A lot of people would think that being a witch is backwards," Edith pointed out. "That you're inherently evil."

"You want to know what, Edith? I can actually see that. People react out of fear to what they don't know. The difference is that people are not bad – or different – just because they have a different color of skin."

"It's the way they're raised, too," Edith said. "They're more prone to get addicted to drugs and sell them. How can you think that's good?"

"That's just ignorant," I argued.

"I don't think I like the way you're talking to me," Edith said.

"Well, I don't think I like this whole conversation," I replied. "Maybe you should just go."

"Fine," Edith said. "Just remember, though, your way of thinking isn't the only way of thinking."

"I can't even look at you right now, Edith," I said. "You make me sick."

Maybe it was the anger talking. Maybe it was the fatigue, I don't know. All I did know is that I needed Edith out of my sight. Edith acquiesced to my request, but not before she shot me one more, hard frown and a parting verbal shot.

"Just forget about her, Bay," she said. "She's not worth your worry."

"Maybe you're not either," I replied harshly.

Edith was gone by then, though. I have no idea if she heard me. I focused on my laptop – or at least I tried. My frustration with Edith – and everything else – was blocking my workflow, though. Finally, I slammed my laptop shut in aggravation.

"Bad morning?"

I jumped when I heard the voice, turning to see Sam standing in the open doorway of my office. "What are you doing here?"

"I was going to have a meeting with Brian, but he postponed it," Sam said easily. "He had something else come up. I saw your car here and I thought I would ask you to lunch."

That was the last thing I wanted to do. "I'm busy," I said. "Maybe some other time."

"You don't look busy."

"Well, I am."

"What's the harm in lunch?" Sam prodded. "I think we need to clear the air between us and I think, if food is involved, it can only help."

He was trying to be charming. Still, he had a point.

"Fine," I said. "Let's go to lunch."

"Great."

I could think of a few words I would use to describe this prospect and 'great' wasn't one of them.

TWENTY-FOUR

I let Sam pick the spot for lunch. I wasn't surprised when he chose Miss Sally's Sandwiches, a small deli on the corner of Main Street – about two blocks east of Hypnotic. The deli was small enough to be quaint, but big enough for us to get a corner table out of earshot from everyone else.

Once we placed our orders, Sam fixed me with a friendly smile. "So, do you want to tell me what's wrong?"

Did he want me to tell him about the sad little ghost that was haunting my days or the racist white one that was haunting the paper? Or that I was worried that Landon had left town and didn't plan on returning? Those didn't sound like viable options, so I decided to lie.

"I'm just tired," I said. "I didn't sleep well last night."

"Trouble with your boyfriend?"

"No," I said evasively. "Just a bad night of sleep. Everyone gets them."

"Sure," Sam said easily, biting into the pickle on the side of his plate. "You seem especially agitated, though."

"How would you know? I could be like this on a daily basis. You don't even know me."

"Point taken," Sam said. "So, how about I try to get to know you?"

"Why?"

"Why? Because you seem to dislike me."

"Maybe I just dislike the fact that you're stringing Brian along even though you know that this isn't going to work," I suggested. "Maybe I just don't like the fact that you're soaking him for money on an endeavor that was never going to work?"

"Fair enough," Sam said. "I'm not going to lie, the odds of being able to expand The Whistler to three days of publication a week are slim. My job is to make sure that we've explored every avenue and that's what I plan to do."

"Great," I muttered. "Bully for you."

"I think something else is going on with you," Sam said pointedly.

"Really? What?"

"I think that maybe you're having some family problems," Sam said, prodding me to open up.

"I'm always having family problems," I replied honestly.

"How so?" Sam leaned forward, intrigued.

"Whenever you deal with family, there's going to be drama," I replied simply. "Family knows all your secrets. They know all your weak points. They know how to exploit both."

"So, your family is exploiting you?"

"That's not what I said."

"That's kind of what you said."

"Not even in the slightest," I countered. "I just said that every family has problems."

"And what are your family's problems?"

He was digging.

"Well, for starters, we're having some construction done out at the inn and my Aunt Tillie is obsessing about every little detail," I said. "I've been put in charge of helping her. That's just a series of headaches – the next one worse than the previous one. She's constantly out there getting them all riled up."

"Oh," Sam looked disappointed. "Well, have you tried talking to her?"

"Have you tried talking to a granite statue? Have you tried telling a rock what to do? Because my Aunt Tillie is about as movable as a granite statue."

"She's definitely ... persnickety."

"That's putting it mildly."

"Still," Sam pressed. "It seems to me that there's more going on than that."

"Well, Thistle and Clove are doing their spring ordering, too," I said pleasantly, starting to warm up to the game I was playing. "That always makes Thistle cranky. It's a hard job, because if you order too much, it's just like throwing money out the window. And, on the flip side, if you order too little, then you miss out on strong profits. It's always a stressful time of year for them. Since I live with them, it's stressful for me, too."

Sam didn't seem thrilled with the banality of my answers. He couldn't argue with them either, though.

"Well, maybe they should hire an assistant or something," he offered lamely.

"It's a small business," I replied. "That wouldn't be fiscally responsible."

"I guess not."

I kept my face frozen with faux familial worry, while internally I was practically guffawing. This was more fun than I realized.

"Still, there must be a lot more going on," Sam said finally.

"Oh, there is," I said. I was pretending that I was enjoying unburdening myself but, in reality, I was trying to make Sam lose interest in the Winchester witches. "My father and uncles, who have been gone for years, are suddenly back and they're opening a competing inn. That has my Aunt Tillie in a right snit and, even though they won't admit it, my mom and aunts are off their game, too."

"That must be difficult," Sam said wanly.

"Oh, it is," I said. "I mean, I'm glad my dad is in town. We've kept in touch over the years, more than Thistle and Clove have with their fathers, that's for sure. Still, it's like I'm being disloyal to my mom if I spend time with him and it's like I'm being mean to my dad if I try to avoid him."

"And what do you want?" Sam asked resignedly.

"I want everyone to get along," I said simply. "That's not an option, though, so we're all just feeling it out. It's really hard, especially with my Uncle Warren getting engaged. Clove has barely seen her father and now he's getting married. She's going to have a new stepmother. That's got her all freaked out."

"Yeah, I can see how that would happen," Sam agreed.

"It's just one thing after another with my family," I said. "Aunt Tillie will start planting her pot field soon – and that's always a constant fight. She claims she has glaucoma, but she really just likes it."

Okay, maybe I was going too far now.

"Well, the police don't seem to mind," Sam interjected. "As long as she's not selling it, it's probably not a big problem."

"No, she doesn't sell the pot," I said. "She just grows it and uses it. She sells the wine, though."

"Wine isn't illegal."

"As long as you have a permit."

"And she doesn't have a permit?"

"Um, no."

"Well, that's ... ."

"A big pain, I know," I said. "She just doesn't seem to understand – or maybe she just pretends, I don't know – why we're all so worried about it. They could take her away."

"Would that be such a bad thing? She seems to cause your family a lot of pain."

"Not pain," I countered. "And, yes, it would be a bad thing."

"You don't even seem to like her," Sam pointed out.

"She's my aunt, I love her," I said. "I don't always like what she does, but she's family."

"Oh, sure," Sam said, warding off the sudden fury that I was turning on him. "I didn't mean anything by it."

"She's family," I repeated. "She's trouble, but she's still family. You don't turn your back on family."

"I know," Sam said in a placating manner. "Your family is just a lot of drama."

"Isn't every family?"

"I guess."

I took a big bite of my sandwich, pausing to regroup. I didn't have a lot more to complain about that wouldn't tip off Sam to the big family secret. A sudden presence a few feet to the right of me caught my attention. I shifted in my chair, expecting to see the waitress standing there – but finding Landon instead. I swallowed hard, my mouth going dry at the sight of him.

"This is the third restaurant I've checked for you," Landon said, grabbing an empty chair from a nearby table and pulling it up next to me. "I didn't realize you were having a lunch date."

"It's not a date," Sam said hurriedly. Landon's sudden appearance had thrown him for a loop. "I was just trying to get her out of her bad mood."

"Really?" Landon fixed Sam with an icy glare. "And why were you in a bad mood?" Landon turned to me, grabbing a handful of potato chips off my plate and popping one in his mouth.

"She didn't sleep well last night," Sam answered for me. His nerves were clearly getting the best of him.

Landon kept his gaze fixed on me. His ice blue eyes were mesmerizing. "That makes two of us."

"I should probably let the two of you do ... whatever it is you do," Sam said, getting up from his chair, tossing some money on the table to cover the bill. "I'll see you later, Bay."

"Bye."

We both watched Sam leave the restaurant. Once he was gone, Landon turned back to me. "Having lunch with the enemy?"

"He wanted to know about the family," I murmured.

"And what did you tell him?"

I smiled to myself. "I told him every banal thing I could think of. Ordering at Hypnotic. Aunt Tillie bothering the contractors. My mom and aunts having trouble with the Dragonfly."

"So you tried to bore him into submission," Landon mused. "That was probably a smart move."

"Yeah, he was getting really bothered by what I was telling him," I agreed. "You came at the perfect time, though. I was running out of things to tell him."

"So you're glad to see me?" Landon asked curiously.

"Always."

Landon smiled despite himself. "I wasn't sure – after yesterday. I didn't mean to yell at you."

"I know. I didn't mean to yell at you either."

"I know."

"I wasn't sure," I broke off. "I wasn't sure when you didn't come over last night if you would ever ... ."

"What? Come back?" Landon looked surprised.

"Yeah."

"Bay, you've got to stop doing this," Landon sighed wearily. "I'm not just going to take off and run. I thought we could both use a night apart for things to cool down. It was a bad idea. All I thought about was you all night. I'm not just going to pick up and leave. You've got to believe that. I don't know why you're so ready to believe that I'll just walk away – but I'm not going to. It's going to be easier, for both of us, if you just get that into your thick head."

"Fine," I grumbled.

Landon reached over and took the other half of my sandwich off my plate and bit into it. "So, what else is going on?"

"Not much," I said. "Edith is a racist."

"Edith? The ghost at The Whistler?"

"Yeah. I told her about Erika and she told me that she basically got what was coming to her because she ran from slavers."

"You can't fix ignorance," Landon shrugged. "Ignore her. She sounds like a real piece of work anyway."

"Yeah, she is," I blew out a sigh.

"Anything else?"

"No. What about you?"

"We asked the Coast Guard to run some extra sweeps," Landon said carefully. "They didn't find anything."

"No boat?"

"No boat."

"I don't know what else to do," I admitted helplessly.

Landon placed his hand over mine soothingly. "Well, we'll figure it out."

"We will?" I asked.

"Yeah, we will," Landon said, rubbing his thumb over my hand as he continued to munch on the sandwich. "We'll figure it out together."

"Okay," I said relief washing over me.

"You still smell like bacon."

"I know."

"I still like it."

"I know."

"Want to go take a nap?"

I doubted he had a nap on his mind, but that sounded exactly like what I needed right about now.

TWENTY-FIVE

Landon and I spent the afternoon in bed – and only part of it was spent sleeping. After the bacon smell energized him – again – I finally managed to drift off into a sound sleep. I had no idea if it was the feeling of his arms wrapped around me – or the way our heartbeats slipped into the same rhythm when they were close – but I was finally relaxed enough to just let go so sleep could claim me.

When we woke up, the light filtering in through the window was starting to wane.

"What time is it?" Landon mumbled.

I glanced at the clock. "Time to get up."

"Why?"

"We have to go up to the inn for dinner."

"Why?" Landon sounded a little whiny this time.

"They're cooking a special dinner. The contractor and his family are going to be there. I invited them, so I have to be there." I glanced over at him, his hair spread out on the pillow – kind of like a halo – and sighed. "You don't have to come if you don't want to."

Landon made a lazy trail with his hand down my bare back. "No, I'm coming."

"Are you sure?" I cocked an eyebrow as I looked down at him. "You could stay here naked and I could just climb back in bed with you in a couple of hours?"

Landon looked intrigued by the suggestion but shook his head. "I need sustenance. That half of a sandwich I ate earlier isn't keeping my energy level up. And, as long as you smell like bacon, I'm going to want to keep my energy level up."

"I'm starting to get a complex about the bacon," I admitted.

"Let's just hope they're not serving pork, huh?"

Isn't that the truth?

An hour later, we had both showered and dressed. Landon had balked at the shower until I told him that my mother would know we had spent the afternoon having sex if he didn't.

"Won't she know anyway?" He asked as we walked up to the inn.

"Probably," I said. "We don't need to give her reasons to know, though."

"I guess," Landon shrugged. "They always seem to know, though."

"They're weird that way," I agreed.

"Weird being the optimum word," Landon said, linking his fingers with mine and pulling me close. "Still, it was a good afternoon, so I don't care if they find out or not."

"Are you staying all weekend?" I asked hopefully.

"Are you going to smell like bacon all weekend?" Landon winked at me.

"I have no idea," I replied honestly. "I wouldn't count on that if I were you. It could go away at any time."

"Well, it's a good thing that I like you for more than the bacon then, isn't it?" Landon smiled widely before dropping a kiss on my forehead.

We let ourselves in the back door, taking care not to be too loud in case Aunt Tillie was watching *Jeopardy* – which she was. She didn't bother to look up when we entered. "I see you two made up."

"How did you know that?" I asked.

"I told you, I know ... ."

"All and see all, yeah, I heard you the first three thousand times you said it," I finished for her.

"I told you that he would be back," Aunt Tillie said. "So there was no reason for you to be all mopey this morning."

Landon smirked in my direction. "You were mopey?"

"I was not," I lied.

"She was all depressed and sad," Aunt Tillie countered. "I felt so bad for her I almost lifted the curse early."

"Don't do that," Landon said hurriedly. "Make her suffer."

Aunt Tillie finally tore her gaze from the television. "Why don't you want me to lift it?" She looked suspicious.

"I don't think she's learned her lesson yet," Landon replied smugly.

"He likes the smell," I interjected. "It turns him on."

I was actually hoping that little tidbit would be enough to have Aunt Tillie rethinking the curse.

"Men are odd," Aunt Tillie said finally. "You smell like frying swine and you can't keep them off you. Why do you think I always made your Uncle Calvin cook?"

Landon's smile widened to encompass his entire face. "See. It's not just me."

"No," I agreed. "It's all men. I heard Marcus and Thistle going at it like rabbits last night."

Aunt Tillie pursed her lips. "I should've picked a different smell."

"Well, hindsight," I said breezily, grabbing Landon's wrist and pulling him into the kitchen behind me. "Don't encourage her," I hissed.

"What?" He asked innocently. "I was just making conversation."

I rolled my eyes but couldn't hide my small grin. Maybe I was going to miss the bacon smell, too? Just a little.

"Well, there you are," my mom said when she caught sight of me. "I was wondering if you would bother coming to dinner tonight."

"We're not even late," I protested.

"I was talking about last night," my mom said pointedly.

"Oh."

"What happened last night?" Landon asked, showing more interest in the food that was being dished onto plates than anything else. "What is that?"

"It's braised pork chops," Marnie said. "We've been brining all day."

Landon's eyes lit up. "Pork."

"And potatoes and vegetables and fresh bread," Twila added.

"It looks delicious."

"It is," my mom said, smiling at him warmly. When she turned back to me, though, her smile vanished. "And why didn't you bother to show up for dinner last night? Or at least call to say why you weren't coming?"

"I was just tired," I said lamely. "I went to bed early."

"Oh, really?" My mom looked nonplussed. "Because your aunt said it was because you and Landon were in a fight and you were pouting. When I saw you this morning, it looked like you hadn't slept in days. You look more ... rested now."

"You were in a fight?" Twila asked Landon pointedly.

"We had a disagreement," Landon clarified. "It's fine now."

"Well," Twila patted Landon on the arm. "As long as you apologized."

"How do you know it was my fault?" Landon asked curiously.

"It's always your fault," Thistle offered helpfully from her spot next to the sink.

"Good to know."

We helped carry all the dishes out to the table. Brian and Sam were already seated – and Chief Terry and Dean were there, too. At the center of the table, Dirk Langstrom was already sitting next to a pretty woman in her thirties, who I assumed was his wife. He also had an elderly man sitting on the other side of him.

"I'm glad you could make it," I greeted Dirk warmly.

"Thank you for inviting us," Dirk said, getting to his feet. "This is my wife, Kate. And this is my grandfather, Kenneth. He was visiting for the weekend. I hope that's okay."

"It's fine," I said quickly.

"Welcome," Twila said brightly. "We made a special dinner, just for you."

"Are those what I think they are?" Chief Terry asked, his eyes practically bulging out of his head.

"Yes, it's the braised pork chops," Marnie said. "We know how you love them. I suggested we make them just for you."

"You suggested?" My mom cocked an eyebrow.

Marnie ignored her.

Chief Terry smiled happily. "You folks are in for a real treat," he said. "This will be the best meal of your lives."

My mom and aunts preened under the compliment. I couldn't help but notice that they were all suddenly jostling for the open spot next to Chief Terry. To no one's surprise – at least not mine – my mom ultimately won the spot. "I'm glad you could make it," my mom said warmly.

"It's been a quiet week," Chief Terry said. "I wouldn't have missed this for anything."

Landon exchanged an amused glance with me, pulling my chair out and waiting for me to get settled before he sat down in the one next to me. Aunt Tillie slid through the door from the dining room and climbed into the chair at the head of the table – between my mom and Landon – and looked around expectantly. "Let's eat."

"And who are you?"

Everyone at the table turned to see that Kenneth Langstrom, all white hair and pronounced wrinkles, was suddenly staring at Aunt Tillie like she was on the dinner menu.

"I'm Tillie," Aunt Tillie said, suddenly flustered by the attention. "Who are you?"

"I'm Kenneth Langstrom."

"Is that supposed to mean something to me?" Aunt Tillie regained her verbal footing pretty quickly.

"He's my grandfather," Dirk interjected quickly.

Aunt Tillie fixed her gaze on him. "And who are you?"

"He's the contractor," I reminded her suspiciously.

"Oh, I didn't recognize him without the hat," Aunt Tillie said. "Why are they here?"

"Because I invited him," I said stonily. "Don't be rude."

"Why did you invite them?"

"Because I thought they deserved a nice meal after all the work they'd been doing," I said.

"Oh," Aunt Tillie replied. "I guess that's okay."

"Good," I replied, sliding her a disappointed look.

Everyone took the opportunity to dig into their food. The only sounds at the table for the next few minutes were exclamations of joy and sloppy chewing noises. After everyone had settled down a little bit, Brian finally broke the silence at the table.

"Ladies, this could be the finest meal I've ever eaten."

"Could be?" Chief Terry looked incensed. "What have you eaten that's better?"

"Yeah," Aunt Tillie asked pointedly. "What?"

"She's feisty," Kenneth cackled from his spot next to me. "I like her."

"Be careful, Kenneth," Thistle said sagely. "She bites."

"She can bite me any time."

Dirk looked embarrassed by his grandfather's utterance. "Gramps."

"What?" He asked, his blue eyes twinkling. "We're all adults here. Am I right?" He turned to me expectantly.

Who was I to argue? "You're right."

"Never tell a man he's right," Aunt Tillie ordered. "It goes to their head. Both heads."

"Aunt Tillie!" My mom looked scandalized.

"Oh, pipe down and eat your dinner," Aunt Tillie grumbled.

I glanced over at Landon, who was busy shoveling food into his mouth and watching this evening's dinner show. He didn't seem bothered by the conversation at all. "You don't find this odd?" I whispered.

"For this house? No odder than usual."

I shrugged and went back to eating.

"So, what did you girls do today?" My mom asked.

"More inventory and ordering," Clove said. "We're almost done."

"Well, that's a big job," Twila said. "It's good you're almost done."

"It's taken them a week," Aunt Tillie argued. "I could've done it in a day."

"You could've done it in a day?" Thistle challenged. "When was the last time you did inventory?"

"That doesn't matter," Aunt Tillie sniffed. "It just wouldn't have taken me a week. You guys just get distracted by stupid stuff and it takes you longer than it should."

"Beauty and brains," Kenneth said, winking at Aunt Tillie. "A devastating combination."

Aunt Tillie blushed suddenly. No, really.

"Gramps," Dirk said angrily and shook his head. "That's not appropriate."

"Where's the bacon?" Brian asked suddenly.

"What bacon?" My mom asked. "There's no bacon."

"No, I smell bacon."

Thistle scowled. "There's no bacon."

"Am I the only one that smells the bacon?"

"No," Sam wrinkled his nose. "I smell it, too."

I kicked Landon under the table. "See."

Landon sighed. "It's probably just the pork," he said.

"It's not the pork," my mom said. "What is it?"

"It's just the pork," Aunt Tillie said succinctly. "Will you people just eat your food and shut up?"

Kenneth turned to me, a wide smile plastered on his face. "I like them bossy."

I could feel Landon shaking with silent laughter on the chair next to me. "I think your Aunt Tillie has an admirer?"

Aunt Tillie pointed at Landon menacingly. "You eat your dinner."

"Yes ma'am."

Still, though, I didn't miss Aunt Tillie straightening at the head of the table and watching Kenneth with a mixture of curiosity and guile.

Uh-oh.

TWENTY-SIX

"That was my favorite family dinner ever, I think," Landon said when we were walking back to the guesthouse.

"How do you figure?" Thistle asked bitterly. "We still smell like bacon. If this lasts much longer, I'm not going to be able to walk."

"Why?" Landon asked curiously. When realization dawned on him, though, he quickly changed the subject. "I think your Aunt Tillie likes old Kenneth."

"Yeah, that was interesting," I agreed. "I've never seen her show any interest in a man before."

"What about your uncle?"

"He died before I was born."

"Huh," Landon mused. "Maybe this will be just the distraction she needs."

"That might be a nice change of pace," Thistle said. "I hadn't thought of that."

Landon wrapped his arm around my waist. "Ready for bed?" He asked suggestively.

"Really? You just ate a pound of pork and the bacon still turns you on?"

"Actually, no," Landon said. "Well, maybe. I was actually just ready for bed, though. That pound of pork is making me sleepy. I didn't sleep well last night. Remember? And that nap was nice this afternoon, but a whole night of sleep sounds great about now."

I couldn't argue with that.

The next morning, I woke up to Landon cursing from his side of the bed. "What's wrong?" I sat up, looking around the room in a panic. "Who's here?"

"No one is here," Landon said quietly. "It's gone."

"What's gone?"

"The bacon," Landon complained. "The bacon is gone."

I lifted up my arm and sniffed myself. I blew out a sigh of relief when I did. "Thank God!"

Landon threw himself down on the bed next to me dejectedly. "I'm going to miss it."

"You'll live."

We showered together – which involved a little fooling around – and were sitting in the living room deciding what to do with our day when Thistle ran out into the living room. "It's gone," she said excitedly.

"Don't remind me," Landon grumbled.

"Yeah, Marcus is pouting in there, too," Thistle said. "Why don't you two go throw a pity party together while we celebrate?"

"You want me to go get in bed with Marcus?" Landon didn't look pleased with the suggestion.

For her part, Thistle looked intrigued. "I don't know. Why don't you go in there and try it and I'll tell you if it works for me or not," she suggested.

Landon fixed her with a hard glare. "That's sick."

"No sicker than someone jumping me every five minutes because I smell like bacon," Thistle shot back.

Landon merely rolled his eyes.

Clove's bedroom door opened and she practically danced out. "I don't smell like bacon anymore," she announced.

"We know," Thistle said. "We were just talking about how we were going to celebrate."

"We're not going to celebrate," Clove countered. "You and I are finishing inventory."

"That can wait until Monday," Thistle said.

"No," Clove shook her head. "We have to have our ordering ready to go on Monday to make sure we get everything in time."

"Oh, well," Thistle sighed. "A business woman's work is never done."

Once they were both gone, Landon turned to me. "What do you want to do today?"

"I have to stop by the paper and pick up my laptop," I said. "I left it there yesterday and I never went back to the office after lunch."

"Do you have to work this weekend?"

"Not really," I said. "I just need the laptop in case."

"Okay," Landon agreed. "Why don't we go into town together? I'll drop you off at the paper and I'll check in with Chief Terry and then we'll do something together this afternoon?"

"Like what?"

"I have a few ideas," Landon said, running his hand up and down my arm suggestively.

"I don't smell like bacon anymore," I said.

"So?"

"Well, I thought that was what was turning you on?"

"The bacon was just an added bonus," Landon said. "Trust me, I don't need it."

For some reason, I did trust him.

When we got to town, Landon parked in front of the police station. "Are you going to come here and get me when you're done?"

"No," I shook my head. "Why don't you come to Hypnotic when *you're* done? I'll help Thistle and Clove while you're there."

"It could take me a few hours," Landon warned.

"That's fine."

We exchanged a quick kiss before parting and then I headed straight for The Whistler. I had already decided that I was going to ignore Edith if she appeared. Maybe she sensed that, because she didn't make her presence known.

I packed up my laptop and left The Whistler, taking the time to enjoy the warming day and the clear blue skies overhead. That's one of the things you miss about the country when you're in the city – clear skies and clean air. I was enjoying my five-block walk when something caught my attention out of the corner of my eye. It was Sam and he was coming out of Mrs. Little's pewter unicorn shop.

Crap.

I glanced around, furtively moving under the awning of Mrs. White's bakery shop to disguise my presence as quickly as possible. The last thing I wanted to do was run into Sam.

I took the opportunity to give him a long, hard look from my hiding place. He really was attractive. Not in the same way as Landon or Marcus, who were both ruggedly handsome and impressively built. It was more like he was handsome in a slick way, like Brian was. It was no wonder Clove was attracted to him.

Sam was talking to someone, although I couldn't see exactly who it was. He kept turning back and looking through the open door of the shop while chattering away. I watched with interest as a woman finally stepped through the door, letting it swing shut behind her. My breath caught in my throat when I recognized the woman. It was Karen.

The two of them were gesturing wildly to one another, although I couldn't hear what they were talking about. I tried to calm my nerves. This was probably just a coincidence. She was a designer and he was a ... whatever the hell he was. They were probably just talking nonsense about the town.

The problem was, they seemed to know each other. There was a level of intimacy to their conversation that could only be observed from far away. For some reason, and I don't know why, watching them converse was sending a chill down my spine.

I remained where I was until they parted ways, both going in separate directions. Once I was sure they were gone, I picked up my pace and headed straight for Hypnotic. By the time I got there, I was out of breath.

Thistle sensed something about my mood the minute I walked through the door. "What's wrong?"

I bent over at the waist, struggling to catch my breath. "I just saw something," I gasped.

"What?"

"Karen and Sam were talking to each other down by the unicorn store," I said.

"So?" Thistle didn't look half as intrigued as I was feeling.

"You don't think that's weird?"

"That Sam and Karen were talking to each other on the street? No," Thistle shook her head. "Why should I? They were probably just talking about the weather or something."

"What if they weren't?"

"Okay," Thistle said carefully. "What would they have been talking about that should worry us?"

I shook my head. "I don't know," I admitted. "They seemed to know each other, though. Like they were friends or something."

"Maybe they've crossed business paths before," Clove suggested. "That's not out of the realm of possibility."

"No," I agreed. "I just ... it gave me a weird feeling."

"Do you think they're having an affair?" Clove asked hopefully. "Maybe the wedding won't happen after all?"

"I don't know if that's it," I said, biting my lower lip.

"Then what?" Thistle looked exasperated.

"I don't know," I snapped. "There's just something about it that bugged me."

Thistle cocked her head. "Okay," she said finally. "We need to find out how they know each other."

"Why?" Clove asked.

"Because it's important to Bay," Thistle replied simply.

"So how do we do it?" Clove asked. "How do we find out how they know each other?"

"We ask your dad," Thistle said grimly.

"No," Clove shook her head vehemently. "No way."

"We have to," I said quietly.

"What am I supposed to ask? Hey, Dad, is there any reason why your girlfriend would be talking to the guy we're not supposed to like even though he's done nothing to prove to us that he's untrustworthy?"

"No need to get snippy," Thistle said. "We'll just go out to the inn on the pretense of looking around to see how it's coming along and ask some questions about Karen. It will be no big deal. I promise."

"Really? Because whenever our family does something, it always turns into a big deal," Clove countered.

She had a point.

"It won't this time," I said. "I promise."

"See, I know you actually mean that," Clove replied. "The problem is, I also know that, even with the best intentions, our family always manages to screw things up. And sometimes in a big way."

She had another point.

"It won't be like that this time," Thistle said. "Trust me."

"Why should I trust you?"

"We're family."

"Pick another reason."

"Because you need to know now just as much as we need to know," I suggested.

Clove sighed. "Fine," she ceded. "If either one of you embarrasses me, though ... ."

"We won't."

"If either one of you makes things worse between my dad and me," Clove continued, fixing us both with a hard glare. "I'll never forgive you."

"It's going to be fine."

I mostly meant that, too.

TWENTY-SEVEN

Ten minutes later, we were all piled into Thistle's car – which was pointed toward the Dragonfly – while Clove continued to lament her bad luck.

"You know what I've realized?" Clove was in the backseat and, while her gaze was pointed at us, I had no idea who she was actually talking to. It was a toss-up at this point.

"What have you realized?" I asked idly.

"Every bad decision I've ever made in my life has been made because of the two of you," Clove replied. "Every single one."

"That's crap," Thistle argued. "How do you figure?"

"I'm co-dependent," Clove mused. "You two are always saying it. Usually, I brush it off because I think you're just teasing me to tease me. But, you're right. I am co-dependent. Whatever you two say goes. I knew this was a bad idea the minute you mentioned it and, yet, here I am. I'm going with you to ask my dad if his fiancée is up to something because Bay saw her talking to a guy she doesn't trust on the street. This is just ... stupid."

"What are you rambling about?" Thistle glanced in the rearview mirror irritably.

"Nothing," Clove sighed dramatically. "You obviously don't care about my feelings."

"Obviously," I said dryly. "When we get out to the Dragonfly, why don't you just stay in the car and we'll go ask your dad ourselves?"

"Oh, yeah," Clove scoffed. "How is that going to go? Hey, Uncle Warren, what's that woman doing with the guy I think sees ghosts but don't know if he sees ghosts?"

"You're just a little ray of sunshine today, aren't you?" Thistle grunted.

"If you don't like my attitude, then don't talk to me," Clove shot back.

"Why do you always have to make things more difficult?" Thistle asked. "Why can't you, just once, agree to the plan and not sit there and gripe about it?"

"Me gripe? You're the queen of gripe."

"I'm the queen of the world," Thistle countered. "Get that straight."

"Let's not argue," I interjected quickly. "It's just going to make the next hour go by that much slower."

"Fine," Clove sniffed. "I'll stop if she stops."

Thistle rolled her eyes and fixed me with a hard stare. "When she falls off the deep end, you're going to look back on this day and realize you saw all the catastrophic signs at this exact moment."

"I'll keep that in mind."

"That doesn't sound like she's stopping," Clove said petulantly from the backseat.

"You guys make me feel tired," I muttered.

When we parked outside the Dragonfly, Thistle turned in her seat so she could meet Clove's hostile gaze head on. "I know you're pissed," she said carefully. "I promise we'll be smooth about this. He won't even know what we're doing."

"You can't promise that," Clove replied bitterly.

"I can promise to try," Thistle said through gritted teeth.

"Fine."

"Fine."

I glanced between the two of them warily. "Fine," I agreed. This had the potential to be a huge cluster of crap if it went sideways.

Once we were on the front porch, Thistle turned to me expectantly. "Do we knock?"

"I don't know," I shrugged. "It's a business."

"It's not open yet, though," Clove said. "It might be rude not to knock."

"So, knock," I said.

"You knock," Clove said nervously. "I don't want to knock."

"This is a stupid discussion," Thistle said.

"Like all the rest of our discussions are classy and smart," I replied.

"She has a point," Clove said.

"Oh, I'll knock," Thistle said finally, pushing in front of us impatiently. Just as she raised her hand to rap on the door it opened, and Uncle Warren was standing in the entryway curiously.

"What are you guys doing?"

"Arguing about who was going to knock," I replied honestly.

"Or if we even should knock," Thistle said sheepishly.

Uncle Warren cocked an eyebrow as he regarded Thistle. "And you drew the short end of the straw?"

"No," Thistle shook her head. "I just got tired of arguing about it."

Uncle Warren bobbed his head in understanding, like Thistle's explanation had been something other than nonsense. "Do you guys want to come in?"

"Sure," I said quickly, before Clove could say something that would make us look even stranger than we already did. "Wow," I said when we were in the lobby. "This place just keeps getting better and better. I see you got furniture."

"Yeah, you like it?"

I ran my hand over the oak front desk appreciatively. "It's really nice."

"I like the colors you picked," Clove said, glancing around the room. "The blue is nice and welcoming, but it's not too dark to be oppressive and it's not so light that it will be hard to keep clean."

"It took us forever to agree on colors," Uncle Warren said, his voice easy, his eyes wary. "I like what we finally settled on, though."

"Yeah, it's great," Thistle said. "I like paint better than wallpaper. Wallpaper annoys me."

"Isn't the Overlook filled with wallpaper?" Uncle Warren asked, confusion crossing his face.

"Yeah," Thistle said. "I like the hardwood floors and stuff, but I've never really been a fan of wallpaper."

"Well, you could ask your aunts to take it down," Warren suggested.

"Yeah, that won't go over well," Thistle said. "They fight change."

This conversation couldn't get much more boring or forced.

"So, what are you going to do for decorations?" Clove asked nervously. "Paintings?"

I was wrong.

"As fascinated as I am about the decorations that we're considering, I don't really think that you're here to talk about watercolors versus oil prints."

We really are horrible at this. If we were spies, we'd be the first ones tortured for information. Heck, they wouldn't even have to torture us. We'd roll over for a big pile of chocolate.

"We just wanted to see the inn," Clove said hurriedly.

"Really?" Uncle Warren arched his eyebrows speculatively. "Because it seems like you have an agenda – one that none of you seem too eager to pass on to me. So, in the interests of saving time, why don't you just say what you came here to say?"

"No, we really wanted to see the inn." Clove looked like she was about ready to jump out of her own skin.

Uncle Warren turned to me expectantly. "Maybe you should tell me what you want?"

"Oh, um ... well, it's really nothing." Nervousness was making my hands sweat and I could feel a red flush creeping up my cheeks.

"We want to know what you know about Karen," Thistle finally blurted out.

"Subtle," I mumbled.

"Oh, man," Clove whined. "You said you weren't going to do it this way."

"It's not like I had much of a choice," Thistle argued. "We're horrible liars."

"Isn't that the truth," I mumbled.

"Why are you asking questions about Karen?" Uncle Warren asked warily.

"We're just curious," I said quickly. The words sounded hollow to my own ears, so I figured they sounded empty to Warren's.

"Bay saw her talking to this guy downtown, this Sam Cornell," Thistle said. "She doesn't trust him and we just wanted to make sure that nothing weird is going on."

"What the hell?" Clove looked exasperated.

"We're caught," Thistle shrugged. "Continuing to lie is going to get us nowhere."

"Okay," Uncle Warren blew out a sigh. "Let me get this straight, Karen was downtown talking to a guy you don't like and now you want to know about Karen? Even though she hasn't done anything wrong?"

"Pretty much," I agreed.

"Have you considered that Karen was just making small talk with someone in town? This is Hemlock Cove, after all," Uncle Warren was smiling, but the expression didn't make it all the way to his eyes. "Some people just chat on the street."

"They seemed friendly," I replied uncomfortably.

"Friendly how?" Warren asked tersely. "Like they were dating or something?"

"No," I said hurriedly. "Just like they knew each other."

"Maybe she ran into someone she knows," Warren said. "I don't see why you guys are all worked up about this."

"We're not worked up about this," Thistle said. "Bay is worked up about this and we just came with her because, well, apparently we're all joined at the hip."

"I see," Warren said, a true smile warming his face. "I think you guys watch a little too much television. Not everything is some conspiracy."

"That's what I told them," Clove said primly.

"Oh, well, thanks," Thistle grunted angrily.

"Well, I did tell you that."

"Bay, why don't you like this man?" Uncle Warren turned to me.

"I don't trust him," I said evasively. "He's up to something."

"What?"

Clove jumped in, explaining about Sam's connection to The Whistler and about how he had been questioning us about our family. She left out the part – thankfully – where I was certain Sam had seen Edith. No one wanted to explain that.

When she was done, Uncle Warren didn't look any more enlightened than he had when she began. "So he's curious about your family? He's staying at the inn, right? If I met your family for the first time, I would be curious. Especially about Aunt Tillie."

"There's just something about the way that he's doing it," I offered lamely.

"Well, when I see Karen for dinner tonight I'll ask her about it," Warren said earnestly. "I think you guys are barking up the wrong tree, though."

"I agree," Clove said.

Thistle rolled her eyes. "You're really starting to irritate me."

We said our goodbyes – including a lame apology to Uncle Warren for being so suspicious – and once we were outside, Clove let loose with a string of curses that would have made Aunt Tillie magically tie her tongue for a week.

"I told you that this was going to make us look stupid," she snapped. "Did you believe me? Of course not."

"Oh, it was fine," Thistle brushed off her diatribe. "He just thinks we're being juvenile. If that's the worst of our problems then it's a good day for us."

"You embarrassed me," Clove countered. "You embarrassed me in front of my dad."

"It's not a big deal," Thistle argued. "We embarrass you every day. You'll get over it."

"I don't want to get over it."

"Oh, just shut up."

I tried to silence Thistle and Clove's argument in my busy mind – but I wasn't entirely successful. So, instead of squelching the noise, I decided to focus on the external setting of the Dragonfly as a coping mechanism.

While our mothers were kitchen witches, Clove, Thistle and I were earth witches – meaning we find comfort in nature. I was hoping to use that element to drown the never-ending argument that Thistle and Clove were currently engaged in.

The ploy was working – well, kind of – when Erika suddenly popped into view in the middle of the driveway. "There you are," she said brightly. "I've been looking for you everywhere."

"Erika," I said in surprise. "What are you doing here?"

Erika's attention had been diverted to Clove and Thistle – who hadn't heard her arrival. "Why are they fighting?"

"They like it."

"That's silly."

"What can I say? We're a silly family."

"Huh," Erika shrugged. "Do they ever stop?"

"Only when they're sleeping. So, why are you here again?"

"Oh, I was looking for you," Erika said. "I needed to tell you something."

"What? Did you find the boat again? The boat with the other children?"

"No," Erika shook her head. "I found another girl, though. One like me."

"One like you," I faltered. "Do you mean … ?"

"A ghost. She's a ghost like me. She wants her mommy. I can't make her stop crying. Finally, I decided to bring her to you."

"Where is she?" I glanced around nervously.

"She followed me, but she's scared," Erika said. "She doesn't know what to do and she thinks you might be mean."

"Why does she think I might be mean?"

Erika shrugged. "Because the people on the boat were mean to her."

"The boat? She was on the boat with you?"

"No, the other boat," Erika said.

I swallowed hard. "The other boat? She died on the other boat?"

"Yeah," Erika said. "She really wants to see her mommy. Can you get her mommy?"

"I need to see her, Erika," I said calmly. "Can you get her to come out?"

"I'll try." Erika didn't look convinced at the probability of the task, but she floated over to a clump of trees and bent down. I couldn't hear what she was saying, but after a few minutes, I saw another girl move out into the light with her.

I plastered a smile on my face, all the while my heart dropped. This little girl clearly wasn't on the boat with Erika. She had long blonde hair, tied into pigtails on each side of her head, and she was wearing modern denim overalls. Whenever she had died, it had been recently.

"Hi, sweetheart," I greeted her cautiously. "Can you come over here and talk to me?"

I noticed that the argument behind me had ceased. Clove and Thistle were fixed on me, but they weren't moving. "Another ghost?" Thistle asked.

"Yeah."

"From Erika's boat?"

"No," I shook my head grimly. "Definitely not."

"Erika says you can help me," the little girl said piteously. "Can you help me?"

"I'm going to try," I said honestly. "What's your name?"

"Gracie. Gracie Campbell," she said quietly. "I just want my mommy."

I didn't blame her. Quite frankly, right now, I wanted my mommy, too.

TWENTY-EIGHT

"I need your help."

I barged into Chief Terry's office dramatically. I had left Gracie and Erika – who didn't like the idea of driving in a car in the slightest – at Hypnotic with Clove and Thistle. It had taken awhile, but I had finally gotten enough information out of Gracie to give Landon and Chief Terry a place to start their search.

"Do you knock?" Landon looked surprised by my sudden appearance.

"The door was open."

"We were in the middle of a conversation," Landon pointed out.

I glanced over at Chief Terry, who seemed a little too amused by our verbal interplay. "What are you smiling at?"

"I just like that you're driving someone else crazy for a change," Chief Terry said. "It takes the onus off me."

"Well, not for long," I said.

Chief Terry's eyes shifted from bemusement to alarm quickly. "What's wrong? Is it your mom? One of your aunts?"

"Aunt Tillie?" Landon asked grimly.

"No, they're fine," I said. "Well, at least I think they're fine. This is about something else."

"What?" Landon asked suspiciously.

"So we were out at the Dragonfly," I started.

"When?" Landon jumped up angrily. "You said you were stopping by the paper and then spending the afternoon with Thistle and Clove until I was done here."

"I did," I replied irritably. "I just saw ... that doesn't matter right now. It turned out to be a big nothing. Anyway, when we were leaving the Dragonfly, Erika found us."

"Who is Erika?" Chief Terry asked curiously.

"She's a ghost," I replied carefully.

"A little girl ghost," Landon supplied.

"The one you had me searching the lake for?" Chief Terry looked nonplussed. "The one that died running away from slavers? What does she want now?"

"She's not the problem."

"She's not?"

"Well, she is," I corrected myself. "I have to find a way to help her move on and I have no idea how I'm going to do that. How do you help a hundred-and-sixty-year old ghost get closure? I can't even think about that right now, though. We have bigger problems."

"We do?" Landon didn't look thrilled with the statement.

"Erika wasn't alone when she showed up at the Dragonfly," I said.

"Who was with her?" Chief Terry asked curiously.

"Another little girl."

"One from her boat?" Landon looked confused. "Wasn't much of a freedom ride, was it?"

"No," I shook my head. "This little girl was not on Erika's boat. She's from the other boat. The one Erika told us about."

"She died recently?" Chief Terry was tense again.

"Yeah."

"How can you be sure?"

"Well, she was blonde, white and wearing OshKosh overalls," I replied succinctly.

"That doesn't mean she died recently," Chief Terry said warily. "Kids wore OshKosh decades ago."

"She's a new ghost," I said. "Erika said she was on the boat."

"How did she die?" Landon asked. "Wait, I don't want to know."

"You don't?"

"Okay, tell me," Landon said grimly. "Not knowing is worse than knowing. Tell us."

"I don't know how she died," I admitted. "She didn't want to talk about what happened on the boat, which makes me think it was pretty bad."

"What did she want to talk about?" Chief Terry asked.

"She's a little freaked out and upset," I replied. "Basically, she just wants her mommy."

"Well that's just ... sad," Landon said quietly. "So what do we do?"

"We find out about her," I said simply. "She said her name is Gracie Campbell. If I had to guess, she's about eight years old, but I would expand the parameters when you do your search. It's hard to pin it down with kids that age."

"You want us to see if there's a missing girl named Gracie Campbell?" Chief Terry asked wearily.

"Yes."

"And then what?" Landon asked.

"Well, if we can find a real girl that's missing, can't we just fudge some details to get help looking for the boat?"

"Fudge some details?" Chief Terry raised his eyebrows. "Is that a technical term?"

"No," I bit my lower lip. "Can't you do something if we prove that the little girl is real and that someone is looking for her?"

"How am I going to explain to the Coast Guard that a ghost told us she died and then we found her in a missing person file?" Chief Terry asked.

"I don't know," I shrugged helplessly.

Landon grimaced. "Let's take it one step at a time," he said. "Let's see if we can find Gracie Campbell first and then decide what to do when and if that happens."

"I guess we have to start somewhere," Chief Terry agreed.

"I THINK I MIGHT HAVE HER."

I glanced up and met Chief Terry's steady gaze. "Really?"

Chief Terry and Landon had been going through missing person files for the past two hours. Occasionally, they would call me over to ask if any of the children in the files they were looking at looked familiar but – so far – the search had been a big bust.

I moved around Chief Terry's desk and glanced at his computer screen. The sight of Gracie Campbell's face – her living face – was staring back at me. "That's her."

"Her name is Grace Ellen Campbell," Chief Terry said, reading from the information file attached to the photo. "She's ten years old. She was reported missing a little over a week ago."

"Her mother?" I asked resignedly.

Chief Terry shook his head sadly. "No. According to this, her mother was injured in a car crash that killed her father four months ago. She's been in foster care since."

"Foster care? But you said her mom survived. She's looking for her mom."

"Her mother has been in a coma since the accident," Chief Terry explained. "She was put into the foster care system for the time being. It doesn't look like she has any other living relatives besides the mother and until a determination can be made on the mother's viability, the kid stays in foster care."

"Not technically," I said, my voice barely a whisper. "She's not in the foster care system anymore."

"No," Chief Terry agreed. "Not anymore."

Landon walked back into the office, returning from his coffee hunt, and glancing up at us as he did. "Find something?"

"We found her," Chief Terry nodded. "It's complicated, though."

Landon moved to read over Chief Terry's shoulder. After a few minutes, he turned to me expectantly. "Well, this is just … ."

"Terrible?"

"Disgusting," Landon said. "Someone took this little girl because they knew she was vulnerable. They knew that a lot of people wouldn't be looking for her. Then they killed her."

"So, is this enough to get more patrols on the lake?"

Landon rolled his shoulders, trying to rub out the kinks as he did. "I don't know," he said honestly. "We have to think of a valid reason why."

"What do we do until then?"

"We talk to the foster mother," Landon said grimly. "I want to do some research on her, make sure she's not involved in this."

"You think she's involved?" I was horrified.

"I don't know," Landon cautioned. "I can tell you that I'm not going to let her get away with it if she is."

His face was fierce with determination.

"I've got a friend at the Coast Guard," Chief Terry said, rubbing his chin tiredly. "I'm going to talk to him and let slip that we've had a couple of residents commenting on a strange boat off the coast."

Landon looked intrigued. "A strange boat?"

"I'm going to let him think that maybe there are drug traffickers out there or something," Chief Terry said. "It's not perfect, but it's something at least. This way, they'll be on the lookout and more apt to stop boats in the channel."

"How does that help?" I was confused.

"Because, if there's a big drug bust out there, the Coast Guard will get all the glory," Landon said knowingly.

"So, why not just tell them our suspicions?"

"Because," Chief Terry answered. "They'll think we're crazy. We've got to make it look like it's their idea, not our idea."

"Don't you think all this subterfuge is just a little paranoid?"

"Really? Coming from you and your wacky cousins?" Landon challenged me.

He had a point.

"Okay, you guys know what to do in this situation better than I do," I said. "I'm going to run back over to Hypnotic and see how Clove and Thistle are getting along with Erika and Gracie."

"Now, when you say you're going to be at Hypnotic, does that mean I'll find you traipsing around the countryside in about an hour when I come to pick you up?" Landon's question was pointed.

"It's not like we were doing anything dangerous," I countered. "We were just going out to see Uncle Warren."

"What you still haven't told me is why?"

"We wanted to ask him some questions," I replied irritably. "Is that a crime?"

"When you tell me you're going to be one place and you end up in another, that's a crime," Landon said.

"No, it's not," I shot back. "It's running an errand with my cousins."

"I'm not going to fight about this," Landon warned.

"Good," I raised my eyebrows in challenge. "I would hate for us to fight about something trivial. Again."

Chief Terry started chuckling.

"This isn't funny," Landon turned on him.

"Watching you two fight all your hormones? It's damned funny from where I'm sitting."

Landon flushed. "Hormones? This has nothing to do with hormones."

"Oh, please," Chief Terry waved off Landon's anger. "Boy, every time you look at her I can feel the hormones. It's kind of sweet. Gross and uncomfortable, but sweet all the same."

I smirked at Landon victoriously.

"I wouldn't be so full of yourself, missy," Chief Terry turned to me. "You're just as bad."

"That's just a bald-faced lie," I said.

"I agree," Landon grumbled.

"Of course," Chief Terry said. "There are no hormones involved here. I'm totally wrong. Sorry. I don't know what I was thinking."

"So, I'll see you in an hour?" Landon asked, purposely turning his back on Chief Terry as I started to move out of the office.

"Yeah, I'll be there. I promise."

"Good," Landon said. "I might want to have a talk with you about ... those hormones later tonight."

I smiled despite myself. "Yeah, well, okay."

"Hey," Chief Terry barked. "Let's not get all flirty in front of me. It makes me uncomfortable."

"You were the one that brought up the hormones," Landon pointed out.

"Yeah, but I don't want to see you two talk about doing stuff about them," Chief Terry said. "She's always going to be ten years old to me and that makes you a dirty old man. Are we clear on that?"

"Yeah, we're clear," Landon said shortly.

Chief Terry turned to me. "Clear?"

"Does that mean I don't have to hear about your hormones where my mom and aunts are concerned?"

Chief Terry looked scandalized. "That is none of your business, young lady."

"Oh, it's not so funny when it's your hormones, is it?"

"This conversation is over," Chief Terry said suddenly. "You go do whatever it is you do with your cousins and you, Landon, you go back to doing some actual work."

"Got it, chief," I laughed as I walked out the door. I was halfway down the hall when I heard Chief Terry speak again.

"How do you put up with her?"

"I don't know," Landon answered. "It must be all the hormones."

TWENTY-NINE

After a night of exploring our hormones – no bacon smell included – Landon and I woke up refreshed and relaxed.

"It's hard to believe that I can feel this good when things are so bad right now," I admitted, snuggling into Landon's side the next morning.

"We can't stop living, Bay," Landon said, dropping a kiss on my forehead. "We're going to find Gracie and we're going to find the people that hurt her. We can't do it all in one day, though."

"But there are other kids out there."

"I know," Landon said. "The problem we have is that we don't know if that boat is even in the area anymore. We don't have any specifics about the boat. You said Erika can't read. We don't know the name of the boat. We don't even know if it is in Michigan waters or international waters. For all we know, the boat has docked in Canada at this point and is long gone."

"Well, you're a joy in the morning," I grumbled.

I felt Landon's chest quake with laughter next to me. "You're the biggest grump of all in the morning and you're making fun of me?"

"I'm not grumpy in the morning."

"Right," Landon sighed. "You're all sweetness and light."

"What time is it?" I bolted up suddenly.

"Why?"

"I have to get down to the inn," I said. "The contractors are coming and I promised that I would stop by to make sure Aunt Tillie isn't ... well, being Aunt Tillie."

"That's a tall order," Landon said.

"Well, if you get up and get showered right now, I can see a big pile of peanut butter pancakes in your future," I teased him.

Landon looked interested. "Your mom's peanut butter pancakes?"

"Well, I'm not cooking for you."

"How come your mother and aunts can all cook, but I found you and Thistle eating tuna straight from the can for dinner two weeks ago?"

"Not all gifts hit every generation," I said lightly, climbing out of bed.

"Gifts? Cooking is a gift?"

"When you're a kitchen witch, like them, yes."

"And what kind of witch are you?"

"I'm an earth witch," I said. "Thistle and Clove are, too."

"What does that mean?"

"It means we can call upon the elements and we're at home in nature essentially," I replied distractedly. I always got a little uncomfortable when Landon probed too far into the witch thing. It made me nervous.

"Call upon the elements? Like that wind monster?"

We didn't speak about the events from a few months ago very often. I knew Landon was still uneasy with what he had seen.

"Kind of," I hedged.

"Your mothers were involved in that, though," Landon pointed out.

"They can call upon the elements," I replied, meeting Landon's searching gaze worriedly. "That's not a great strength for them. They funneled their power into the spell that Clove, Thistle, Aunt Tillie and I conjured."

"So you created the wind monster?"

"We all did," I said.

"And who gave it form?"

I grimaced. I had wondered if he had noticed that. "Aunt Tillie."

"How can you be sure?"

"Truthfully? Because when it passed by me I realized I recognized the eyes staring back at me."

"You knew him?" Landon looked impressed.

"No," I shook my head. "I recognized him from pictures."

"Who was he?"

"My Uncle Calvin."

Landon looked flabbergasted. "Was it really him?"

"I don't know," I shrugged. "We conjured the wind out of rage and anger. Maybe Aunt Tillie just gives form to her anger."

"Why don't you ask her?" Landon asked pointedly.

"Maybe I don't want to know the answer," I said. "Or, maybe, I know she doesn't want to answer the question."

"So, you're just going to let it go?"

"Do you have any other suggestions?"

"Ask her," Landon replied simply.

"Why don't you ask her," I suggested. "That sounds like an even better idea to me."

"I'm not asking her."

"Well," I shrugged. "I guess we're in the same boat."

AN HOUR later Landon was plowing into his second plate of peanut butter pancakes and I was finishing off a glass of tomato juice as my mom and aunts busily discussed the contingency of guests that were expected to arrive in two days.

"More pancakes, Landon?" My mom pushed the plate toward him, her eyes twinkling mischievously. "You certainly have an appetite this morning."

"I just love your cooking," Landon said, avoiding the obvious infringement of personal space my mother was currently embarking on. "Bay can't cook. Her idea of breakfast is cereal – or a glass of tomato juice."

Landon made a face when I swallowed another gulp of juice. He was disgusted by tomato juice and had made that opinion fairly obvious every time I drank it over the past few months.

"She's always loved tomato juice," my mom agreed. "I like it, too, but she could live on it. Have you seen her dip pickles in it for a snack? That's really gross."

"Yeah, she does that about once a week," Landon grimaced. "I make her brush her teeth before she kisses me."

"Well, that's nice – I guess." My mom frowned at the over share.

Landon realized what he'd said but it was too late to take it back. "I'm sorry. That was too much information. Chief Terry made it abundantly clear that he didn't want to hear about my hormones and I'm guessing that you don't either."

I kicked Landon swiftly under the table.

"Ow," he rubbed his leg. "What is that for?"

"What are you doing?" I hissed.

"Talking to your mom over breakfast," Landon said ruefully. "Is that a crime?"

"Just stop talking," I muttered.

"You should listen to her," Aunt Tillie said sagely from her spot on the other side of Landon. "You're awfully chatty this morning and it is embarrassing the girl."

"I'm not embarrassed," I countered.

"You look embarrassed."

"Well, look again," I said briefly.

"You still look embarrassed."

"You know what?" I pushed away from the table. "I have actual work to do today, so why don't we check in with the contractors and then you can spend the afternoon telling them about how embarrassed I am?"

"Fine," Aunt Tillie said, suddenly going rigid. "I'll meet you down there in a few minutes."

"Why?" I asked, narrowing my eyes at her suspiciously. "What are you up to?"

"What do you mean?" Aunt Tillie frowned. "I'm not up to anything. Why do you always assume I'm up to something?"

"Because you usually are," Landon said around another mouthful of pancakes.

"You stay out of this," Aunt Tillie warned him off with a point of her finger.

"Fine," I said tiredly. "I'll be down at the construction site. You do whatever it is you're not doing and meet me down there. And you," I turned to Landon. "Keep me up on whatever you find out today."

Landon nodded. "You got it."

"What are you doing today?" My mom asked Landon curiously.

"I'm just working on something with Chief Terry," Landon said evasively.

"Oh, well, if you're seeing Terry, I have some fresh baked donuts to send with you," she said happily. "Let me go pack them up."

"You made fresh donuts? How come I'm just hearing about this now?"

"Because they're for tomorrow," my mom said. "You and your cousins will eat them all if we're not careful."

"You could've set a few aside," I complained.

"There's a plate of chocolate-sprinkled in the kitchen for the three of you," my mom said. "You can take them with you when you go."

"Awesome."

Dirk was already hard at work when I made my way down to the construction site. He greeted me with a warm smile and an embarrassed shake of his head. "I'm glad you're here," he said. "I wanted to apologize to you about what my grandfather said at dinner the other night."

It took me a second to focus and then I remembered Kenneth and his curmudgeonly flirting with Aunt Tillie. The memory wasn't unpleasant.

"It's fine," I waved off his concerns. "Trust me. It was nice to see Aunt Tillie get a little shaken."

"Well, it still wasn't appropriate," Dirk said apologetically. "My grandfather thinks that, because he's old, he can just say or do whatever he wants."

"Aunt Tillie thinks that, too," I said. "It has nothing to do with her age, though, and everything to do with entitlement. She's always been like this – or so I hear."

"Well," Dirk hedged. "Either way, I just want you to know that I had a talk with him and he promised not to do it again."

"I don't understand," I started. "It doesn't matter. It's not like he'll see her again."

"Um, well ... ." Dirk was faltering.

Uh-oh.

"The thing is, my grandfather, he started the business," Dirk explained. "He's still the main owner of the business and, even though he doesn't do any of the work anymore, he still has the ability to come on job sites with us."

I glanced around the area quickly, my gaze falling on Kenneth near one of the trucks. "So he's going to keep coming out here to work?"

"He won't be doing much work," Dirk said grimly. "Except maybe on your aunt."

Something niggled in the corner of my brain. "Did my Aunt Tillie know he was coming?"

"No, I don't think so."

"Huh."

"Huh, what?"

I inclined my head behind Dirk. He turned curiously, just in time to see Aunt Tillie arrive with a box full of donuts. She put the box down on the hood of one of the trucks, opened it, and pulled out a chocolate frosted one and handed it to Kenneth grudgingly. "I figure you deserve one of these, even if you're not really working."

Kenneth smiled, tickled to see Aunt Tillie again. "That hard hat makes you look hot."

"Are you getting fresh?"

"Maybe," Kenneth smiled.

Aunt Tillie glanced at me and frowned. "Well, enjoy your donut."

"Don't you want to have one with me?" Kenneth asked.

"I already ate breakfast," Aunt Tillie stiffened.

"Well then, maybe while everyone else is working, you can show me the rest of the grounds? I bet they're beautiful."

"They're just grounds," Aunt Tillie shrugged.

"You don't want to show me around?" Kenneth looked disappointed.

"I could show you around," Aunt Tillie said begrudgingly. "If you're that interested, it's not a problem."

"Good," Kenneth brightened considerably and held out his arm for her. "Shall we, milady?"

I pushed my tongue to the roof of my mouth to keep from laughing aloud as Kenneth led Aunt Tillie past Dirk and me.

"Don't you say a word," Aunt Tillie warned as she walked by. "Not one word."

I merely shook my head. "My lips are sealed."

But only until I could get some time alone with Clove and Thistle. This was too good not to share.

THIRTY

When I made it to The Whistler about a half hour later, I was still chuckling to myself about Aunt Tillie and Kenneth. I couldn't remember her ever taking interest in a man before – especially one like Kenneth. She seemed to like him, though – against her better judgment – which made me think he might be good for her. He'd certainly be good for Clove, Thistle and I – mostly because he would be a welcome distraction. She would be less likely to torture us if she was distracted by him.

I sat down at my desk and, while I was waiting for my computer to boot up, I let loose a whoosh of surprise when Edith popped into view a few feet from me.

"Well, I see you decided to come back to work," Edith said primly.

"Edith," I replied coldly. I realized I was still angry with her.

"I see you're still pouting about our fight the other day," she sniffed. "I think that's pretty juvenile of you."

"Hmm," I mused absently. I was hoping she would take the hint and go away.

"Are you listening to me?"

"No, Edith," I replied quietly. "I am really not in the mood to listen to you right now."

"Because you don't agree with me? That hardly seems fair."

"It's more than that, Edith, and you know it," I challenged her. "You said some pretty awful things."

"About a girl that you don't even know," Edith shot back. "A girl that died a hundred and sixty years ago."

"Yeah?" I raised an eyebrow briefly. "Well, maybe you and I have a different definition of what's important and what's not important."

"So, that's it, you just don't want to be friends anymore?" Edith looked brokenhearted. I could feel my feelings for her starting to thaw – and then she opened her mouth again. "All over a darkie? You're willing to give up our friendship over a darkie?"

"Edith, don't you have somewhere else to be?" My voice was cold enough to freeze Edith in mid rant.

"You're really upset about this?"

"I am really upset about this," I agreed.

"And you don't think you're being unreasonable?"

"Not in the slightest."

"Well," Edith pursed her lips. "I guess I'll go find something else to do then."

"That sounds great," I kept my attention focused on my computer screen. It was only when I was sure that she was gone that I let the breath that had been pooling in my chest escape. This Edith situation was a whole other problem I wasn't prepared to deal with. It's not like I could just cut Edith out of my life. She was a ghost, she could pop in and out of wherever she wanted whenever the whim hit.

Plus, the real tragedy of the situation was that Edith didn't think she'd done anything wrong. She wasn't purposely being obtuse. I kept reminding myself that she had lived in a different time, so even though she was dead in this one, she didn't know any better.

That argument wasn't making me feel any better. I decided to push the entire quandary out of my mind and focus on other things – at least for the time being. Getting Erika to pass over and finding out what happened to Gracie – and hopefully saving the other children on the boat – were my first priorities. Edith's backwards thinking and hurt feelings were low on my priority list right now.

And, even though I didn't want to think about it, the next edition of The Whistler was going to have to be dealt with. I had already decided to write the main story on the restoration of the Dandridge, so the first order of business was doing a little research on the lighthouse.

I started by Googling the building and reading up on the history of not only the Dandridge, but a bevy of other lighthouses throughout the Great Lakes on a State of Michigan website. Before I realized what was happening, I had wasted three hours reading up on the Dandridge and a few surrounding lighthouses in the area.

"You look deep in thought."

I glanced up to the doorway and grimaced when I saw Sam Cornell standing there. "Just doing some research," I said.

"On what?" Sam seemed determined to wear down my defenses and erode my rampant distrust of him.

"On the Dandridge," I replied. I was equally determined to be professional but distant.

"Oh, you're going with that for the front page of this week's edition, right?"

"I am," I said, watching warily as Sam moved around the side of my desk and stood behind me to read over my shoulder. I was glad that I had actually been telling the truth this time.

"Did you find anything good?"

I was uncomfortable with Sam invading my personal space, but I tried not to show it. That would give him power – and that was the last thing I wanted to do.

"I don't know, define 'good,'" I replied. "I found out when it was built and a little bit of background on the gentleman who initially owned it."

"I thought lighthouses were owned by the state."

"Yes and no," I said. "When the Dandridge was built, the state was building some lighthouses but so were individual businessmen. In the case of Anthony Benson, he was a local entrepreneur who built the Dandridge on family property. When he died, his children sold the parcel to the state and they took over running the Dandridge until it basically fell into disuse in the 1930s or so."

"That's pretty impressive," Sam said. "That you found out that information so quickly."

"It's the Internet," I replied blandly. "It was actually pretty easy."

"When are you going out to the Dandridge for your story?" Sam asked curiously, ignoring my sarcastic tone.

"In the next few days," I replied. "Dean was open to suggestions for dates."

"I'd like to come with you."

"Why?"

"Because I'd like to see the property," Sam replied simply.

"Well, Dean doesn't seem particular about people going out there to look around," I suggested. "You can go out there on your own at any time."

"So, you're saying you don't want me to go out there with you when you go?" Sam looked amused.

"I don't need your help to do my job," I said simply. "I'm capable of doing it myself. If you want to see the Dandridge then you are capable of doing it yourself."

"I don't understand why you're so combative where I'm concerned," Sam said petulantly.

"I don't believe that was combative," I replied stiffly.

"Neither do I," Landon said, breezing into my office and jostling Sam – just a little – while he tried to maneuver him out from behind my desk and back toward the doorway. "If you want to see combative, I'd be more than willing to show it to you outside," Landon suggested.

I glanced up at Sam, who had gone two shades paler when Landon wandered into the room. He looked uncomfortable with Landon's sudden appearance. "Mr. Michaels."

"Agent Michaels," Landon corrected him.

"Agent Michaels," Sam repeated uncomfortably. "I wasn't aware you were visiting Ms. Winchester today."

"I try to visit Ms. Winchester every day," Landon replied airily. "I find I miss her after a few hours."

"Really?" I glanced up at him in surprise.

Landon shrugged. "Must be all those hormones."

"You better not let Chief Terry hear you say that."

"Yeah, I've definitely learned my lesson about that," Landon agreed.

I watched Sam out of the corner of my eye. He was shuffling nervously in the doorway. He obviously wanted to leave, but he also didn't want to give Landon the impression that he had scared him away. He was torn. Landon must have noticed, too, because he fixed Sam with a hard stare. "Are you still here?"

"I happened to be having a conversation with Ms. Winchester when you interrupted," Sam said boldly. "Rudely interrupted, I might add."

Landon rolled his eyes and turned back to me. "What are you doing?"

"Looking up history on the Dandridge."

"Find anything good?"

"Just some history tidbits," I replied.

Sam was practically dancing in the doorway he was so uncomfortable now. "We were having a conversation," Sam said. I had to give him credit. He wasn't giving up. He wasn't exactly winning, but he wasn't giving up either.

"Now we're having a conversation," Landon said pointedly, wagging his finger between him and me for emphasis.

"I ... fine," Sam blew out a sigh. "I don't want you to think I'm rewarding you for bad behavior, but I also believe in respecting law enforcement."

"Good, you can go now," Landon dismissed Sam.

Sam cast one last glance in my direction, although it was an unreadable one. When he was gone, I turned to Landon with a dubious look. "That was mean."

"I don't like him."

"I don't like him either, but that was still mean."

"I don't like him hovering over you," Landon admitted.

"Hovering?"

"You know, invading your personal space."

"You sound jealous."

"I am not jealous," Landon countered. "I'm protective. There's a difference."

"If you say so," I smirked.

"Don't go thinking so much of yourself," Landon warned me. "I am not jealous."

"So you said."

"No, really."

"Okay," I nodded.

"So do you want to hear what I learned or just sit there and let your head get bigger and bigger?" Landon asked irritably.

"I don't know, it's a hard choice," I teased him.

Landon glared at me, although there wasn't any malice in the gesture. He was just playing the game.

"Okay," I blew out a sigh. "What did you learn?"

"You're not going to like it," Landon said, moving back around my desk and shutting the office door to make sure no one could hear us.

"Why am I not going to like it?" I asked suspiciously.

"Because it's not good news."

I steepled my fingers on top of my desk and waited.

"So, Gracie was placed with a foster mother named Stella Smith," Landon started.

"Smith?" I already didn't like the sound of that.

"Yeah, it's an alias," Landon said grimly. "Stella managed to pass all the background checks put forward by the state, but they're not exactly strenuous. Your Aunt Tillie could pass them, too, and we wouldn't want her influencing the minds of the youth of America today."

"Stella has had three children in her care," Landon continued. "The first, a boy, was only with her two weeks before his mother got custody back. Then, besides Gracie, there was another little girl named Ava. She is eight."

"Where is Ava now?"

"No one knows."

"What?"

"We can't find Ava. I have the state police doing interviews and going door-to-door, but right now both Ava and Stella are gone."

"Where were they living?"

"Flint," Landon said.

"I don't know if that's good or bad," I shook my head.

"I don't think it's either," Landon said. "From Gracie and Ava's perspective, though, that's one of the worst areas in the state to have to go into foster care."

"Why?"

"A lot of people are struggling in that area right now and sometimes, well, things fall through the cracks."

"Like two little girls?" I asked bitterly.

"Yeah, like two little girls."

"What happens now?"

"We've got people out looking for Stella."

"Do you think she's on the boat?"

Landon looked momentarily lost. "I honestly don't know. She could be. She could be in the wind, too. Stella Smith didn't exist until a year ago. That's obviously not her name. She could be anywhere and running God knows what scam."

"How did she get approved?"

"It's a thankless job, Bay," Landon said. "It's basically a job that's full of good people – but bad people find their way into the system, too. You can't keep them all out."

"I feel sick."

"I know," Landon murmured, kneeling next to me and rubbing the back of my neck.

"What happens now?"

"Now? Now we try to find Stella and we try to find the boat."

"And if we can't?"

Landon grimaced. "We have to find one or the other, Bay," he said tiredly. "If we don't, then we have nowhere else to look. We need a break here."

I rubbed the bridge of my nose wearily. "I'm so frustrated," I admitted.

"Why?" Landon looked concerned.

"Sam Cornell is sniffing around here. Gracie died. Erika is stuck here until I can figure something out. That Kenneth guy is stalking Aunt Tillie and I think she likes it. It's just so much crap."

"Kenneth? The old guy from dinner the other night?"

"Yeah."

"He's stalking your Aunt Tillie?"

"They took a walk along the property together today," I said. "He obviously likes her and, what's freaky is, I think she likes him, too."

Landon barked out a laugh. "See, everything isn't all bad."

"I just wish everything would stop," I sighed. "Just for a few hours."

Landon raised a dark eyebrow and considered me. "You want some peace and quiet?"

"More than anything."

"Okay, then," he said, standing up decisively. "Be ready for me to pick you up here at five. Don't go anywhere else. Actually be here at five and I'll take you some place to get a little quiet."

"Where?" I asked curiously.

"That's a secret," Landon tweaked my nose. "I think you'll like it, though."

Something told me he was right – and it wasn't just my hormones talking this time.

THIRTY-ONE

I went back to work for a couple of hours. At first, I found it hard to concentrate with the idea of Landon's "surprise" looming over me. Because I found the history of the Dandridge so interesting, though, I lost myself in the research before long.

When I heard a knock on the door to my office, I glanced up in surprise. I was under the impression that Sam had left in a nervous snit right after his encounter with Landon, and Brian hadn't bothered coming in today.

Landon was standing in the doorway watching me curiously. "You seem engrossed in whatever you're doing."

"What are you doing? I thought you weren't coming back until five," I laughed. "Did you miss me that much?"

"It's a quarter after," Landon tapped his wristwatch for emphasis. "I figured you would be climbing the walls because I was late. I'm actually surprised to find you here and not wandering around getting into mischief with Thistle and Clove."

I decided not to rise to the bait. "We do not wander around getting into mischief," I explained to him. "It sort of follows us."

"Like a lost puppy?"

"Pretty much. Just not as cuddly."

Landon held out his hand expectantly. "Let's go."

"Where are we going," I smirked, clicking my laptop shut and standing excitedly. I felt like a kid on Christmas morning for some reason.

"I told you, it's a surprise," Landon smiled.

I reached my hand out, lacing my fingers with his, and let him lead me back out of the building. Landon pulled up short once we were on the other side of the front door to the paper. "You need to lock up?"

"Yeah, give me a second."

Landon watched as I selected the right key from the ring in my pocket and then I heard him growl as I turned around. "What's wrong?"

"What is with this guy?"

I glanced around Landon's shoulder and frowned as Sam made his way up the walkway and toward The Whistler. "Oh, you're leaving?"

"We are," I nodded.

"I was hoping that someone was still here," Sam said hurriedly. "I guess I lucked out."

"For what?" Landon asked.

Sam directed his answer to me instead of Landon. "I was hoping to be able to work for another hour or so inside the building. If you let me in, I'll make sure everything is locked up when I leave."

"I don't think that's a good idea," I said honestly.

"Excuse me?" Sam looked surprised at my answer.

"You don't work here," I reminded him. "You're a paid consultant. I don't think that means you get free run of the building and everything inside when no one else is here."

"Brian said I was to have free rein over the building," Sam reminded me.

"Then maybe you should call Brian to let you in," Landon suggested.

"I don't think this involves you," Sam said stiffly.

"Well, Bay said no," Landon said. "Therefore, why don't you go after the man who invited you here? I agree with Bay. You're not an employee. If Brian wanted you to be able to come and go whenever you want, he would have given you a key."

"It must be great to be you," Sam said coldly. "To be perfect and so above the rest of us."

Landon wrinkled his nose and I felt his body tense beside me. I put my hand on his arm to placate him. "Let's go."

Landon fixed his eyes on me and smiled tightly. "Right, let's go. I believe I have a surprise to make good on."

"So, that's a no on letting me into the building?" Sam asked.

"It's a no," I called back, not bothering to turn around and meet his gaze head on. I could feel the anger radiating off of Sam from ten feet away. I didn't have to look at him to see the abject hatred roiling off of him.

"SO, YOUR SURPRISE is to bring me out to the Dandridge?"

As far as surprises go, I was a little let down. Landon and I were parked on the dirt road on the other side of the structure, and he was watching me curiously. There was a hint of mischief on his face, but he was trying to hide it – so I pretended I didn't notice.

"You just spent the entire afternoon researching the history of the Dandridge," Landon reminded me.

"So you thought you would reward me with a trip to the Dandridge?"

"Yup," Landon said, opening the door of his SUV and sliding out.

I sighed as I did the same. I moved to the front of the vehicle, expecting Landon to join me, but he was busy rummaging through the hatchback of the vehicle. "What are you doing?"

"Just looking for something," Landon said.

I couldn't see him from my position, but he was clearly searching for something important. I decided to go find out for myself when I saw the hatchback lower and snap shut. I watched Landon move around the far side of the vehicle suspiciously.

"I'm starting to lose my patience," I admitted.

"With what?" Landon winked, only infuriating me further.

"This isn't much of a surprise," I said carefully.

"Well, I'll have to try better next time," Landon replied casually, moving up next to me and finally letting me see what he had in his hand. It was a big picnic basket and a blanket.

"What's that?"

"What's what?" Landon asked innocently.

"What's in the picnic basket?" I tried again.

"What's usually in a picnic basket?"

"Food."

"Well, I guess there's food in here, then."

"You cooked?" I was a little worried. Landon made fun of my cooking skills and yet his were even more disturbing.

"Maybe I did," Landon teased.

"What did you cook?" I asked worriedly.

"Fried chicken, potato salad and cake," Landon announced proudly.

"You cooked fried chicken?"

Landon pursed his lips. "Okay, maybe Twila cooked it."

"You went to Twila for food?" I was impressed.

"She seemed like a better option than your mom," Landon replied dryly. "You said you wanted some time alone and I figured asking your mom for help was cheating."

"And asking Twila wasn't?"

"It was less of a cheat."

"You know, the minute you left with that picnic basket, Twila went and told my mom," I said.

"I figured," Landon said. "I should get points for good intentions, though."

"You do," I said, linking my arm through his and letting him lead me to the lawn in front of the Dandridge. "You get special consideration because Twila makes the best potato salad I've ever had. Well, her and Marnie."

"That's what she said," Landon laughed. "Except she said hers was better than Marnie's."

I helped him spread the blanket out and, when we were settled, I peered into the picnic basket excitedly. "Oh, man, you really did get Twila's fried chicken."

"Did you think I was lying to you?"

"No," I shook my head. "I just love her fried chicken."

"Well, from my perspective, everything they make is pretty darn good," Landon admitted. "I've gained ten pounds since I started dating you."

"You have not," I replied. "You forget, I've seen you naked."

"Oh, I haven't forgotten," Landon laughed, grabbing a chicken leg and taking a bite out of it enthusiastically.

"So you just wanted me to tell you that you look good naked?" I asked, taking my own piece of chicken and digging in. "That's a little pathetic. Fishing for a compliment."

"What can I say," Landon said. "Sometimes, a guy just wants to hear that he's not fat."

I giggled. There was something endearing about a flirting man who goes out of his way to give a girl a picnic. He knew exactly what I had needed – before I even did. It didn't hurt that he was incredibly hot – and when he was being sweet, he was smoking. Shallow? Yes. It was also true.

"Well, you look better naked than any other guy I've ever seen," I said, immediately regretting the words as soon as they left my mouth. "I mean, oh crap, that was a stupid thing to say."

Landon waved it off, smiling despite himself. "I find it charming. It's just so ... you."

"I'm going to take that as a compliment."

"You should," Landon smirked, taking a bite of the potato salad. "You were right, this is the best potato salad ever."

"I told you."

"I thought my mom's potato salad was good," Landon said. "This is amazing, though."

"Your mom cooks?"

"She cooks," Landon said. "She's a pretty good cook. She doesn't cook like your family does, though. I don't think anyone cooks like your family does."

"Yes, well, when they want to do something, they're all incredibly driven," I agreed.

"I think that goes for you, Clove and Thistle, too."

"How do you figure?" I laughed. "I work at a weekly that has three stories a week – and two of those are advertorials."

"That's what you do," Landon countered. "That's not who you are."

"And who am I?"

"Someone who cares," Landon replied simply. "That's your gift, Bay. You care. Sometimes you care too much. You're loyal, stubborn and you care. Sometimes, that's a mix that drives me crazy – but it's also what makes me crazy for you."

I felt my cheeks color under the compliment. "I don't know what to say," I said finally.

"You don't have to say anything," Landon said. "That's your biggest drawback. You don't know when to just shut up."

"Are you telling me to ... ?"

I didn't get to finish the sentence. Landon leaned forward and pressed his lips to mine quickly. "Shut up, Bay."

I sank into the kiss, moving closer to Landon and letting his body heat warm me with the golden glow only I could see when we were together. Sometimes, only sometimes, our auras joined. Since auras weren't a strength of mine, I only saw them when I lost control and, since I was from a family that tried to exert control on everyone, that didn't happen very often.

"That is gross."

I jumped when I heard the voice, pulling away from Landon in surprise.

"What?" Landon looked around in alarm. He couldn't see the guest that had just popped into view.

"It's Erika," I said quietly, running a hand through my mussed hair and turning my attention to her. "What are you doing here?"

"Is that your boyfriend?"

"Yes."

"Yes, what?" Landon asked curiously.

"She asked if you were my boyfriend."

"Oh."

"He's handsome," Erika looked Landon up and down. "He should cut his hair, though."

"Have you been talking to my Aunt Tillie?"

"No, but after spending time with Clove and Thistle, I want to."

"Why?"

"She sounds fun."

"Then Clove and Thistle have been telling you vicious lies."

"They said you'd say that."

"I bet."

I glanced at Landon out of the corner of my eye. If anything was going to ruin the mood, watching me converse with empty air had to be at the top of the list. He seemed mildly interested in the half of the conversation he could hear, though, and he wasn't making a move to leave. I took that as a good sign.

"So, what are you doing here?" Erika asked curiously.

"Having a picnic."

"People used to come out here from time to time and do that," Erika mused. "They could never see me. I tried talking to them. It made me sad."

"I'm sorry that happened," I replied honestly. "I can see you, though. So why are you back out here?"

"I was looking for you."

"Why?"

"Because Clove and Thistle told me to go find the boat again."

"Did you find it?"

"What?" Landon asked.

"She went looking for the boat again."

"Did she find it?"

"Why can't he hear me?" Erika asked.

"He's not like Clove, Thistle and I," I replied.

"He's not magical?"

"He's got his own kind of magic," I said purposefully. "It's just not the type of magic that can be used to see you."

Landon smiled at my explanation, even though he hadn't heard Erika's question.

"What kind of magic does he have?"

"He has the kind of magic that helps people," I replied simply. "And he makes people feel better."

"Like the children on the boat?"

"Like the children on the boat," I agreed.

"Good," Erika said. "Because you're running out of time."

"What do you mean?"

"The boat is going to be gone soon. Two days."

"How do you know that?"

"I listened to the people upstairs on the boat. That's what they said. They said they had to be gone in two days."

"What is she saying?"

"She says we're running out of time," I said grimly. "We have two days."

"Two days? Well, crap," Landon climbed up and started packing up the picnic.

"What are you doing?"

"We have to get moving on this," Landon said.

"You believe me?"

"Are you lying?" Landon asked, but he didn't stop packing the picnic back up to wait for my response.

"No," I said. "You're taking a lot on faith, though."

"That's what a relationship is, Bay," Landon said. "I believe in you. So, let's help these kids."

"You're right," Erika giggled. "He does have a different kind of magic."

THIRTY-TWO

After packing up our picnic, we returned to the guesthouse – but found it empty. I realized that Thistle and Clove were probably up at the inn having dinner.

"You want to tell them, don't you?" Landon asked.

"It can wait until morning," I said.

"Are you sure?"

"We're not joined at the hip," I pointed out.

"Really? I wasn't sure," Landon teased, although the mirth in his voice didn't encapsulate his entire face.

"You're worried," I observed.

"Worried? I don't know if that's the right word," Landon said. "I think concerned would be more like it."

"So, what do we do?"

"I called Chief Terry on our way back here and he said he would get out some extra patrols as soon as possible," Landon said. "Until tomorrow morning, though, we're stuck."

"What happens tomorrow morning?"

"Tomorrow morning I drive over to Traverse City and find a way to get my boss to put the full weight of the FBI behind this."

I felt my heart rate ratchet up a notch. "Do you think you can do that?"

Landon shrugged noncommittally. "I have no idea. What I do know is that I couldn't live with myself if I didn't at least try."

"What will you tell him?"

Landon shook his head. "I don't know yet. I guess I'll figure that out on the drive over there tomorrow morning."

"Can't you just call him?"

"I think I'll be more convincing in person," Landon replied honestly.

I bit my lower lip. "Will you stay over there tomorrow night?" I was reluctant to admit that I wanted him close to me. I felt a little pathetic even thinking it.

Landon smirked. "Missing me already?"

"No," I shot back. "I don't care if you stay over there."

"Well, that's good," Landon replied dryly. "But I care. I'll be back tomorrow night, one way or another."

"How can you be sure?" I asked curiously.

"Because, either way, the boat is over here. If we're really working on a timetable, then I have to be over here where I can do some actual good."

"So you'll be back tomorrow night?"

"I'll be back tomorrow night," Landon agreed. "And while I'm gone, I expect you and your cousins to stay out of trouble."

"What's that supposed to mean?" I protested.

"You know what it means," Landon cast me a dark look.

"No, I don't," I pushed out my bottom lip obstinately.

"That means I don't want the three of you concocting some crazy plan about how you're going to solve this without the help of law enforcement."

"We would never do that," I protested.

"You've done nothing but do that since I met you," Landon pointed out.

"That's not true," I hedged, but my memory was suddenly agreeing with him and arguing with me. "Well, it's not totally true."

WITCHING ON A STAR

"You three are going to stay out of trouble, right?" Landon pressed.

"I said we would."

"And you're not going to tip off your Aunt Tillie to do something as a way around that promise?"

Crap, he was catching on to our tricks.

"I promise."

"Good," Landon said, pulling me toward him and dropping a kiss on the top of my head. "I wouldn't be happy to lose you."

"That's a nice thing to say."

"And if you do something stupid," Landon continued. "I'm going to make you wish you'd never met me."

"That's not a nice thing to say."

"You want me to be nice?" Landon cocked an eyebrow and looked down at me suggestively.

I blew out a sigh. "Okay," I said. "But you're going to have to do all the work because I'm really tired."

"I'm up for that," Landon laughed moving toward the bedroom. He stopped abruptly at the door. "There's no bacon in the house, right?"

I frowned. His cuteness factor was diminishing rapidly.

"SO, I HAVE AN IDEA."

"This can't be good," Thistle intoned, watching me from her spot behind the counter of Hypnotic as I paced around the store like a caged animal. I had spent the last thirty minutes catching my cousins up on everything I had learned in the past twenty-four hours.

"I don't want any part of it," Clove announced primly.

"You don't even know what it is," I pointed out.

"That doesn't matter," Clove replied. "I've learned my lesson about doing what you guys want me to do. I'm not codependent anymore."

"Really?" Thistle arched an eyebrow doubtfully. "You cured your own codependence by sheer force of will in two days?"

"I did," Clove agreed.

"Huh," Thistle mused. "You should run a seminar on how to do that. People would pay big bucks to let you cure their codependence."

"Do you really think so?" Clove's eyes sparkled with interest.

"Absolutely," Thistle nodded enthusiastically and then rolled her eyes in my direction when Clove looked away.

"You guys want to help me?" Clove asked.

I pursed my lips to keep from laughing. "Wouldn't that be the opposite of breaking the codependent streak?"

Clove considered the question seriously for a second and then scowled at me. "You're just trying to confuse me."

"Big shocker there," Thistle mumbled.

"What?" Clove asked suspiciously.

"I was asking Bay what her idea was," Thistle changed the subject.

"I told you that I don't want to know," Clove said angrily.

"I wasn't asking for you, I was asking for me," Thistle argued. "Not everything is about you."

"No, apparently it's about you," Clove shot back.

"You're bugging me," Thistle sniped.

"You're both bugging me," I interjected impatiently.

"Oh, yeah," Thistle turned back to me. "What's your idea again?"

"I think we should do a summoning spell," I announced boldly.

Thistle didn't look impressed. "Why?"

"To call the boat."

"Huh," Thistle rolled the idea around her in mind. "Do you think we can do that?"

"I don't know," I admitted. "I think it's worth a try, though."

"A summoning spell only works to call energy," Clove countered. "A boat is an object, not energy."

"We don't know that it only works on energy," Thistle shot back. "We just know we've only used them to summon energy. That's actually not a bad idea."

"It's not going to work," Clove said.

Thistle ignored her. "People are made of energy," Thistle said, her eyes flashing with intrigue as she watched me. "What if we actually combined a summoning spell with a command spell?"

"What's a command spell?" Clove narrowed her eyes.

"She means a hypnosis spell," I said.

"A hypnosis spell?" Clove looked flummoxed. "We haven't used one of those since high school. Don't you remember? We used it on Coach Bailey to convince her we were always on our periods so we wouldn't have to participate in gym and it backfired and she had some sort of meltdown because she thought she was hemorrhaging?"

"We're older now," Thistle replied, although she smirked evilly at the memory. She had always hated Coach Bailey.

"We're smarter now," I added.

"We're not any smarter now," Clove scoffed. "If anything, we're dumber."

"We could ask Aunt Tillie," Thistle said after a moment, although she didn't look thrilled at the prospect.

"No way," I shook my head. "I don't want her involved in this."

"I'm not going to be involved in this either," Clove said angrily.

"Good for you, Sparky," Thistle said and then turned back to me. "Can we do a hypnosis spell if we have no idea who we're trying to hypnotize?"

"It's not going to be a hodgepodge spell," I reminded her. "It's going to be something we create. And, if it doesn't work, then there's no harm done."

"What if it does work?" Clove asked.

"Then we'll save a boatload of kids," Thistle reminded her.

Clove sighed. "I want to save the kids, too," she said quietly. "Say the spell works and we pull them into the dock," she plowed on. "What happens then? Are we going to take on a boatload of human traffickers by ourselves?"

"We'll be able to see if the spell is working in plenty of time to call Chief Terry and Landon," I pointed out pragmatically. "They can be waiting with cops on the docks when the boat arrives. We won't technically have to do anything or be in any danger."

"That's actually not a bad idea," Clove bit her lower lip. "Why don't we tell them now what we have planned?"

"What if it doesn't work, Doofus?" Thistle smacked Clove up the backside of her head. "Then we'll just look like idiots wasting the time of the police when they're trying to track down this boat. We can't pull them off what they're doing until we know it is working."

"And how are Landon and Chief Terry going to explain how we managed to call a boat to shore?" Clove challenged us.

"We'll call anonymously," Thistle said simply.

I pointed in her direction in agreement. "That's exactly what we'll do."

"I don't know," Clove whined.

I ignored her indecision and took the opportunity to answer my cellphone when it rang in my pocket. I recognized Landon's number. "Hey."

"Hey," Landon greeted me. "Where are you?"

"Having lunch with Thistle and Clove at Hypnotic," I lied.

"It's ten in the morning," Landon said after a beat.

"So? I'm bored. I'd rather spend the two hours before lunch with them instead of dodging Sam," I said. "It's just a really long lunch."

"You're not up to something, right?" Landon sounded worried.

"We're not up to something," I snapped, manufacturing some fake ire to sell my point. Thistle flashed me a thumbs up from across the room.

"I'm in Traverse City," Landon started.

"I know."

"I talked to my boss."

"Is he going to help?"

"He's going to try to get increased patrols on the lake," Landon said, although is voice was oddly flat.

"Why don't you sound happier about that?"

"He gave me a lecture about believing anonymous sources."

"Oh," I murmured. "So, if this doesn't work out, it's going to blow back on you?"

"Probably," Landon said tiredly over the phone. "Anyway," he continued. "I don't want you to worry about that."

"Then why are you calling? Did you miss me that much?"

"If I say yes will you roll in bacon grease for me?"

"No," I frowned, all hints of amusement fleeing my features. The bacon thing was getting old really quickly.

"Ah, well, I had to try," Landon lamented. "I just wanted to let you know that I'm going to be late tonight."

"You're not coming back?" Disappointment bubbled up.

"No, I'm coming back," Landon said hurriedly. "I've just decided to have dinner with my brother before I come back over. He has something to tell me and, truth be told, I haven't seen him as much as I used to and I think he's feeling a little bit neglected."

Guilt roiled in my stomach. "I'm sorry."

"It's not your fault." Landon seemed surprised by my sudden apology.

"Well, you're not seeing him because you're constantly over here."

"I like being over there."

"Still," I said, realization dawning in my mind. "I think you should stay over there and spend a few hours with him."

"You do?"

"I do."

"Why are you changing your tune all of a sudden?" Landon asked suspiciously.

"Because I feel guilty about keeping you away from your family," I lied smoothly. "I don't want to be the reason you're not spending time with them."

"And this has nothing to do with some idiotic idea you're scheming up with Clove and Thistle?"

"None whatsoever," I replied succinctly.

Landon was quiet on the other end of the phone for a second. "You're not lying to me, right?"

"I'm not lying," I was starting to get legitimately frustrated with him now. Sure, I was technically lying, but he didn't know that and it was annoying to have him constantly accuse me of things I hadn't even done yet.

"Okay," Landon said softly. "I'm sorry I'm being so ... ."

"Mean?" I suggested.

"I was going for the word suspicious."

"Mean works, too," I said.

"Okay," Landon relented. "I don't want to fight. I'm going to keep in touch with the Coast Guard via cellphone tonight, so if I hear anything, I'll let you know."

"Thanks," I said.

"And you're going to stick close to Thistle and Clove, right?"

"I thought you didn't want me running around with them?"

"I don't want you running around alone more," Landon admitted.

"I'll be with Thistle and Clove," I said, glancing over at my cousins and their bemused faces. "I can promise you that."

"Make sure you keep that promise," Landon said.

"You got it."

"Okay," Landon said finally, although I could tell he was still troubled. "I'm going to let you go."

"Okay," I said with faux breeziness.

"I'll see you tonight."

"I'll see you tonight," I agreed.

I disconnected the phone and turned to Clove and Thistle incredulously. "He's so untrusting."

"That's because you just told him a big pack of lies," Clove said.

"They're not lies," I countered. "I promised I would stay with the two of you and I'm sticking close to the two of you."

"You also said you weren't up to anything," Clove reminded me.

"That's very nebulous," I replied. "That could mean anything."

"Or nothing," Thistle suggested.

"Exactly," I agreed.

"We're terrible," Clove sighed.

"Oh, yeah," Thistle agreed grimly. "We totally suck."

"So, you're not telling Marcus what we're doing either?" I asked sagely.

"No way," Thistle shook her head. "He'd rat us out to Aunt Tillie in ten seconds flat."

"God, we really do suck," I whined, running a hand through my hair in frustration.

"We've always sucked," Clove said. "It's a sign of maturity that we can recognize it now."

I didn't verbally agree with her but, in my mind, I was nodding away. "Let's get to writing a spell," I said decisively.

This had to work. And, if it didn't, we were all going to be in a lot of trouble – and buried under an entire mountain of suck.

THIRTY-THREE

Guilt is a funny thing. When you don't think about it, you can easily ignore it. When you know you're doing wrong, though, it can cripple you.

I was currently in that hazy area in the middle. I kept trying to tell myself that I wasn't really lying to Landon – but I wasn't sure I actually believed my own internal monologue constantly professing my innocence.

"You're going to drive yourself crazy if you keep doing that," Thistle said, watching me from her spot at the sink in The Overlook. We were currently in the kitchen slicing bread. Our mothers had already taken the rest of dinner out to the table.

"I'm not doing anything," I lied.

"You're feeling guilty about lying to Landon," Thistle countered. "It's written all over your face. That's why you keep scrunching your face up in that constipated look when you think no one is looking."

"I'm not lying to Landon," I said irritably.

"I didn't say you were," Thistle said. "I think you think you are, though."

"It's not really a lie, right?" I turned to her hopefully.

"You told him we weren't up to anything," Thistle shrugged. "We're always up to something, so it's technically a lie."

I visibly blanched.

"Of course," Thistle jumped in hurriedly. "He knows we're always up to something, so he was just setting you up for failure. This is really his fault."

Huh. "Yeah, we'll go with that," I agreed, picking up the breadboard and moving toward the dining room. "That was a really good point," I paused before moving through the door. "Thanks."

"That's what I'm here for."

"What are you here for?" My mom asked curiously from her spot at the dining room table. I noticed she was sandwiched in between Chief Terry and Aunt Tillie. I couldn't figure out how she always managed to secure a spot next to Chief Terry when Marnie and Twila were always vying for one, too. I had a feeling it was equal parts bossiness and moxie.

"To tell Bay what she wants to hear," Thistle shot back easily.

"That's what you're here for?" My mom furrowed her brow. "To tell Bay what she wants to hear?"

"Basically," Thistle agreed. "And to bring sunshine and light to Hemlock Cove with my very existence."

"What are you two up to?" My mom narrowed her eyes suspiciously.

"Why do people always ask us that?" I grumbled.

"Because you're always up to something," Marnie offered. I noticed that Dean was eating dinner at the inn again, and he was sitting between Marnie and Clove. He was watching the family exchange with keen interest.

"We're not always up to something," I argued.

"Clove," Marnie turned to her daughter. "What are you three up to?"

Clove colored under Marnie's sudden attention. "Why are you asking me?"

"Because whatever they're up to you know about," Marnie said.

"You three can't keep a secret from one another. And you're the snitch, so that's why I asked you."

"I wonder where we learned that from." I said with snarky delight.

"I'm not a snitch," Clove replied angrily.

"Sit down and eat your dinner and stop embarrassing me," my mom ordered, plastering a fake smile on her face as she turned to Chief Terry. "So, what's new in Hemlock Cove these days?"

Chief Terry glanced at me nervously. "Not much," he said. "Just the usual stuff. Some Coast Guard patrols in the area searching boats over some anonymous tip and, oh, Rob Quinlan got arrested again."

"What for?" My mom asked curiously.

"He moved Old Man Preston's car."

"That doesn't sound like something worth arresting him for," Twila mused.

"Old Man Preston didn't give him permission," Chief Terry supplied.

"Oh, well then," Twila said. "So it's just a normal day for Rob, huh?"

"So, he's a car thief?" Sam asked from his spot at the far end of the table.

"Car thief is a bit of a stretch," Chief Terry said. "He has trouble remembering what's his and what's not his."

Sam looked surprised. "That's called a thief."

"He's just misunderstood," Chief Terry brushed off Sam's judgmental assumption. "Everyone in town knows that Rob has sticky fingers."

"And you just accept that?" Sam looked incredulous.

Chief Terry fixed Sam with a hard stare. "You're looking at it like it's the big city," he said. "This is a small town, and we're loyal to one another."

"Even a car thief?" Sam didn't pick up on the cold cues Chief Terry was casting about.

"He doesn't always steal cars," Thistle said. "Sometimes he steals horses."

"And tractors," I added.

"And there was the time he stole the Shepherd family's storage shed," Clove interjected.

"He stole a storage shed? Why?"

"Maybe he had things to store," Chief Terry shrugged. "He gave it right back when we went to get it."

We all glanced up at the door separating the dining room from the lobby when the distinct sound of someone clearing their throat interrupted the flow of conversation. I was surprised to see Kenneth – a big clump of wildflowers clutched in his hand – standing at the door.

"Sorry I'm late," Kenneth said, his gaze fixed on Aunt Tillie.

"I didn't know you were invited," my mom hedged curiously.

"He wasn't," Aunt Tillie huffed.

"I thought there was an open door policy on dinner here," Kenneth glanced around the room for support, his craggy face falling on me finally. "Isn't that right?"

Something about Kenneth's earnestness tugged at my heart. I wanted to help him – and it wasn't just because he kept toppling Aunt Tillie from that mountain she liked to preach from.

"That's usually the rule, Kenneth," I said carefully. "Maybe there's not enough food or something?" I turned to my mom challengingly.

"Of course there's enough food," my mom openly chastised me. "There's always enough food."

"Then there must be some other reason Kenneth isn't invited to dinner," I mused. "What would that be?"

My mother frowned at me. "Kenneth is always welcome at dinner," my mom said finally. "Kenneth, take a seat."

"Great," Kenneth replied excitedly, stripping off his coat and slinging it over the back of the open chair on the other side of me and dropping his flowers on the hutch behind us. "Where's your boyfriend?"

"He's in Traverse City having dinner with his brother," I said.

"Oh, that sounds nice," he said, his eyes twinkling. "I guess I'll be your boyfriend for the night."

"I guess so," I laughed.

Aunt Tillie was practically fuming at the head of the table. "Don't you get fresh with her," she warned Kenneth. "She's way out of your league. Everyone here is way out of your league."

"You didn't say that when he asked you on a walk earlier," I reminded her. "In fact, I believe the last time I saw you the two of you were strolling arm in arm around the grounds like teenagers in love."

Aunt Tillie glared at me.

"Why didn't I know about this?" My mom asked. As a bossy control freak, she was incensed by the prospect of something happening on the grounds that she didn't know about. In truth, we were all like that, though.

"You put me in charge of the construction," I said. "I thought that meant I was in charge of the construction people?"

"How is that relevant?" My mom narrowed her eyes at me. I could tell she thought I was trying to trick her – which I totally was.

"Kenneth owns the construction company," I continued. "That makes him one of the construction workers."

"I'm not talking about the construction," my mom said through gritted teeth. "I'm talking about your Aunt Tillie's date with Kenneth."

"It wasn't a date," Aunt Tillie exploded. "And you have a big mouth," she swung on me. "I told you to keep it to yourself."

"That was before Kenneth showed up to woo you in front of everyone," I teased. "I figured that was essentially letting the cat out of the bag."

"I never got that expression," Twila mused dreamily from her spot in the middle of the table. "What does that even mean? Letting the cat of the bag? Why would you have a cat in a bag?"

"I want to get back to the guy that steals everything in town but no one seems to care," Sam interrupted pointedly. "That sounds like a pretty interesting story."

"It's not," I said angrily. "If you write something about Rob then everyone in town is going to be totally pissed off."

"Is it the job of a newspaper to placate the populace?" Sam turned to Brian curiously.

Brian looked uncomfortable with the sudden attention. "I have to agree with Bay on this one. I've seen Rob stealing stuff all over town –

including that tarp they use to cover the gazebo. Everyone just pretty much ignores him – and they still love him. If we go after him, we would lose advertisers."

"I don't understand," Sam challenged. "You're saying that you're ignoring stories on purpose?"

"Not all stories," Brian said. "Just stories that are going to anger people."

"So that's the basis for news now? Fluff?" Sam's knuckles had turned white he was clenching his flatware so hard.

"Simmer down, son," Chief Terry ordered. "You're freaking out about nothing. Rob isn't a danger to anyone but himself. There are other things that are a lot more important going on in this town than Rob and his sticky fingers."

"Like what?" Dean asked curiously.

"Oh, um, just stuff," Chief Terry said evasively, exchanging a wary look with me and then turning back to his dinner. "This dinner is marvelous, ladies. Well done."

"How is your dinner?" Kenneth asked Aunt Tillie saucily. "It looks good. You make it look good."

Aunt Tillie glared at me. "This is your fault."

"I'm not the one befuddling Kenneth's mind with love thoughts," I teased her. There was mirth in my voice, but I kept an eye on Sam as he continued to fume at the other end of the table.

"This whole town is crazy," Sam said. "You're all so secretive. You try to hide things," he turned to me pointedly. "You should all know you're not fooling anyone. I know that you're all keeping secrets."

"What are we trying to fool people about?" Marnie glanced at Sam dubiously.

Sam looked surprised when Marnie pointed the question at him. "I didn't mean ... I didn't say ... I don't know ... ."

"Then maybe you should shut up and eat your dinner," my mom suggested coldly. She had no idea what was going on, but I could tell she didn't like the way Sam was looking at me. Quite frankly, I didn't like it either.

"I think we should all shut up and eat our dinner," Chief Terry agreed. "It's a great dinner and we're ruining it with all this chatter."

"Totally," Dean agreed, shoveling another forkful of mashed potatoes into his mouth. I think he was just enjoying the dinner theater – like most people did. He obviously wasn't picking up on the hostile overtones everyone else at the table was casting about.

"It's like all the women in this family have a magical way with food," Kenneth said, winking at Aunt Tillie. "I bet you taught them everything they know."

"Of course I did," Aunt Tillie said. "Not that they listen to my wisdom most of the time."

"You did not," my mom argued. "You never cooked. Our mom taught us how to cook."

"And where is she?" Kenneth asked curiously. "I bet she's just as pretty as Tillie here."

"Not even close," Aunt Tillie harrumphed. "Everyone knows I'm the beauty in the family."

My mom rolled her eyes. Since she was the one that looked like my grandmother, I had a feeling she took offense to the statement. "My mom died years ago," she explained to Kenneth. "And she was the beauty of the family."

"You're just saying that because you look like her," Marnie said. "I agree with Aunt Tillie."

"Of course you do," Twila said. "You look like her."

"Who do you look like?" Dean turned to Twila.

"I look like our Aunt Laverne," Twila said. "She was the real beauty in the family. She was also the best cook."

"Everyone is beautiful in this family," Kenneth said, trying to head off the argument and appease Aunt Tillie.

"Eat your food, Kenneth," Aunt Tillie ordered. "Shut your mouth and eat your food."

"Your wish is my command."

I raised my eyebrows as I glanced between Aunt Tillie and Kenneth. This just kept getting more and more interesting. One glance at my mom told me she was thinking the same thing.

"Kenneth, what happened to your wife?" My mom asked suddenly.

"She died of a heart attack almost twenty years ago," Kenneth said, his voice lowering a notch.

"I'm sorry," my mom said. "You must have loved her a lot."

"I did," Kenneth agreed. "I will always love her. That doesn't mean I can't find something to love in someone else, though."

Aunt Tillie looked uncomfortable and pleased at the same time. When she caught a glimpse of my smirk she returned the expression with a glower of her own. "Eat your dinner," she ordered.

"Yes, ma'am," I pursed my lips to keep from laughing out loud. "Your wish is my command."

Thistle snorted into her green beans appreciatively.

"Stop it," she ordered.

"Stop what?" I asked innocently.

"Whatever it is you're doing," Aunt Tillie said.

"Okay."

"I mean it."

"Okay."

"I'm not joking."

"Okay."

"Stop it!"

THIRTY-FOUR

"I still think this is a bad idea," Clove said defiantly.

We were back at the guesthouse and getting dressed for our evening excursion. Like with all of the rest of our late-night adventures, we decided to dress completely in black – including a hat to cover my blonde hair.

"You always think it's a bad idea and yet you always go," Thistle said. "Why is that?"

"I blame you," Clove said pointedly.

"You always do," Thistle replied cheekily.

"Can we get back to the point where this is a bad idea?"

"No," Thistle shook her head. "We're not looking at it as if it's a bad idea. We're looking at it as if we're trying to save kids. Remember that."

Clove sighed. Even she couldn't argue with Thistle's rationalization. "Fine," she said. "When this goes wrong, though – and it always goes wrong when we do crap like this – I'm going to bring it up for years to come."

"You always do."

"That is, if we don't die," Clove continued.

"We're not going to die," I scoffed. I was seventy-five percent sure I was telling the truth.

"We're not going to die," Thistle agreed. "And we actually could save lives."

"Fine," Clove said. "I said I was going and I'm going. Let's get this over with."

Thistle smiled like she always did when she managed to bully Clove. I think that's what keeps her skin looking so young. Meanness cleans your pores, I guess.

We took Thistle's car out to the Dandridge – mostly because it was dark and it wouldn't stand out in the inky black of night as easily. "Should we park on the access road or in the parking lot and hike in?" Thistle asked.

"Access road," Clove piped up immediately. Hiking through the dark wasn't exactly high on her list of things she wanted to do. I wasn't as sure, though.

Thistle glanced at me. "What do you think?"

"Parking lot," I said finally. "The car will stand out more if we abandon it on the side of the road at night."

"Plus, if someone's out there, they've probably parked there, too," Thistle said knowingly. "This way, we can sneak up on the property easier. I agree. Parking lot it is."

"Why does my vote never count?" Clove pouted.

"It counts," Thistle countered. "You just got out-voted."

"So, it didn't count," Clove said.

"Do you ever stop whining?" Thistle complained.

I ignored both of them as we parked and exited the vehicle. Thistle popped the trunk and rummaged around for a few seconds, coming out with two flashlights. "You came prepared?"

"You sound surprised."

"Well," I hedged. "Usually we just figure things out on the fly."

"That's why I put the flashlights in the trunk," Thistle said grimly. "I figured we would need them sooner or later and – look – I was right."

I took one of the flashlights and Thistle kept the other. Clove followed close at our heels as we started to move up the trail. "How come you two get to hold the flashlights?" Clove complained.

"The two people at the front get the flashlights," Thistle shot back. "Do you want to be in front?"

"No," Clove said hurriedly. "You can keep the flashlights."

"That's what I thought," Thistle said knowingly.

It took us about fifteen minutes to hike to the Dandridge. When I saw the silhouette rear up in the night sky, I clicked the flashlight off instinctively. Thistle followed suit almost immediately.

"What are you doing?" Clove hissed.

"Shhh," Thistle admonished her. "Just listen for a second."

We all stood in silence for a few moments, soaking in the night air. I could hear a few birds nestling and – far off – the sound of the waves rolling in behind the lighthouse. I couldn't hear anything else, though.

"I don't think anyone else is out here," Thistle said finally.

"That's good, right?" Clove asked nervously.

"I don't know," Thistle shrugged. "I guess it's just easier. I don't really think Dean would care if we're out here – but explaining to him what we were doing would be ... complicated."

"Where do you want to do the spell?" I asked.

Thistle moved farther into the clearing surrounding the Dandridge and considered my question. "I think the dock is the easiest place."

I followed her gaze, the moonlight illuminating the aged wooden structure and the dark expanse of water beyond it. "That's as good of a place as any," I agreed. "Plus, it's out in the open."

"Which makes us easier to see," Thistle reminded me.

"It makes the boat easier to see, too," I countered.

"True," Thistle agreed. "Let's go."

We picked our way to the dock, being careful to avoid any errant rocks that might cause us to trip, and then filed down to the square end at the edge of the water. "It's a beautiful night," I breathed in the spring air appreciatively.

"At least it's not raining," Thistle agreed, pulling three candles out of the bag she had brought and placing them in a triangle on the dock.

Clove helped her light them and then turned to me expectantly. "Let's get this over with. I want to go home."

We stood in a circle, joined hands, and closed our eyes. The spell we had written earlier in the day required different threads of power. We had all agreed who would handle each thread earlier in the day. Hopefully, if this worked, we would be able to call the boat to us – or at least create a trail to follow to find the boat. I wasn't a hundred percent sure how it would work. It was really just a hope and a prayer at this point.

We started to chant as one.

In this here, the darkening hour, we call upon the ancient power.
Help us find a ship in the night. Give us power. Help us fight.
There are young souls in need. Direct our power so they don't bleed.
We join together now, clasped hands, earnest hearts.
We ask for aid.
Answer us now.
Give us the knowledge we seek so we can help the meek.

WE GLANCED AMONG OURSELVES CURIOUSLY. Nothing appeared to be happening. For a second, it looked like the energy had convalesced, but instead of shooting out over the water it simply rose above us and dispersed.

"Did you ever think," Thistle started tiredly. "That we're the worst rhymers ever?"

"It's not as easy as it should be," I agreed.

"Our moms are much better at it," Clove agreed. "And even Aunt Tillie. We just suck at it."

"Don't ever tell her that," Thistle said hurriedly. "Her head will just get bigger."

"She's a little distracted right now," I said, still scanning the area randomly, hoping for some sign that our spell – however weak – had worked. "Didn't you notice that she and Kenneth left the inn together after dinner?"

"Snuck out would be more apt," Thistle countered. Her head was jerking from left to right as she searched the horizon, too. She didn't look like she was having any luck either. "I think they were going on a moonlit walk."

"I like him," Clove said decisively. "I think he could be good for her."

"He could be good for us, too," Thistle said. "If she's fixated on him she can't get distracted by us."

She had a point.

"I don't think it worked," I said finally.

"We could try it again," Thistle suggested.

"If it didn't work the first time it's not going to work the second time," I sighed dejectedly.

"Well, let's just look around," Thistle said. "Just to make sure."

"Okay," I agreed. "We'll have to split up."

"Split up?" Clove's voice rose an octave. "I don't think that's a good idea."

"The quicker we look around the quicker we can go home," Thistle said sagely. "I would think that would appeal to you."

"Fine," Clove grumbled. "But I'm not going alone. We only have two flashlights."

"You can go with Thistle," I interjected quickly.

Thistle glared at me. "Or she could go with you."

"I think you two make a better team," I argued. "I'm the oldest, so I should be the one to go alone. You know, more knowledge and all."

"Oh, so now you're fighting about who gets stuck with me? I hate you both."

"You'll live," Thistle said. "You can come with me," she sighed finally. "We have less knowledge, after all."

I moved off the dock to the left, exchanging one last look with

Thistle as she and Clove moved off to the right. I slipped into the woods, clicking the flashlight back on as I did.

The terrain was rough, so I moved slowly. Even though the foliage had died over the winter, it was quickly regrouping and would be out of control within a few weeks. My foot snagged in the root of a nearby tree causing me to stumble – but not lose my footing completely. I bent over with the flashlight to make sure that I wasn't going to fall when I pulled it out. When I straightened back up, I gasped as Erika flashed into view.

"Turn off the light."

"What?"

"Turn it off."

I did as I was told, even though I wasn't sure why. There was an urgency to her voice that I couldn't deny. Once the light was gone, I was plunged into darkness because of the heavy canopy over my head. I couldn't see Erika. I couldn't see anything.

"You found the boat," Erika said. "I knew you would."

"Where is it?" I kept my voice low.

"It's over there."

"Over where?" I strained my neck, but all I could see was black.

"Over there." I got the distinct impression that Erika was pointing – but it's not like I could see the gesture.

"I can't see without the light," I said finally.

"If you turn the light on, the people on the boat will see you."

"I still don't understand," I said finally. "Where is the boat?"

I was surprised when I felt a flutter by my hand. It was like a wave of cold washed over me. "I will lead you," Erika said. "You're going to have to trust me."

I didn't have a lot of options – so I did just that. I cast one last glance over my shoulder, hoping to catch a glimpse of Clove and Thistle. They weren't there, though, so I let the flutter tug me farther into the woods and toward a boat I wasn't even sure really existed.

THIRTY-FIVE

"I don't understand what I'm looking at," I whispered. My visual field was still encumbered by the dark, but it was now also enhanced with some weird squares of light that I couldn't quite define.

I realized rather suddenly that my voice had taken on a tinny tone – and that the sounds of a forest at night had been replaced by a hollow echo. "Are we in a cave?"

"Yes," Erika whispered. "It's a really big cave."

"I don't understand," I started and then paused to listen again. "I still hear the water. Is the boat in a cave?"

"It's a really big cave," Erika repeated. "Maybe it's not a cave, maybe it's more like a hole in the rocks."

"What rocks?" I was so confused.

"The rocks on the wall of the water," Erika replied simply.

I searched my memory. A cliff, I realized. She was talking about a cliff. "Is there an inlet into the cliff?"

"What's an inlet?" Erika asked.

This was getting us nowhere. "What are those lights?" I asked finally.

"That's the boat."

I narrowed my eyes to focus, breathing in evenly and trying to calm my nerves. I could do this.

"Open it to me, let me see, let me see," I whispered quietly, letting the refrain wander through my mind. I could feel the magic building and expanding and suddenly things came into sharper focus.

We weren't in a cave, which was a relief. I didn't think there was a cave on the lake side of Hemlock Cove that could've fit a boat – especially a large barge like I was looking at now – inside comfortably. What we had entered was a weird cove that was actually sheltered from the outside by three walls of rock. In other words, you would only see a boat if you knew it was already there.

The barge itself was large – and old. It looked like an industrial trawler, one that was regularly on the lake moving equipment from the west side of Michigan and the east side of Wisconsin to areas north of us. There was nothing about it that was distinctive. It looked like a regular workboat – which was probably why the increased patrols hadn't picked it up. Well, that and the fact that it was hidden in a cove.

"I bet this is why they built the Dandridge here," I said finally. "This cove."

"They built the lighthouse here because of the cove?" Erika asked curiously.

"It was a way to hide boats," I said. "A natural way. One that wasn't obvious."

"Is this where my boat was?"

"Probably," I said grimly. "They probably took shelter from the weather here – and from other patrol boats. I would bet they had scouts out on the channel to tell them when it was safe to leave."

"Do you think I died here?"

I glanced over at Erika. I could see her features now, but I wasn't sure that was a help or a hindrance. "Probably," I replied finally.

"So, what do we do now?"

I considered the question. "I'm going to try and get on that boat."

"Alone?"

"Yeah," I said. "I want you to go find Clove and Thistle and get them over here. Tell them to call the police. Thistle has a phone and I didn't bring mine – which seems like a terrifically stupid idea, at this point. I'm going to need help."

"Gracie can do that," Erika said. "I want to stay with you."

"We don't have time to look for Gracie," I said. "Just go get me help. Make sure you tell Thistle to call the police before she comes. I'll be fine." I was hopeful that I was telling the truth.

Erika looked dubious, but she winked out – leaving me alone to gather my courage. "Just do it," I prodded myself. The longer I sat here and thought about it the harder it was going to be to motivate myself to infiltrate the boat.

So I moved.

I kept to the shadows and started circling the barge. There had to be a way to board it – and I was hoping it wouldn't involve me having to swim. When I got to the far side, I found that another dock had been erected – one that looked a heck of a lot newer than the one at the Dandridge. I inspected it for a second, but I didn't linger. I followed the walkway of the dock until it ended at the metal wall of the trawler, scanning the side of the barge for a ladder. I saw it, about a foot back from where I was standing. I took a deep breath and started to ascend.

I tried to climb as quietly as possible. I had no idea what I would find on the deck of the boat, but I'd made up my mind and I was doing this either way. If I was lucky, the boat would be empty and I would be able to explore it – find the cargo I was looking for – and escape from the boat just in time to meet up with the cavalry and save the day.

Wait. Did that sound narcissistic?

When I made it to the top of the boat I ceased my forward momentum and waited. I couldn't hear anything. The only sound was the lapping of the water beneath me. I swung myself over the lip of the boat, dropped to the other side, and remained crouching while I waited again. Still nothing.

Finally, I straightened up and looked around. The top of the barge was cluttered with the usual stuff you would expect to find on an industrial boat. It was obvious no one was being kept up here. I saw a set of stairs to my right and moved toward them. I stopped at the top of the stairs and debated switching the flashlight back on. Ultimately, though, I decided against it.

I held on to the railing to my right and took it one step at a time, listening as I dropped, and hoping that I wouldn't find anything horrific at the bottom of the steps. Once I was safely in the bowels of the boat I practically choked on the smell that overwhelmed me. It was a mixture of urine, body odor and ... something else. There was a musty, rotting smell that accompanied the other unwelcome odors I first detected. Oh, God, I realized, it smelled like a rotting body.

"Gracie," I practically choked on the solitary word.

"I'm over here."

I heard her voice before I saw her floating in the corner. "I ... ."

"My body, it's over here." Gracie pointed to a tarp in the corner. It was clear there was something underneath it – and I knew what that something was. I didn't want to see it up close.

"We'll take it ... you ... off here soon," I said calmly, fighting the sudden urge I had to throw up where I was standing.

"You can't fix me?"

"No," I shook my head.

"I didn't think so."

"It's going to be okay," I promised her.

"I know," Gracie shrugged. "They can't hurt me anymore."

"Where is everyone else?"

"Over here," Grace moved, beckoning for me to follow her. She led me down a dark hall, one that had three different doors – those ones that had wheels to open them instead of handles – and paused outside of the farthest one. "They're in here and they're scared."

I moved to the door, tugging on the handle. It didn't budge. I gripped it harder and pulled again, this time the handle swung around – squeaking loudly as it cranked over. Once I got it to the point where it wouldn't turn anymore, I pushed on the door and held my breath as it swung open several feet.

I glanced up and down the hallway one last time – blowing out a sigh of relief when I realized that it was still only Gracie and I – and then slipped inside of the room.

I don't know what I expected, but the horror I walked into was beyond all reasonable thought. Five different heads all jerked up when I entered. I glanced between them all briefly, counting three girls and two boys, and then moving toward the closest child.

Up close, he was filthy. He looked to be about seven years old and he had blond hair and green eyes. His ski-slope nose was dusted with freckles and his eyes were empty of both warmth and light.

"Who are you?" He asked dully.

"My name is Bay," I said. "I'm here to get you out of here. All of you."

"Really?" The boy didn't look like he believed me. He had probably forgotten what hope really was.

"Really," I nodded, frowning as I saw that he was bolted to the floor with a metal chain. "Crap."

"You can't get it off?" The boy asked.

"I'll get it off," I said grimly. I searched the room with my eyes but kept my body still so as not to frighten him. "Are there keys anywhere?"

"They keep them with them," Gracie said helpfully.

I wrinkled my nose tiredly. I knew Chief Terry would be coming – and I could only hope he would be here soon – but I wasn't going to keep these kids chained to the floor one second longer than I had to.

"We'll just have to do it another way," I said grimly.

"What other way?" The boy whispered.

"Magic," I widened my eyes in mock play. I was trying to relax the kids, but I was telling the truth. I ran my hand over the padlock securing the chain to the floor, whispered a quick spell and pulled on the end of the padlock. It sprang open and I yanked it off.

The little boy's eyes widened in surprise. "Wow."

"Yeah, wow," I agreed.

"I'm going to go get everyone else and then we're going to leave," I said.

"Where are we going?" The boy asked.

"Away from here," I said. "After that? We'll figure it out. I just need to get you away from here for right now. Okay?"

"Okay."

I moved to the next child, the other boy, and muttered the same spell. All of the children looked terrified, but I didn't have time to cajole them all into trusting me. I had to get them out of here. The trust would come later.

Once they were all free, I watched as they all huddled together and watched me through a bevy of untrusting and sad eyes. I had to do something to prod them out of this room. "I bet you guys are hungry."

They looked interested now – each and every one of them. "I promise you as much food as you can eat if you follow me out of here." I moved toward the door, casting a glance back over my shoulder. "Whatever you want. Ice cream. Pot roast. Hamburgers."

That did it. The kids all moved toward me. Once they were at my back, I turned around one more time. "Just do me a favor. Try to be really quiet."

"Are the bad people here?" One of the little girls asked, her lip quivering.

"I don't think so," I said. "They weren't here a few minutes ago but they may be back."

The kids looked scared again. "The police are on their way," I said. "My cousins are out there – and my cousin Thistle is badass. I'm going to get you out of here. I promise you that."

I swung back around and pulled the door open wider so we could leave this hell and step out into the light. When the door swung open, I stepped back inadvertently as two figures stood in the doorway.

"It's the bad people," Gracie murmured at my side. "They found us."

Apparently they had – and I was surprised at the two faces that were currently frowning at me with open distaste.

"Well, I have to say, I wasn't expecting either of you."

"I think we're the ones that weren't expecting you," Dean said, stepping through the door menacingly.

Karen followed him, her features cold and angry. "What are you doing here, Bay?"

Now what?

THIRTY-SIX

"How did you get them loose?" Dean asked angrily, taking a step toward me.

I could feel the children shrinking in terror behind me, so I projected a warming spell around them in an effort to still their fear. "Magic."

"Magic?" Dean looked nonplussed. "Really? You have a skeleton key or something? You can pick a lock for some reason?"

"No," I shook my head.

"How did you find this boat?" Karen asked. She was pacing closer to the door – and she didn't look happy.

"I was out for a walk and just stumbled upon it," I lied. "When I saw the boat, I just wanted to check it out. I thought it was abandoned."

"Where are your cousins?" Dean asked. He didn't look like he believed me, and he was searching the room curiously – like Thistle and Clove were hiding in a corner or something.

"Home."

"Really? You came out for a walk at the Dandridge alone? At night?"

A thought occurred to me. "I wasn't alone. Landon was with me."

Dean's face crusted over with anger. "Where is he?"

"She's lying," Karen said. "If she was out here with him he would be here now. Do you really think an FBI agent would be running around in the dark with this idiot? She's just trying to stall."

"I guess we should kill her now then," Dean said. "We'll dump her with that other brat when we get a couple hundred miles north."

"Her name was Gracie," I said angrily clamping my mouth shut when I realized that I had shared too much information.

"How do you know that?" Karen asked suspiciously, taking a step forward. "How could you possibly know that?"

I heard one of the children behind me whimper. I had to stall until help arrived. "I know a lot of things," I said boldly. "We've been looking for this boat for a while."

"This particular boat?" Dean asked worriedly. "I knew it."

"Why do you think you kept running into us up here?" I continued, avoiding Dean's question. "We were looking for the boat. We were looking for the kids."

"You didn't do a very good job of looking," Dean scoffed. "We were right here the whole time."

"I didn't know about the cove," I admitted. "It's kind of frustrating to think that we could've ended this days ago."

"We can end it now," Karen suggested. "I'm all for that."

"Why did you guys stay here so long?" I asked hurriedly, trying to distract both of them. "You could've escaped and no one would have been the wiser."

"We couldn't leave," Karen said bitterly. "The Coast Guard has been all over this area for days. We were stuck."

Whoops. I decided to change to a different tactic. "So, opening the Dandridge was just a big fat lie?"

"Actually, no," Dean said. "I have every intention of refurbishing the Dandridge. It's going to be our home base. It will be a nice little business for the town and a great way to hide what we're really doing."

"Your home base for what?"

"For this," Dean gestured at the small faces behind me.

"I don't know what this is," I admitted. "All I know is that you have five children shackled on a boat and another dead child out in the hallway."

"Gracie," one of the kids behind me whispered. "She didn't find a new home?"

I frowned. "Is that what you told them? That Gracie found a new home?"

"You would prefer that we tell them the truth?" Karen's voice was icy. "I don't think that would go over well."

"Where are you taking them?"

"North," Dean said evasively. "We have people waiting for them there."

"To what end?" I pressed. I just needed to keep stalling.

"We're finding them new homes," Karen replied. "They're all orphans. We're part of a rescue group."

"Really? What kind of rescue group chains kids in the belly of a barge?"

"Yeah, I didn't think you would buy that one," Karen laughed. "I had to try, though. I guess that's not going to sway you from your *Scooby-Doo* moment, huh?"

"Not really," I replied dryly. "If I'm going to die, I want to know why."

"You mean you haven't figured it out?" Dean looked surprised. "If you haven't figured it out, why are you here?"

"I told you, I was out for a walk and stumbled on the boat."

"I think we're beyond that," Dean prodded me. "Why don't we lay all of our cards on the table and see where we stand?"

"Okay," I agreed. "We've been looking for the boat for days," I said honestly. "We didn't find it until tonight."

"Who is we?" Karen asked.

"What?" I internally cringed.

"You said we found it tonight. I want to know who the 'we' is."

"I told you, Landon was with me."

"And why isn't he with you now?"

"We got separated," I said. "When he can't find me, he'll be calling the police out here to conduct an extensive search."

Dean and Karen exchanged worried glances. "I think you're lying," Karen said finally. "I think you're out here with Thistle and Clove."

Crap on toast.

"Speaking of Clove," I said. "What's the deal with you and Uncle Warren? Is he in on this, too?"

"I don't know what you mean," Karen said innocently. "We're in love."

"I think you're with him to make sure that people aren't suspicious about why you're in town," I countered. "I don't know much about him, but I can't believe he'd be involved in this."

"I'm in town to decorate the Dragonfly, and when I'm done, I'll be decorating the Dandridge," Karen said. "That's the truth. And, no, Warren doesn't know anything about this. Are you kidding me? He's as naïve as the rest of you. I am telling the truth, though, when I say that I originally came out here to decorate the Dragonfly."

"And, what, you just stumbled on a human trafficking ring?" I probed. "That's seems ... unlikely."

"It does, doesn't it?" Karen mused. "It only seems unlikely to you, though, since you've discovered the truth. Once you're gone, though, no one will suspect me."

"And you'll be able to help Warren while he's trying to console Clove," I replied sagely.

"Oh, I don't see Clove surviving the night," Karen laughed hollowly. "If you know what's going on, so do your annoying little cousins."

"They don't know that it's you," I said hurriedly. "They only know about the boat."

"Then they know too much," Karen said simply.

"They're not the only ones that know about the boat," I said quickly.

"Who else?" Dean asked dangerously.

"Landon. Chief Terry. A few other people."

"That's why there's increased patrols, isn't it?" Dean asked. "It's all because of you."

"It could be," I agreed.

"Well, the question is, how did you find out about our little ... operation?" Karen asked.

"Operation? Is that what you call kidnapping children away from their families and shipping them off God knows where to do God knows what?"

"If it's any consolation," Karen said matter-of-factly. "We are taking them to new families."

"Really? Somehow I have my doubts."

"No, we really are taking them to new families," Karen said earnestly. "Families that have peculiar interests, but families all the same."

I felt sick to my stomach. "You mean sexual deviants, don't you?"

"Among other things," Dean said. "We don't really ask questions of the buyers. We don't care why they want the merchandise – we just procure the merchandise."

"This is an awful big operation for two people," I said. "I mean, you have to kidnap the kids, transport them to the boat, pilot the boat and deliver the kids. I don't think only two people could handle it."

"We're not alone," Karen conceded. "It's a big operation. That's why it's so profitable. We're not the only boat."

"I figured."

"What's important now, though, is where Thistle and Clove are. Why don't you tell us that now so we can get on with this?"

"I don't know where they are," I shrugged. "We separated at the dock. For all I know, they could be back at the inn now."

"You think they would just abandon you and leave you out here?"

"We're not all that close," I replied.

"Oh, please," Karen scoffed. "You three share a brain. It's ridiculous."

"We don't share a brain," I challenged.

"Not for long, that's for sure," Karen agreed. She turned to Dean decisively. "We need to find out where the other two troublemakers are."

"She won't talk," Dean said. "I told you something was up when I had dinner with them earlier. They were acting odd – even for them. I thought it might have something to do with that Sam guy – but I was nervous when that Fed wasn't around. Aren't you glad that I thought ahead and got us a little insurance?"

I didn't like the sound of that one bit.

"Actually, I am," Karen agreed. "They're going to come in handy."

"Who?"

"Why don't you go and get our other guests and we can all have a little conversation together?" Karen suggested.

"Gladly," Dean turned on his heel and stalked out of the room.

I watched Karen warily. I was debating about whether or not I could take her – and keep the kids safe – when I heard a sound that stopped my heart.

"You take your hands off me right now! You have no idea what I'm capable of! I will turn you into a bug and squash you with my own foot – and then I'll feed you to my pet scorpion."

"You didn't," I moaned.

Karen smirked. "No, I didn't. Dean on the other hand, well, he took advantage of the two of them being outside by themselves. They were pretty easy to incapacitate," Karen continued. "What with them being so old and all."

I clenched my jaw grimly when I heard the scuffle outside the door. When Dean pushed Aunt Tillie and Kenneth into the room, I wasn't surprised.

"What are you doing here?" Aunt Tillie looked flabbergasted.

"I could ask you the same thing," I replied blandly. "Well, this just sucks."

"Feels rather normal to me," Aunt Tillie sniffed. "It's like we've been here before."

"That doesn't mean I like it," I grumbled.

"It will be fine," Aunt Tillie responded calmly. "Trust me. These people aren't a threat to us."

"Now," Dean said, stepping back into the room. "Let's talk about where your cousins are. And then we'll talk about exactly what kind of threat we really are."

I didn't overtly flinch when Dean pulled a knife out of his pocket, but internally my heart started pounding.

Crap. Crap. Crap.

THIRTY-SEVEN

"So, I'm guessing when you got yourself into this mess you didn't exactly think things through?" Aunt Tillie was angry.

"You're in the same mess I am," I reminded her.

"I was kidnapped by a crazy man," Aunt Tillie corrected me. "And he came up behind me and cheated, and this was after he complimented our cooking to throw me off his trail, so that doesn't really count. You climbed on this boat alone and by yourself. That makes you queen of the stupids."

"I knew there were kids on here," I complained bitterly. "I was trying to help."

"Good job."

"Will you just shut up," Karen ordered. She was sitting on a crate by the still-open door. Dean had left the room to find Thistle and Clove, but not before leaving Karen with a loaded gun and a lot of time to think. "Just shut up, all of you."

"I didn't say anything," Kenneth offered helpfully. He was sitting on the floor with the kids grouped around him while Aunt Tillie and I had positioned ourselves a few feet in front of the rest of the group.

"Well, keep it up," Karen said.

"Did you have any idea she was involved in this?" Aunt Tillie asked, narrowing her eyes at Karen evilly.

"I had no idea either of them were involved in it," I admitted. "I just knew there was a boat out here with kids on it. The only thing I knew about her was that I saw her talking to Sam on the street – and that made me suspicious. Other than that, though, I only knew about the boat."

"How did you know that? Erika?"

"Yeah," I sighed.

"Who is Erika?" Karen asked darkly. "Let me guess, another cousin I have to round up?"

"Yes," Aunt Tillie replied with as much sallow distaste as she could muster. "I think that's a good thing for you to do. You go and find Erika and kill her and we'll wait here."

Karen furrowed her perfectly manicured brow. "You want me to go and kill someone?"

"Erika," Aunt Tillie said. "She's evil. You'll get along."

"She's not evil," I argued. "That's a really ugly thing to say."

"This is all her fault," Aunt Tillie said. "If she hadn't found you and realized what an easy mark you were, we wouldn't be here."

"Easy mark? Like you could've told her no."

"I could've told her no," Aunt Tillie sniffed. "I'm meaner than you."

"You're not as mean as you pretend to be."

"Apparently you don't know me at all," Aunt Tillie lamented. "I'm mean, really mean," she said pointedly, tilting her chin in Karen's direction.

"I'm still confused who Erika is," Karen said. "If she's the one that caused this whole situation, then we're going to have to find her."

"Good luck with that," Aunt Tillie said.

Karen got to her feet threateningly. "I don't think I like your attitude."

Aunt Tillie wasn't impressed. The gun Karen was waving around wasn't exactly filling her with fear – although I was on the fence about it. "I know I don't like your attitude," Aunt Tillie said.

"What is that supposed to mean?"

"You're a bitch."

I shook my head tiredly. "Really? That's the way you're going to approach this?"

"I only know one way to approach things," Aunt Tillie shot back. "The right way."

"How do you live with her?" Karen muttered, plopping back down on the crate. "It's no wonder the three of them are so screwed up when you're their role model."

Aunt Tillie pursed her lips angrily. "And who was your role model? Mrs. Hannigan?"

"Who?" Karen looked confused.

"Watch a movie," Aunt Tillie scowled. "At least my girls aren't kidnapping children and chaining them in a boat and giving them to Hecate knows who for profit."

"I'm a capitalist, what can I say?" Karen looked unconcerned with the comment. "You wouldn't believe how few people want to hire a decorator – and when they do, they don't want to pay me."

"Maybe you're just a bad decorator," Aunt Tillie suggested.

"You know this is out of hand now, right?" I turned to Karen searchingly, trying to pull her focus off of Aunt Tillie. "You can still save yourself in this mess."

"Oh, yeah? How does that work?"

"We'll tell the police you helped us save the kids," I offered, although it was an empty promise. "You would get consideration for that."

"Consideration? You mean I'll get life in prison instead of the death penalty? That doesn't sound like a win to me," Karen replied snottily.

"Michigan doesn't have the death penalty," Kenneth interjected.

"Yeah, but she's transporting kids through international waters," I replied distractedly. "That makes the case federal – and the feds don't like child-trafficking pricks. They like killing them."

Karen glowered at me.

"That's not helping," Aunt Tillie said through gritted teeth.

"Maybe you're not as dumb as you look," Karen smiled at Aunt Tillie. It was an ugly and mean smile, but a smile nonetheless.

"I wouldn't be so sure," Aunt Tillie challenged. "I miss the days of public dismemberment in the square. I think that's what you deserve."

"Oh, well, that's helping," I scoffed.

We all jumped when the metal door opened again and Thistle and Clove tumbled into the room, followed closely by an aggravated Dean. Thistle's grave eyes met mine. She was trying to tell me something, but I had no idea what.

"Where did you find them?"

"Stumbling around the woods like idiots," Dean said. "I almost missed them, but there were a bunch of fireflies out there and I wanted to check them out – it was like they were on fire or something -- and that's why I went in that direction. I didn't see any fireflies, but I did find the two of them."

I raised my eyebrows at Thistle questioningly.

"The flashlight died," she said simply. "Then, when Clove started freaking out, I wanted to die. It seemed like the easiest solution."

"I wanted to leave," Clove said. "I wanted to go and get Chief Terry, but Thistle wouldn't leave without you."

The loyalty warmed me. The stupidity of the gesture made my heart sink. "Didn't Erika find you?"

"Who is Erika?" Dean asked irritably.

"Another family member," Karen supplied. "They won't tell me much about her but, from what I gather, we have her to blame for this whole mess."

"And she's out there right now?" Dean looked incensed. "Well, this is just great. I thought we had them all rounded up."

"Guess not," Karen shrugged. "You'll have to go find her."

"Why me?" Dean whined. "I just found them. Maybe you should have to go and find this one."

"I am not walking around in the woods in these shoes," Karen gestured to her expensive boots. "These boots are made for fashion – not walking."

"That's your fault, not mine," Dean said. "I'm tired. I'm not going back out there again."

"Well, I'm not going out there," Karen said grimly.

Aunt Tillie raised her hand suggestively. "I'll go look."

Karen rolled her eyes. "Like we're going to trust you?"

"It seems to me, you don't have a lot of options," Aunt Tillie countered persuasively.

"Just sit down and shut up," Dean ordered. "You two go join your crazy family."

Thistle begrudgingly moved to my side, running a hand through her purple hair wearily. "Erika found us," she whispered in my ear and then turned around evasively to face Dean and Karen.

"So, now what?" Karen asked. "Should we shoot them?"

"Well, that's going to be loud," Dean said.

"We're in a boat," Karen reminded him.

"Yeah, but apparently there's someone else named Erika out there."

Karen and Dean lapsed into an argument of their own, which allowed me the chance to question Thistle more fully. "Did you call the police?"

"Yes," Thistle nodded.

"So, they're on their way?" Relief washed over me.

"I got Chief Terry's voicemail," Thistle answered stiffly.

"Well, that will be helpful," I grimaced. "If he checks his voicemail tonight."

"We had a choice," Thistle replied irritably. "We could've gone back into town and tracked him down – leaving you here to die alone – or we could've continued looking for you. We decided to look for you."

"That doesn't look like it's working out too well," I mused.

"I had no idea Aunt Tillie was here, too," Thistle said. "How did she even get here?"

"Dean took them from the inn because he thought there was something weird going on at dinner tonight," I explained.

"There always something weird going on at dinner," Clove said.

"Well, weirder than usual, I guess," I shrugged. "What does it matter? We're all here now."

"One big happy family," Thistle said sarcastically.

"No one needs your sass," Aunt Tillie warned Thistle. "We've got to come up with a plan."

"What plan?" Clove asked worriedly.

"There's only two of them," Aunt Tillie said. "We outnumber them."

"Barely," Clove said. "Plus, you're forgetting the gun."

"And the knife," I added.

"They have a knife?" Thistle didn't look pleased.

"Yup."

"They're not very smart, though," Aunt Tillie said. "That's in our favor, too."

"We also have five kids and Kenneth to protect," I reminded her.

"Yeah," Thistle smirked. "You want to keep Kenneth safe, right?"

"Do you really think now is the time for that?" Clove sounded shrill.

"It might be our last shot to tease her," Thistle said pragmatically. "I can't just let it pass me by."

No, that definitely was not in her nature.

"Do you think Chief Terry will come?" Clove's eyes swam with unshed tears.

"He'll try," I replied honestly. "I don't think we can rely on him, though."

"We can only rely on ourselves," Thistle said grimly.

"That's the way it should always be," Aunt Tillie said. "I have a plan."

"Oh, good," I said. "This always ends well."

"Maybe you can make them smell like bacon and they'll eat each other," Thistle offered.

"Yeah, I didn't think that one out," Aunt Tillie admitted. "I'll do better next time."

"Good to know," Thistle replied listlessly.

"Good to know what?"

"That there will be a next time," Thistle said. "I'm actually looking forward to it."

Aunt Tillie patted Thistle's arm kindly. I thought it was a move to comfort her in the face of our likely demise. It was a nice change for her. "You say that now," Aunt Tillie said. "You won't be looking forward to it when it happens, though."

Well, there is also comfort in knowing that some things stay the same.

"Did you hear that?" Dean stopped arguing with Karen and cocked his head.

"What?" Karen looked exasperated.

"Someone is out there." Dean moved away from Karen and slipped back around the door, disappearing into the hallway.

"Well, look at that," Karen mused. "Erika must have found her way to us. That's convenient."

Thistle and I exchanged wary glances. Or maybe Chief Terry had found us, after all?

The unmistakable sounds of a scuffle met our ears. Karen's eyes flashed in surprise, and she turned toward the door. As much as I wanted to wait and see if Chief Terry would swoop in and save us, I knew that I couldn't take that chance. Thistle must have read my mind. We both rushed toward Karen while she was distracted and jumped her from behind.

Karen swung around wildly, trying to dislodge the two of us from her back. Thistle was vicious, though, and she haphazardly jammed her fingers into Karen's eyes while I attempted to choke her into submission.

Karen inadvertently pulled the trigger on the gun but, thankfully, the bullet was about four feet above our heads. Clove joined the fray at that moment, trying to rip the gun from Karen's hand. When Karen refused to give it up, Clove did the only thing she could think of - - she sank her teeth into Karen's wrist.

Karen howled in pain, dropping the gun into Clove's waiting hand. Clove took a step back and watched Thistle and me expectantly.

"Are you going to do something?" Thistle asked, yanking Karen's hair as hard as she could.

"I did," Clove said, "I got the gun."

"Something else," I gasped, snapping my arm into Karen's throat as hard as I could.

Aunt Tillie moved toward us and I watched in wonderment as she peered into Karen's glassy and terrified eyes. She raised her hand and slapped it against Karen's forehead. "Sleep. Sleep, you bitch."

Karen's body went suddenly slack and she dropped to the floor.

Thistle and I didn't immediately let go of her. When we were sure she was down, we carefully took a step back and regarded her warily.

"If you could do that, why didn't you do it two minutes earlier?" Thistle asked angrily.

"I thought you had it under control."

"Obviously not," Thistle said dryly.

I held up my hand for the two of them to stop. "Do you hear anything?"

"No," Thistle shook her head.

"Is that good or is that bad?" Clove asked.

"I don't know," I said. "It could go either way."

Thistle glanced at the kids and Kenneth worriedly. "You stay here with Kenneth and the kids," she ordered. "We'll check the hallway out."

"That sounds like a good idea," Clove agreed.

Thistle grabbed the gun from her hand and stopped Clove's oncoming argument with one look. "We may need it more than you."

"Fine," Clove grumbled.

I peered around the door, glancing up and down the hallway nervously. I could feel Thistle gripping my arm from behind, but I tried to ignore the shooting pains her fingernails were generating. I gasped when I saw a figure slumped against the wall down the hallway.

"Landon."

"What?" Thistle pushed me the rest of the way out the door and we both raced down the hallway toward Landon's prone body. He didn't stir when we got to him.

"Is he dead?" Thistle asked.

I was scared to find out. I reached my hand up timidly and waved it in front of his face. He was breathing. "I think he's just unconscious," I said finally.

"Where's Dean?"

"That's a really good question." I glanced around, but the hallway appeared to be empty except for us.

Landon stirred and his eyes snapped open. They fixed on me after a few seconds of wandering. It took him a second to speak. "I'm going to kill both of you."

"Get in line," I muttered.

"Where is everyone?" Landon's voice was tinged with a hint of weakness – something I wasn't used to.

"Back there," Thistle waved at the open door. "We told them to stay with the kids until we were sure it was safe to come out."

"You found the kids?" Landon said, rubbing the back of his head tenderly. "That's something, I guess."

I pulled his head toward me and carefully felt along the backside of his scalp. I felt a lump quickly growing. "How many of me do you see?"

"One," Landon groaned. "I'm fine. Trust me, one of you is all I can take."

"Which way did Dean go?" I asked.

Landon shrugged. "I'm not sure. Leave it for the professionals."

"The professional is on the floor and we just found him unconscious," Thistle replied arrogantly.

"Chief Terry is coming," Landon said. "I called him before I got on the boat."

"How did you even get here?"

Landon's face clouded over. "I ... ."

"That's a really good question."

Dean's voice sent shivers down my spine. I stiffly turned to find him standing at the bottom of the staircase, the knife in his hand, watching the three of us.

"Crap," Thistle complained. "This really shouldn't surprise me."

"How many of you are there?" Dean's face was starting to bloom with color. It looked like Landon had gotten a few good blows in during the fight.

"We're a tribe," I replied. "Even we have lost count."

I felt a swirl of energy behind me and knew that Erika had arrived. Landon's gaze travelled to my back and he frowned. I had no idea what he was seeing, but I couldn't turn around and see for myself without leaving all of us vulnerable to Dean.

"It's the bad man."

"Gracie," I breathed. "Where did you go?"

"To find Erika," Gracie said. "I didn't know what else to do when the bad people found you."

"Good girl."

"Who are you talking to?" Dean asked angrily.

"She's talking to me," Thistle tried to divert Dean's attention.

"I thought your name was Thistle? Stupid name, by the way," Dean scowled.

"Tell that to my mom," Thistle replied bitterly. "She doesn't listen when I tell her that anymore."

"What do we do now?" This voice belonged to Erika.

"We need to make him pay." Gracie's voice was chilling. The fact that Dean was standing by her body probably had something to do with it.

"You want to make him pay?" I asked Gracie.

"More than anything."

"Me, too," Erika said. "They should all pay."

I couldn't agree more. I glanced over at Thistle; she nodded gravely and clasped my hand in her own.

"Wait," Landon struggled to sit up straighter. "What are you two doing?"

"Giving them what they want," Thistle said calmly.

The power started to build between us, our joined hands fueling the energy – while Gracie and Erika supplied the rage.

"What's going on?" Dean asked nervously, taking a step toward us.

"I would run if I were you," Aunt Tillie said, stepping into the hallway behind us. "You're not going to like what's about to happen."

"What's about to happen?" Landon asked worriedly. "Is that wind monster coming back?"

"Retribution," Aunt Tillie said, glancing at Erika and Gracie knowingly. "Go take your revenge, girls."

Erika and Gracie seemed to grow in countenance, and an ethereal red haze pooled between them. Dean's eyes widened in abject terror when even his limited brain couldn't fight the tableau forming in front of him.

Thistle and I leveled our eyes on each other. "Solid," we said in unison.

Erika and Gracie, now six feet tall, took solid form and descended on Dean. His screams echoed through the hallways as two formerly small girls – fueled by unending rage and grief – exacted a revenge that spanned a hundred and sixty years and a million tears.

THIRTY-EIGHT

When Chief Terry arrived, Dean was still alive – although I had a feeling he wished otherwise. Chief Terry slapped a pair of cuffs on him and handed him off to one of his officers as he moved toward Landon.

"Are you okay?"

"I'll live," Landon rubbed the back of his head ruefully. "That guy is stronger than he looks."

"I thought I told you to wait for me?" Chief Terry looked angrier than I had ever seen him.

"I couldn't wait," Landon said, glancing at me guiltily.

Chief Terry sighed. "I get that," he said. "I probably would have done the same thing in your situation. Still, though, this is going to be a huge mess of paperwork."

"Yeah," Landon agreed.

"Which means," Chief Terry glanced behind us to make sure no one was in hearing range before finishing. "You need to get your stories straight now."

"What stories?" Thistle asked curiously.

"Well, for starters, how did Tillie get here?"

"That buffoon kidnapped me outside of the inn," Aunt Tillie replied gruffly.

"And Kenneth," Thistle added.

"Who is Kenneth?" Chief Terry asked curiously.

"Her boyfriend."

"He's not my boyfriend!"

"That old guy that was hitting on her at dinner tonight? He's here, too?" Chief Terry rubbed his face in exasperation.

"Who are you calling old?"

Chief Terry ignored Aunt Tillie's imminent wrath. "Well, that's easy to explain then. Where is Kenneth?"

"In the room with Clove and the kids."

"What kids?" Chief Terry practically exploded.

"There are five kids in there," I pointed to the open door. "I found them shackled to the floor."

Chief Terry's face drained of color. "Are they okay?"

"I think they need food," I said. "They're scared, too."

"I bet."

"Why don't we shuttle them out to the inn," Thistle suggested. "Our mothers would love nothing else but to fill them full of food – and maybe get them a bath – and that will distract them from coming down here."

"That's a really good idea," Chief Terry agreed. "Plus, questioning them here isn't going to be easy. Okay, let's get the kids," he said to Thistle. "You two," he pointed at Landon and me. "You figure out the rest of the story – and you don't tell it to anyone but me."

"Got it, Chief," Landon grunted, climbing to his feet and slinging an arm around my shoulders to keep his balance.

"Oh, this is just going to be a nightmare," Chief Terry grumbled before he followed Thistle and Aunt Tillie down the hall. "Someone is going to owe me a big, fat German chocolate cake when this is all over."

"I'll make you one," Aunt Tillie offered.

"Not you," Chief Terry argued.

"Fine. I'll order my nieces to do it for me."

"And short ribs, too?"

"You're awful demanding for a guy that showed up late," Aunt Tillie reminded him.

AN HOUR LATER, I was standing with Landon on the dock outside of the Dandridge. Emergency personnel and a crime tech team from the state had descended on the boat. Chief Terry had warned us that the Coast Guard was on the way, too, and he (strongly) suggested that we get out of the immediate area until he could take our statements.

After a cursory check-up by the first responders, I had led Landon to the dock so he could sit down and regain his full faculties. I also wanted us far away from the congregated hordes when Landon finally blew his top.

We had been sitting on the dock for ten minutes – and he hadn't said a word. I was starting to get uncomfortable.

"Maybe you should go to the hospital," I suggested finally. "Just to be sure."

"I'm fine," Landon said quietly, staring out at the rolling lake.

The silence that followed was too much. "You want to go out to the inn to get something to eat?" Or are you looking for a way to walk away without crushing me? I didn't ask the second question out loud.

"Why did you get on the boat?" Landon asked, ignoring my initial question.

"I wanted to get to the kids," I replied simply.

"And how did you think that would end?"

"With me getting the kids off the boat."

"Did it even occur to you that there might be someone else on the boat? Someone with a gun? Or a knife?"

"It occurred to me," I replied blandly. "I was just hoping it wasn't the case."

"You were hoping it wasn't the case?" Landon shook his head irritably. "What were you guys doing out here anyway?"

"Just looking around," I lied.

Landon gestured to the candles that we had left at the end of the

AMANDA M. LEE

dock when we had performed our spell earlier. "You want to change that story?"

"We were trying to find the boat," I admitted. "We were casting a spell to call the boat to us."

"What?" Landon practically exploded. "That is the dumbest thing I've ever heard!"

"Don't yell at me!"

Landon sucked in a deep breath to calm himself. "What were you planning on doing when the boat arrived?"

"We thought we would have time to call the police if it actually showed up," I admitted. "The spell didn't work, though."

"That's because the boat was already here," Landon supplied angrily.

"Well, we didn't know that," I said.

"You were really going to call the police?" Landon looked dubious.

"We really were," I replied honestly. "We're not stupid."

Landon rolled his tongue into his cheek and bit down on it. "We'll discuss that at a later date."

I wrinkled my nose, pinching the bridge above it to keep from exploding myself. "How did you even find us?"

"I went out to the inn, but you were already gone – and so was your Aunt Tillie, which had all your mothers in a tizzy. They thought she was off doing something unseemly with Kenneth and wanted me to find them."

I laughed. I couldn't help myself. "I'm sure that was just what you wanted to do with your night."

"I had other ideas, that's for sure," Landon said, looking me up and down and then turning back to the lake. "I checked the guesthouse, but you guys weren't there."

"We weren't planning on being gone that long," I explained. "I thought we would be back long before you got back into town."

"I knew," Landon said, his voice low. "When you weren't there, I knew you were out here. It was like ... it was like being vindicated when I found Thistle's car in the parking lot. I had every intention of storming down here and dragging all three of you kicking and screaming back to the inn – and then telling your mothers what you were up to as punishment while they filled me full of cake."

"How did you find the boat, though?"

Landon finally turned back to me, his gaze solemn. "A little girl was on the dock."

"What?" I was confused.

"I couldn't find you," Landon said. "I was so angry when I was coming down here and then, when you weren't here, I was worried."

I let him continue, watching him breathlessly.

"And then there was a little girl here," Landon said. "She just popped in out of nowhere."

"Erika," I exhaled loudly.

Landon nodded. "She told me you were on the boat and you were in trouble. She told me that bad people were on the boat with you. I knew it was too much to hope that the bad people she was referring to were Thistle and Aunt Tillie."

"So you came to the rescue," I finished for him.

"No," Landon shook his head. "I called Chief Terry and made sure he was on his way out here and then I climbed on a boat and got myself knocked out and you rode to the rescue."

"Not me," I said, dropping to the dock next to him and running a hand through his hair gently. "Erika and Gracie."

"When I saw her," Landon said, still averting his eyes from mine. "I kept telling myself that it was my subconscious. It couldn't be real, you know?"

"Oh, I know," I agreed wearily.

"On the boat, though," Landon said. "I saw her just kind of pop in behind you and she had that other little girl with her. And then I saw … I saw a big pool of red. I kept telling myself I was imagining it, but I wasn't."

"I'm sorry," I offered lamely.

Landon turned back to me, his angry eyes softening in the moonlight. "For what? For being stupid and climbing on a boat without knowing if it would kill you?"

"Sure," I said. "I am sorry about that," I stressed. "I'm sorry that you saw things you didn't want to see tonight. That's what I was talking about."

Landon chuckled. "I'm not."

"You're not?"

"It helps me understand you a little more," Landon admitted. "It helped me understand your family. It's going to make your family meeting my family a little easier, I think."

"Yeah," I agreed, dropping my head on his shoulder. "Wait. What?"

"Oh, yeah, I haven't had a chance to tell you yet," Landon smirked. "The other thing I was doing out at the inn was making reservations. My family is going to be here in a few weeks for a visit – my mom really wants to meet you – and I thought it would be good for everyone if they spent the week at the Overlook. That's the big news my brother wanted to talk about over dinner."

Oh crap.

Landon watched as the color drained from my face. "I think it's funny that the prospect of meeting my family scares you more than human traffickers on a boat. That's not weird at all."

"I'm not scared," I scoffed. I was terrified.

Erika picked that moment to pop into existence next to me. Landon jumped in surprise. He could still see her. That was interesting. "Gracie is gone."

"What do you mean she's gone?" I asked.

"She went away."

"You mean her body?" I asked sadly. "The police will make sure it gets home, Erika. I promise."

"She went with her body," Erika said.

"I don't understand."

"When the police pulled the tarp off her body there was this bright light and then she was just gone."

"You mean she passed on," I said quietly.

"She went to the better place?" Erika's eyes lit up hopefully.

"She did."

"When will I go?"

"I ... "

"What is that?"

I glanced over and saw Landon pointing to the sky. I narrowed my eyes to see what he was looking at. It was a shooting star. "Make a wish," I whispered to Erika.

She watched the star for a second and then screwed her eyes shut in concentration.

I watched the star, expecting it to wink out on the horizon, but instead it changed direction and started heading toward us. Landon scrambled to his feet as the star neared, pulling me with him and trying to shade me with his arm. I fought his efforts and watched the star as it alit on the end of the dock.

The blinding light caused me to close my eyes for a moment. When I opened them again the star was gone and there was a woman standing on the edge of the dock. She was dark, like Erika, and her clothes belied an era more than a hundred years past.

"Mama!"

I turned to Erika, surprise etched on my face. Mama?

"Erika," the woman opened her arms as the ghostly apparition of her daughter raced into them. "I've been looking for you for a very long time. I couldn't find you. Not until now."

Landon marveled at the spectacle in front of us, but he didn't say a word. He left that to me.

"You're Erika's mother?"

"I am," the woman straightened up and met my gaze kindly. "Thank you."

"For what?"

"Fulfilling her wish."

"What was your wish?" I asked Erika curiously.

"To go home."

"Are you taking her home?" I glanced back up at the woman who was running her hand down her daughter's small head lovingly.

"I'm taking her to a new home," the woman said carefully. "She'll be safe there. No need to worry."

"I'm not worried," I said. "Well, I was worried when I didn't know how to get her to you, but I'm not worried anymore."

"You have a good heart," the woman said. "People are watching and they know that. They're always willing to help. Don't forget that."

"I don't understand," I admitted.

"You will. Some day."

The woman kept Erika close as they started to fade, but Erika pulled away and took a step toward me questioningly. Her mother ceased shimmering and watched curiously. "I'll miss you," Erika said. "You were the only one that could see me and you saved me. You got me to my mama."

"You got yourself to your mama," I said, my voice hitching. "And you saved those other children."

"Not Gracie," Erika said sadly.

"You could never have saved Gracie."

"Neither could you," Erika said. "Remember that."

"Why?"

"Because you worry about too many things," Erika said, a small smile playing at the corner of her mouth. "You can't fix everything."

I smiled as the tears started to fall and Erika moved back toward her mother. "Have a good ... life," I whispered.

Erika smiled brightly. "You, too. I'll be watching every time you wish on a star – so wish on a lot of them."

Then they were gone.

EPILOGUE

A few days later, everyone was congregated at the inn for dinner. The children had left the day before – even though my mom had suggested adopting them all – and were on their way to new homes.

After some research, Chief Terry found that all of the children had been conveniently "lost" in the state foster system. The state police had raided the office responsible for placing all the children and taken three people into custody.

After a few hours of questioning, the office drones had rolled over on the entire operation. Within a twenty-four hour period, the Coast Guard had conducted five different raids and saved twenty-five more children – including a little girl named Ava. The story had made national news – and the front page of The Whistler that week, of course.

Karen and Dean had been taken into custody and were facing federal charges – including the death penalty. Gracie's mother had died in the hospital, and I could only hope that she had passed on to wherever it was that Gracie had gone when she blinked out of our world and travelled to another.

It had been a busy few days, so I had no idea how Uncle Warren was taking the revelation about Karen. I had a feeling another uncomfortable visit to the Dragonfly was in our immediate future. That was a concern for another day, though.

My mom and aunts had insisted on a celebratory dinner once their first big group of the season had vacated the inn. We had another small lull – but only for about three days before the season really got into swing.

"This smells great," Chief Terry said enthusiastically as my mom slipped a dish of short ribs onto the table in front of him.

"Well, you did request it," my mom winked as she sat down in the chair next to him two seconds before Marnie could try and snake it from her. Twila scooted into the seat on his left and Marnie shot her a hateful glare before finally sitting in a chair farther down the table.

"He earned it," I corrected.

Landon slung his arm around the back of my chair and rubbed my shoulder appreciatively. "So a head wound doesn't equate earning it?"

"Yeah, you guys had a really busy couple of days," Brian said. "You're heroes again."

"I wouldn't call us heroes," Clove said. "Just concerned citizens." She flashed a smile in Sam's direction and he returned it warmly.

Thistle rolled her eyes. "I would call us heroes."

"Of course you would," Aunt Tillie said.

"Where's your boyfriend?" Thistle asked pointedly.

"He is not my boyfriend! How many times do I have to tell you people that?"

"Just until it starts sounding like the truth," Thistle replied sweetly.

I decided to change the subject. "So, I guess the refurbishment of the Dandridge is off the menu," I said. "That's too bad. Dean may have been a psycho, but that was still a great idea."

"It's actually moving forward," Chief Terry said nervously, casting a glance in Sam's direction at the end of the table. "Another interested party stepped forward to continue on with the project."

"Who?" Landon asked suspiciously.

"That would be me," Sam said, a wide smile spreading across his face.

"You?" Thistle looked nonplussed. "Why you?"

"Well, after careful consideration, I've come to the conclusion that expanding The Whistler's distribution just isn't a viable option," Sam started.

"Humph," Aunt Tillie muttered. "We could've saved you some time if you would have listened to us from the start."

"Yes, well," Sam brushed off Aunt Tillie's statement. "I found that I love the area so much that I don't want to leave. With this opportunity opening up at the Dandridge, I thought a change of occupation might be in order."

"I think that's a great idea," Clove said warmly. I could already see visions of white dresses and hot sex with Sam dancing in her head. "That means you'll be living here now."

"I think it's a stupid idea," Thistle grumbled. "What do you know about running a business?"

"More than you when you opened your store I would suspect," Sam said pointedly.

Thistle blew out a raspberry and stuck her tongue out at Sam.

"I find it interesting that you decided to land here," Landon said, staring daggers into Sam. "This doesn't seem like an area where a big city guy like yourself would want to live."

"This area has a lot to offer," Sam replied. "Who doesn't love nature?"

Clove raised her hand quickly and then nervously pulled it back down.

"And then there's the rich history of this area," Sam pressed. "I can't wait to explore it some more."

"Well, good luck then," I said briefly, shrugging off the chill that ran through my body at his pointed words.

"I assume that means you'll be getting your own place?" Aunt Tillie asked hopefully.

"I'll be moving into the living quarters at the Dandridge," Sam agreed. "It's going to be a few weeks before that's ready, though. I have some things to take care of down state but I'll be back in a few weeks when all that is taken care of. It will really be perfect timing."

"Well, that sounds nice," Twila said.

"For who?" Aunt Tillie asked dryly.

"Let's eat," my mom ordered tensely. "This is a celebration."

We all did as we were told, but the meal couldn't exactly be classified as comfortable. When we were done, Landon suggested going for a walk. "Our jackets are in the back."

"I'll get them. You wait for me here." He dropped a kiss on my brow and then slipped back into the inn, leaving me alone in the front foyer. I wasn't alone for very long, though.

"That was another interesting dinner."

I turned and fixed Sam with a tight smile. "Well, at least you can say we're all interesting."

"Among other things," Sam agreed, his eyes probing.

"What other things?" I asked innocently.

"Well, I mean, I keep learning more and more about you guys the more time I spend here," Sam said coyly. "For example, several nights ago I was walking around the grounds at night – just to get some fresh air – and I saw a group of people in a weird clearing."

My heart started pounding in my chest. I knew I had heard someone else out there that night.

"I would expect nothing different from a coven of witches, though," Sam said, smiling widely. "So, yeah, I'm really looking forward to living here."

I felt all the air whoosh out of me as a lightheaded-fog descend on my brain. *Crap.*

Printed in Great Britain
by Amazon